LIVID

LIVID

◆ ◆ ◆

a novel

Cai Emmons

Red Hen Press | *Pasadena, CA*

Book Design by Mark E. Cull

Library of Congress Cataloging-in-Publication Data

Names: Emmons, Cai, author.
Title: Livid: a novel / Cai Emmons.
Description: First Edition. | Pasadena, CA: Red Hen Press, [2022]
Identifiers: LCCN 2022016964 (print) | LCCN 2022016965 (ebook) | ISBN
  9781636280752 (paperback) | ISBN 9781636280769 (ebook)
Subjects: LCGFT: Suspense fiction. | Novels.
Classification: LCC PS3605.M57 L58 2022 (print) | LCC PS3605.M57 (ebook)
  | DDC 813/.6—dc23
LC record available at https://lccn.loc.gov/2022016964
LC ebook record available at https://lccn.loc.gov/2022016965

Publication of this book has been made possible in part through the generous financial support of Nancy Boutin.

The National Endowment for the Arts, the Los Angeles County Arts Commission, the Ahmanson Foundation, the Dwight Stuart Youth Fund, the Max Factor Family Foundation, the Pasadena Tournament of Roses Foundation, the Pasadena Arts & Culture Commission and the City of Pasadena Cultural Affairs Division, the City of Los Angeles Department of Cultural Affairs, the Audrey & Sydney Irmas Charitable Foundation, the Meta & George Rosenberg Foundation, the Albert and Elaine Borchard Foundation, the Adams Family Foundation, Amazon Literary Partnership, the Sam Francis Foundation, and the Mara W. Breech Foundation partially support Red Hen Press.

First Edition
Published by Red Hen Press
www.redhen.org

LIVID

"While men were always getting furious, they calmed down in the end. Women, who appeared to be silent, acquiescent, when they were angry flew into a rage that had no end."

—Elena Ferrante, *My Brilliant Friend*

PART ONE

1

It wasn't my proudest moment, but not one cell in my body regrets it.

2

The summons to jury duty came as a surprise because I'd only been back in this small Northwestern town for a few months. I thought I'd slipped in unobtrusively, pulling a "geographical" as some therapists like to call it, a false belief that a change of location will change one's state of mind. I knew better, but one always hopes. Initially I was annoyed by the nasty legal tone of the summons, and I cast about for a legitimate reason to be excused, but there was none—or none that would stand up in the eyes of the law. No dependents. No financial hardship. As a self-employed accountant my work is flexible. So, I resigned myself—the odds were I wouldn't be chosen anyway.

The appointed day, just shy of the summer solstice, was absurdly sunny and likely to be hot, hardly the kind of day one wants to be stuck in a courtroom. I made my way through the labyrinthian courthouse to a large windowless anteroom where I sat with a slew of other potential jurors—well over a hundred of us—escaping into one of my Thinkathons in which I meander around the serpentine pathways of my brain. My father kept coming to mind, though I wished he wouldn't. He had been on all sides of the law—and would have plenty of opinions about me serving on a jury. Not that I would listen.

We filled out questionnaires with personal and demographic information—age, marital status, educational status, length of time at our current residence—and they divided us into groups of thirty to forty. Each group was assigned a bird name: the Larks, the Owls, the Tanagers, the Sparrows, the Robins. I was an Owl. Eventually the Owls, Robins, and Tanagers were called and ushered, in strict single file, like

sheep in a dour conga dance, down a maze of corridors and through security and up a staircase until we arrived at the courtroom for voir dire.

It took me a moment, as we settled into the spectator benches,
to register the defendant, who sat alone at a table in the front of the
courtroom. A woman! No one had mentioned we were here to decide
the fate of a woman. I expected, were I to be chosen, to weigh in on
the fate of a man, some person raised in a broken family of limited
means, someone who'd had an inadequate education and no parental
encouragement, a person with little impulse control and maybe a drug
problem and certainly a short fuse. In all honesty, I hadn't given a lot
of thought to who the defendant would be, but it was disappointing to
realize I'd fallen prey to the usual stereotypes.

The woman was attractive in a rough way, with profuse blonde-
brown hair gathered into a bun that lay in a tumor-like lump at the
back of her neck. Her eyes, a feral blue, gazed ahead at some distant
point, as if she had recently returned from a solo trip at sea and hadn't
yet realized there was no longer a need to scan the horizon. Her bare
forearms rested on the table, bony-sharp as tools; even the sinewy apparatus of her shoulders and neck appeared taut and useful. She wasn't
old, indeterminate thirties—everyone seems younger than I am these
days—but her skin had been worked over, thickened and textured as
if it was used to sealing things out, a skill I recognize. I imagined her
having sprung from a rural frontier—Montana or Maine or maybe
Alaska—somewhere north with callous winters, ornery plumbing,
intermittent electricity, heating via an insatiable wood stove, a place
where life's central mission was survival.

What riveted me most was her regal comportment. Her spine was
unusually straight, and she was unflinching, despite the number of
evaluating eyes on her. I had to admire her refusal to cower in the
face of humiliation. Occasionally a tremor disturbed her face so
the muscles jigged like iron filings under a magnet. Her power was
undeniable. Her charisma. *I have to know you,* I thought. *I already do.*
An armed and burly sheriff's deputy was stationed just behind her,
somewhat laughable as she appeared neither dangerous, nor ready
to flee.

I glanced around at the people near me to see how they were reacting. They were all expressionless, apparently bored. On my left was a
young person of indeterminate gender, tattoos the length of their arms
and creeping up the front of their neck like an invasive species. On my
right was a heavy guy with rippling gut and infringing buttocks who
I imagined was a trucker. There were several demurely dressed wom-
en who might have been teachers or office administrators, a couple
of smug people I was sure were professors, a snaggle-toothed man in
jeans who was the only one smiling, some young men in shorts and
baseball caps I guessed were students, their female counterparts in
yoga pants. No African Americans—not in this oh-so-white town—a
handful of Latinxs and Asians Americans, but most of the assembled
company were Caucasian.

I had chosen this town because I'd lived here before, and it was
easier to return than to go someplace new. There was the possible
problem of running into Drew, my ex-husband, but the difficult things
that had transpired between us were ancient history, overshadowed by
what had happened more recently and far more grievously back East.
Shawna things—we don't need to get into that. Since my arrival here in
mid-March I'd taken on a few late-filing tax clients; I'd been trying to
make my shabby bungalow more habitable; and I'd reconnected with
a couple of old friends, mainly Val, my lesbian teacher friend. But the
overarching project of powering through grief and finding something
that could be called "meaning"—that eluded me. I'd always known it
wouldn't be instantaneous.

I was surprised I'd forgotten that this town was overrun with young
white males from the university. Insouciant and entitled, these youth
ran stop signs and darted out of side streets, music blaring from their
car windows; they paraded obliviously down the sidewalks immersed
in their phones, apparently thinking they were immune to misfortune.
Their numbers seemed to have multiplied in my seven-almost-eight-
year absence, and my intolerance of them had risen exponentially. I
had to constantly remind myself it was inadvisable to lash out.

The courtroom we'd settled in was aggressively drab, everything
a different shade of brown—the judge's raised oak bench, the dark-

er wood of the gallery seats, the beige-brown acoustic tiles of walls and ceiling, the spot-forgiving speckled carpeting—but all that brown couldn't disguise the room's intensity. You could feel ghosts oozing from the walls, whispering of the myriad dramas that had unspooled there, suggesting the rage the room had witnessed, the cutthroat competition, the battles pitting freedom against punishment. If you'd been in that room alone and listened hard enough, I was sure the details of those stories would emerge, reputations made and broken, lives saved and ruined.

We sat in silence that wasn't really silence, the asthmatic ventilation system rasping, high heels clicking officiously down the length of the linoleum floor of the hallway just outside, attorneys arriving at their respective tables and sifting through papers. It was like waiting for a play to begin, but the actors were already on stage. The defense attorney had a thick-waisted body reminiscent of Tweedle Dee. His suit was badly tailored and covered his body like a tarp; the heat was already getting to him so every few minutes he mopped his brow. The prosecutor was a woman wearing a brown suit that made her look as if she'd been cut from the walls. She paged through a folder, occasionally handing something to her male assistant. A sage, if cynical, prosecutorial decision, I thought, to pit woman against woman.

"All rise!" said one of two sour-faced, gun-packing bailiffs.

Another woman bustled into the room. Clad in wannabe-male attire—a pantsuit and necktie—she was one of those women young enough to still believe she would someday rule the world.

Everyone rose with startling obedience, including me, surprising myself as I've never been a believer in kneejerk compliance. The judge, robed and also female, swept in on a gusty current. She took her place at the bench, high above us all. Perhaps the world was changing, I thought, if so many women had arrived at the top of the legal pecking order. This woman, the judge, was short and stout, almost square, with a wedge of dark hair that rocket-blasted straight up from her scalp. Every move she made announced her ease with power. She pounded her gavel.

"Docket number 5037. The State of Oregon versus Jessie Snell. Murder One."

No one gasped, but I wanted to. This queenly defendant had committed murder? She looked tough, but not *murder-tough*. I'd never been in the presence of any woman who had committed murder. I'd met plenty of cold women, acerbic women, bitter women, catty women, even downright mean women, but had never met a woman—as far as I knew—who had killed another human being.

Potential jurors were summoned by name and number and directed to the hot seat for questioning. The defense attorney, called Counselor Vitale by the judge, took the lead, delivering his questions while remaining beside his client, occupying his seat as if he were the benign host of a late-night talk show, even a friend, sure the whole room was delighted with him.

Soon it became clear he meant business. *Have you or any of your family members ever been the victim of a violent crime? Is it credible that a woman would stay with her husband even if she was afraid of him? Do you believe a husband can rape his wife? What do you think of the #MeToo movement?* These were not surprising questions for a trial like this, but occasionally he scrutinized a juror's questionnaire with laser focus, customizing his inquiry as if he'd noticed something dangerous. *What was your high school friend imprisoned for? I see you're a hunter—why do you like hunting? Did your friend report her rape?* I began palpating the delicate spots in my own background, thinking about the things I had said and not said on my questionnaire.

Identities and entire world views came to light instantly under the spotlight of Vitale's questioning. The apologetic woman with the concave chest. The professor who tugged his earlobe as if concealing something. The retired woman whose inability to stop talking flagged a bad listener. The man whose rolling eyes spoke of deep hostility. The anxious, hypochondriacal woman who was convinced she was allergic to something in the courtroom. People couldn't disguise themselves no matter how hard they tried. I knew how easily I myself could be slotted into a type: middle-aged, mildly overweight (read: lazy), introverted, the kind of person whose creative thinking might be limited due to working in a profession that requires proficiency with numbers. Would Counselor Vitale notice my jaded world view? Would he see my keen intelligence? Would he spot in my countenance any evidence of recent wounding? It seemed quite clear to me I wouldn't be chosen.

Vitale sized people up quickly—he'd clearly been making a close study of people for years—before handing them over to the prosecutor, Ms. McCarthy.

McCarthy was more rote than Vitale had been. She fed everyone the same basic questions: *Is there any circumstance that you believe allows a person to break the law or to take another person's life? Do you believe police officers are generally trustworthy? Do you think being under the influence of alcohol or drugs should excuse committing a crime? Are you a feminist?* Was she a feminist herself, I wondered? Would a feminist want to convict another woman? But of course feminism did not preclude that some women might be criminals and should be prosecuted. What struck me as odd was the way she delivered her questions with an attitude of near boredom, as if she had no investment in this case—or as if she saw it as a slam dunk.

The judge, whose face was a study in neutrality, leaned back in her seat exactly as she might in a beachside recliner, the kind of slouching posture a teacher might chide a student for. Being the sovereign there she could do as she liked. The only part of her that moved was her eyelids, which occasionally rose and fell like remote controls on the scales of justice.

Jessie Snell sat a mere ten or fifteen feet from me. Imperious, fierce, righteous, murderous Jessie Snell. Watching her, a splinter of obsession entered me.

After an hour it became clear that the questioning was going to last a long time, and I sank into another Thinkathon, my attention drifting to other quadrants of my life. The lawnmower I needed to purchase to take control of my scrappy lawn. Edna, who had emailed me after more than a year of being out of touch. The berries I would pick up from the farmer's market if it was still open when we were dismissed. For the record, I regard thinking, simply sitting idly and letting my mind wander, as a legitimate activity, exactly what the human species was put on this earth to do. By contrast, Drew, my ex, valued moving above all else. *Think on*, I tell my brain, *wherever you go is fine with me.*

"Sybil White-Brown." I was jerked back to the body-place by the sound of my name.

Go ahead and laugh—it's supposed to be funny. My father's name was O'Malley, a name that could get you in trouble in Boston. It certainly got my father in trouble. My mother's maiden name was White and when I was born, that became my middle name. From birth through most of junior high, I was Sybil White O'Malley.

After my father left, my mother, wanting a fresh start, changed all of our names. She could have made us all Whites, but she wanted a complete change of identity, so she chose her beloved maternal grandmother's maiden name. That name, originally Brownstein, had been shortened and un-Jewified to Brown. So, my sisters and I became Browns. Boring but straightforward. Our mother, Sandra Brown, my sisters Sue and Sally Brown. I was the only one with the middle name White—my sisters had other family names. My mother suggested I change my middle name, but I, thinking it was funny, insisted on keeping it, becoming Sybil White Brown, later hyphenated to White-Brown.

"Why do you always need to be so different?" my mother asked me when she was dying. Her voice was unusually soft. What might have been a challenge earlier in her life was then simply a matter of curiosity. "Everything," she said. "The name you insisted on. That funny Western man you married. You always had to do things your own way, while your sisters . . ." Her focus faded. She wasn't, at that point, or maybe ever, bent on answers.

I rose, still dazed. I've never liked the limelight, have always eschewed large groups. Drew and I could not have been more different in that way. He was a man whose life force came from socializing. He was a schmoozer, a magnet for men and women alike. He loved to laugh. Everyone adored him and angled to be in his presence; his liquid-brown eyes, peripatetic as fish, had a way of settling unpredictably and conferring coveted attention. When we became a couple everyone told me I'd won the lottery, implying that I, reserved and zaftig as I was, did not deserve him. When we (read: he) hosted parties during our marriage, which he liked to do on a regular basis, I would socialize for a while, then retire early to the bedroom alone.

I took the designated seat. The gazes of too many strangers' eyes rained over me. Jessie Snell's eyes were packed with questions. *What kind of woman are you?* I wondered the same of her. Had she given all the potential jurors this searing look?

Counselor Vitale regarded me with a sly smile that seemed personal. For a moment I wondered if he recognized me. It was a small town, we might have crossed paths. It was possible he was reacting to the curiosity of my name. He glanced down at my questionnaire. Sweat had begun to creep through his suit jacket, an expanding estuary of personal moisture.

"I see you're an accountant?" He smiled, as if my profession amused him.

"Yes."

"And you've only lived here a few months?"

"Yes. I lived here before, and now I'm just back after spending several years in the Boston area where I was raised."

He nodded. "Divorced, hm. Bad divorce?"

"As divorces go, I guess you could say it was okay."

"Amicable then?"

"Yes, amicable."

Amicable is not entirely accurate, but for the purposes of the proceedings such nuances didn't matter. If I were to say more, I wasn't sure what it would be. More than eight years out I still hadn't developed any succinct way to describe the divorce (not that I was often called upon to do so). I am not given to voluntarily divulging personal details, present situation notwithstanding. I fell in love, then things followed an unpredictable course. The same familiar story as countless other marriages.

"Kids?"

I shook my head. Why was he asking these questions when the information was right there on the form?

"Speak up, Ms. White-Brown. Do you have kids?"

I had the sudden irrational belief he knew something. "No. No kids."

"Have any of your friends or family members been victims of domestic abuse?"

I thought briefly of Shawna, of all that might have happened to Shawna in the years before we met, all those things I'd suspected but never confirmed.

"No," I said.

"Do you believe that sometimes good people do bad things?"

I squinted at him. *Of course,* I felt like saying, *haven't you?* "I'm a reasonably good person, Counselor, and I've done plenty of bad things."

I could have illustrated this point for him. The candy bars I used to "liberate" from the pharmacy when I was in junior high, just to see if I could. The public water supplies I swam in illegally. The occasional speeding. I'm not a scofflaw, but if you want to get technical, we all have rap sheets. But, okay, I knew what he meant.

I smiled to showcase my cooperative spirit. I was saying what I understood to be truth, but as soon as the words exited my mouth they sounded inaccurate, only half-truths. Under oath, even the simplest of questions can seem booby-trapped. What, for example, qualifies as abuse? My older sister Sue, a New York litigator, routinely snipes with her husband, and I used to wonder about what happened between them behind closed doors. But I've never seen any evidence of abuse—broken bones or black eyes or suspicious welts—though once in the middle of the night at a summer house we were renting together on the Cape, a thunderous noise came from Sue's bedroom, and in the morning her husband explained it clumsily, saying a chair had "fallen." What they were hiding, if anything, I have never learned to this day. Among the parents of Shawna's classmates I once had a suspicion of abuse, but nothing concrete ever surfaced. And there was the unknown past of Shawna herself.

"You're single now?"

Wasn't this redundant? "Yes."

"An accountant?"

"Yes." *I already said so,* I thought peevishly, but I did my best to conceal the irritation.

He shook his head, chuckling. "Better you than me. I can barely do my own taxes, let alone someone else's." An appeal to incompetence, cultivated as a trait to win sympathy. "Anything else to add you think might be relevant?"

He put a period on the questioning, apparently satisfied there was nothing I might add that could alter his assessment of me, but the question itself was so wide open, so discretionary, that it prompted me to wonder if there was something I should add. I could tell him I'd always been a world class sleeper, but, since my move, sleep had been a shifty companion. I often didn't fall asleep until around five or six in the morning, when the day, at that time of year, was already bright, and I'd rouse myself at ten only because of residual Puritanical guilt. Perhaps in the courtroom during a long trial I would succumb to sleep too easily and therefore be a derelict juror.

"No, nothing else."

He yielded me up to McCarthy who asked her pro forma questions about what I thought of cops and alcohol, and if I thought law-breaking was ever permissible. Then, instead of asking me if I was a feminist, she wanted to know if I thought women were inherently weak. No, I told her, of course I don't think that! What self-respecting woman thinks such a thing these days? *Excise your condescending smile, Ms. McCarthy. I am not the one on trial.*

I passed muster, at least for the moment, and was instructed to remain in the jury box. A good development or bad, I wasn't yet sure, but as other jury candidates came and went, many of them dismissed—a Gender Studies professor, an aesthetician, a retired high school teacher—a sense of distinction came over me, a sense of belonging even, a certainty that, however long the trial took, it was my destiny to be sitting on that jury.

I allowed myself to float again. It wouldn't be hard to clear my schedule for the next week, or possibly two. I had a few active clients without pressing deadlines. There was the two-day midweek trip to the coast with Val, but its purpose was pure pleasure and could easily be postponed.

Something snared my attention back to the courtroom. The back of the head of the man being questioned. Wavy brown hair laced with gray. Sinewy tanned neck. For a second or two I doubted myself, but my body knew. I could have been shown his pinky nail, his elbow crease, his knee or belly button or instep, and I would have known. Drew, my ex-husband.

How had I failed to spot him in the crowd of jurors earlier? Yes, I'd been in a daze, but how had I missed his name being called and his approach for questioning? Had he intentionally hidden from me amidst the crowd? It was possible. I strained to see more of his face, but I was sitting directly behind him so only when he glanced at the judge did I see a sliver of his clean-shaven cheek. Gone was the beard he had always cherished.

My consciousness was a stealth missile, close to the ground, scouring the terrain, calibrating, recalibrating. The impossibility of this.

He began to speak, his voice deep and authoritative as ever. "Physical therapist by day," he said of himself. "And after-hours I'm a wilderness fiend." He smiled as if he'd said something charming and funny but, out of his element, he didn't provoke a reaction from Counselor Vitale—or anyone else—which gave me a little ping of satisfaction.

I'd prepared for a version of this—in my imagination the scene involved running into him on the street and me passing him by with a cool dismissive nod—but not *this version* in which I was incapable of walking away. I wasn't physically chained here, but I was certainly psychologically shackled. Rising and walking out the door would have elicited far too much attention. Maybe it was even illegal.

"Married?" Vitale asked, ignoring the form again.

"No." Drew paused. "Divorced." I half expected him to turn and point—he had to have seen me.

"Long marriage?"

"Thirteen years."

Vitale nodded as if thirteen years was significant. "How long divorced?"

"Eight years."

"Kids?"

"No." *And whose fault was that?* Was I angry? Disgusted? Hard to tell. I believed I had laid those feelings aside years ago. Mostly what I felt was a bold NO.

How deftly he reduced our years together to a few words (though it's true I'd done the same thing). What mark the divorce had left on Drew, the matter of whether it was amicable, was of no interest to Vitale. Did he think—did everyone think—that divorce didn't mark men in the way it marked women?

Vitale handed Drew over to McCarthy, who queried him with her usual cops and alcohol questions. "Do you believe in gender equality?" she said.

"Of course," he answered, clearly indignant. It was hard to imagine she was learning much from this line of questioning. No one professed to believe in gender *inequality.*

Drew, not rejected, or at least not rejected yet, took his assigned seat in the row in front of me, a little to my left where I could see him better, the slope of his nose, a half-crescent of his generous lips. I'd almost forgotten how long his neck was, capable of swiveling, owl-like, more than 180 degrees.

We were dismissed for a brief lunch break. Not pausing to see what Drew was doing, I raced out ahead of everyone into the scorching sunlight. I purchased an iced coffee and a maple scone. I walked around the same two blocks several times, until it was time to return to court. I tossed the half-drunk coffee and uneaten scone. Back in the courtroom for the remainder of the long afternoon, amidst the courtroom's miasma and the mounting heat, I was aware of only the two of us. He had to be feeling the weight of my gaze on his neck. Was he also playing marriage reruns?

4:56 p.m. The jury was empaneled. Drew was Juror #10. I was Juror #3.

3

I had no business being on that hike. I knew it right away. All the other hikers were two or three decades older than I was, but much fitter, with evenly muscular calves that looked as if they belonged on classical sculptures or anatomical charts. There was a quickness about them—sharp jawbones, dexterous hands, faces observant and hyperactive as rodents—that immediately made me feel phlegmatic. *Moderate to easy,* the flyer had said—the perfect way to introduce my underused body to new rigors in this adopted state of mine where only losers weren't devotees of fitness—but this was a *mountain,* for God's sake, neither moderate nor easy. All the fifty- and sixty-somethings raced ahead. Drew, our leader, who I judged to be about my age (I was twenty-eight at the time, he turned out to be thirty-one), gallantly remained behind with me as I lumbered uphill. He did most of the talking, educating me about the evergreens we were passing, the mushrooms and lichens, the volcanic history of the area. He was impressively knowledgeable about the natural world. I was glad he had things to say as I was far too breathless to speak. After an hour and a half the blisters that had been sneaking up on both heels had intensified to the point where I could think of nothing else and had to stop. I urged him to ditch me and go ahead. After a rest I would head down, I told him. But he wouldn't have it.

"We'll fix you up," he said. "Take off your shoes and sit on that rock."

For a moment I resisted—I have never been someone who takes well to being commanded—but he was the leader and responsible for his hikers so I complied. He was already spreading a towel on the needle-strewn forest floor and laying out ointment and bandages and moleskin. His fingers were exceptionally long and deft, and he lined up his supplies with extreme precision, nothing about him haphazard, not the cut of his dark beard nor the cut of his biceps, and his calves were so smooth they almost looked shaved.

My feet, spread on a rock, were flat and puffy, the feet of an endomorph, a woman allergic to moving, toes now red from being smashed into a pair of new, unbroken boots. I was sure they had to smell fungal, having sweated for hours in such confinement.

He laid a hand towel in front of me, dipped a washcloth into the stream we had just crossed, and knelt in front of me, lifting the foot with the biggest heel blister and cradling it. I could have laughed and cried from the shock of his hands holding my foot.

"Nasty," he said.

Ordinarily I would have found a wisecrack about foot fetishists or Jesus, but the shame of my deplorable lack of fitness blocked all access to witticism. An awkward silence ensued while he cleaned both of my feet, applied ointment and bandages to the blisters and moleskin in places that looked vulnerable to new blisters. Then—and this is the thing I went over and over later—he began to massage my feet, right there beside the path, the occasional hiker passing us, the stream burbling like some calming white noise machine, the other members of our party probably already nearing the summit, as if he was performing a perfectly natural sacrament, as if time was no issue. Did he do this routinely on all the hikes he led? I couldn't tell. Maybe he was being dutiful. No doubt he pitied me.

His knuckle pressed into my sunken arch as if to coax it higher. "We don't pay enough attention to our feet," he said, without a trace of irony.

Then, argh, this is the worst part to recall: Despite the scourge of my humiliation—my sorry feet, the poor shape I was in, the certainty he pitied me—I was overcome by an irresistible moan. I tried to disguise it by turning it into a sigh. He tapped my arch, quickening the blood; he rolled the neglected foot muscles as if they were delicacies, and separated each toe as if to help it individuate. I could no longer conceal my reaction and I let myself go, capitulating to the unexpected pleasure of touch, a hunger satisfied, the delight of stepping into a warm bath. I heard myself groaning and a part of me was horrified, but still I could not stop. Who knew touched feet could deliver such ecstasy to the entire body? Overlooked indeed.

When he was done and I was putting on my shoes, embarrassment consumed me—if I'd known then that he was a physical therapist the situation might have made some sense, but he hadn't said so and the situation made no sense at all—and while I agreed to finishing out the hike—how could I not after what he'd done?—I told myself that I would say goodbye to this man at the end of the day and recoup my pride, and I would never have to see him again.

4

I exited the courthouse into a day still robust with cloying summer sunlight and pawed at the depths of my purse for sunglasses, gusts of wind blowing cigarette butts past my feet, attorneys and court officials and cops and maybe some jurors swarming past me. Never had I so fervently wished for invisibility. The dark glasses provided a modicum of relief, but *for Christ's sake,* there was Drew, who I'd thought was behind me, perched on a low wall on the courthouse plaza. He was staring directly at me and after a moment he beckoned with his head.

I descended the steps and went to him, and he rose and we bobbled there in silence before sharing a stiff embrace initiated by him. Then we stepped back and assessed each other. He was still six inches taller than I, so in order to regard his face I had to look up.

"Crazy," he said.

I nodded.

"So you're back," he said. "I heard the rumor from someone."

"For now." As if I had other grand plans.

"How long have you been here?"

"A few months."

Traffic spun by on the avenue not far from us. Several hours of late June sunlight still lay ahead. All I wanted to do was sleep. Squinting against the sunball, I sidestepped into his body's penumbra.

It has always been my habit to meet mayhem with stillness, sifting my options while I maintain the frozen stance of a light-shocked deer. But others become quickly alarmed by my paralysis, so I've learned to work against instinct, forcing myself to speak or move.

"Why didn't you mention me when you were being questioned?" I asked. "I was sure you would."

"You didn't mention me either."

"I didn't see you until you were up there. I swear to God. Is this legal, both of us on that jury?"

"I don't see why not. We're not related. Not anymore." One side of his full mouth inched up so I glimpsed a glint of gold on one of his molars. "But if you want to be excused you can tell the judge you hate my guts and couldn't possibly work with me." He grinned, testing, asking me to confirm or deny my hatred.

I couldn't weigh in on that. I wasn't sure. I said nothing.

"You look good," he said. "You've lost weight."

I nodded. Of course he would notice my weight loss, body-obsessed as he was. I would never forget the way he used to grab the flesh of my belly or thigh in the waning days of our relationship, as if he could knead it away, my extra weight a source of tension between us, him telling me repeatedly my life would be better without it. When things tanked in Boston, I lost weight, but not because of any steely self-discipline Drew would have admired.

"You look the same," I said.

"Grayer."

I shrugged. "I'll stick it out. She interests me."

"Which she?"

"Well, all of them, but I meant the defendant, Jessie."

He nodded slowly and turned his head to the traffic as if someone was making a bid for his attention. "She scares the shit out of me."

His vehemence surprised me. "Really? Why?"

His lips juddered in and out. "We shouldn't discuss the case," he said.

He was right. We had sworn we wouldn't. The judge had said this unequivocally. We were not to discuss the case with anyone including the other jurors. We were not to research it. After she said these things she made eye contact with each of us to underscore her point. Did we understand? Did we plan to violate? Her gaze burned hot, the wide-reaching scope of her attention not a place you wanted to dwell for long. If you violate these orders you will be censured, she warned.

"I have to go," I said, turning abruptly and hastening across the plaza to the crosswalk.

Waiting for the light to change, I couldn't resist a glance backward. He was still watching me, or at least his gaze was pointed in my general direction. I pivoted and hopped into the street, barely avoiding a Beamer whose young male driver blasted his horn. I boomeranged back to the curb as if I'd been hit, then the light changed and I lurched into the street again, almost running then stopping myself, aware he might still be watching, knowing he was probably assessing my rump as he'd always done, noting how the weight loss had winnowed it to positive effect. I'd always thought my buttocks was an immutable body part, and throughout my life I'd made a point of ignoring it—though sometimes it leapt into unexpected prominence from a storefront window, and it often felt, especially when I was showering or getting dressed, a little too bouncy and doughy or even gelatinous—but it had turned out to be more amenable to change than I'd thought. I didn't like to be thinking this as I crossed the street; I honestly didn't give a damn what Drew thought.

At home I yearned for the light to disappear. Already sleep-deprived, I craved sleep. I was in bed before the sun went down, but I rattled and tossed, wide awake, so finally I got up and went out to my tiny fenced backyard and sat in one of the Adirondack chairs with a bottle of wine, hoping the alcohol would make me drowsy. But the night was stimulating—the cool air and the impertinent mosquitos who were not deterred by the cooling and the noises from Brenda's chickens and a scuttling but invisible presence at the back of my own yard. I was berating myself yet again, all these years later, for having allowed myself to get involved with Drew in the first place, when even back then I'd known better.

In fairness to myself, however, I didn't fall for him right away. In fact, I resisted him quite strenuously, wary of a quality in him I'd observed on the hike. He had been flirtatious with those fifty- and sixty-something hiker women. Surprised, they flirted back. It was sickening to watch. There had to be something wrong with a person who dispersed his charm so indiscriminately. After the hike he called me. Seeing his name, I didn't pick up, assuming it was a duty call. But he persisted, leaving messages begging me to call back.

"I know you like me," he said when I finally picked up. "Don't try to deny it."

Even over the phone he had a way of pressing himself into a room, trying to exert control.

"How could you possibly know that?"

"Your foot told me. The way it relaxed as soon as I touched it. And your groaning."

"I didn't groan."

"You groaned. I was there. I heard it. Right there in the woods in the middle of a hike."

"I'm a human being."

"That's why I like you."

"I think you're used to having everyone fall for you, but I'm not going to be one of your cabal."

He laughed at my use of the word cabal. We had this conversation, or one very like it, a ridiculous number of times. He would tell me with utmost assurance that he knew I wanted to get to know him better. Who likes to be told that? *I'm* the authority on what I feel, and I wasn't about to hand that authority over to him. Nevertheless, I kept picking up the phone for those inane looping conversations, which is to say I wasn't as immune to his charms as I wanted to be.

Look at me. I'm no siren. Twenty plus years ago I had youth on my side, good skin, and my hair has always been a solid asset, long and thick as it is, and back then it was a good deal shinier, but as a package I'm basically ordinary, and I was ordinary even in my late twenties. Do you know the Chekhov play, *Uncle Vanya*? The character Sonya, who is not thought of as a catch, says, referring to herself: *You have beautiful hair. You have beautiful eyes. That's what they always tell a woman who is not beautiful.* I identified with Sonya; despite my admirable hair and skin, why would Drew pursue me when he could have had anyone?

It was his singing that finally wore me down, the jaunty songs he left on my voicemail. Familiar tunes with silly lyrics.

> You are the very model of a wary female specimen
> You're guarded and suspicious and loathe to trust just any man
> But stop and look and notice that I'm really quite a nifty catch
> Healthy and attractive and I see in you a perfect match
> Your body turns me on and I know you are intelligent
> You delight in conversation as long as it is relevant
> So please will you consent to spend a little spate of time with me?
> A dapper single man who is capable of love, you'll see.

Or:

> She will not agree-ee to see me
> She thinks that I'm be-ing a heel
> How can I convince her to give me a chance
> To show her all that I feel?
>
> Bring back, bring back
> Oh, bring lovely Sybil to me, to me
> Bring back, bring back
> Bring lovely Sybil to me.

I agreed to go for coffee. We sat across from each other at a tiny tinny table that wobbled each time we laid down our cups, the barista calling out orders in a shrill voice that pierced our space as if she was right at the table with us, the huffing espresso machine, the torrent of surrounding conversations, the din of traffic gunning past the stop sign outside. Despite the noise and chaos, I sat on an island of calm. His luminous presence enshrined me, the broad white smile, kind but slightly mocking my intransigence. It was a posture that would come to be familiar: him sitting in his mountaintop temple smiling out indulgently at one of his acolytes. The push and pull of him, the thrall. He was a force to be resisted—or succumbed to. We weren't exactly sparring, but our back-and-forth held some suggestion of battle. By then I'd been resisting him for a few weeks.

"I guess people don't often refuse you?"

His smile denied nothing. "So, who are you, Ms. Mystery?"

Ms. Mystery. A laughable thought. It might have been possible to fabricate an alluring new self to paste over the boring version of me (the East Coast woman who had moved West in her mid-twenties for a graduate degree in English, wanting a profession, yes, but more pointedly driven to escape the location of her upbringing). Wary, I shared with him the basic facts. He probed for more, and I made him into a fisherman, tugging the line on an unexpectedly resistant catch.

He matched my wariness with wariness of his own, a few vague descriptors of himself, the ranch he hailed from in Eastern Oregon, the physical therapy work he did. "A Body Specialist," he called himself.

A vast unfished sea opened between us. It could have held anything.

"So, the physical therapy explains your expertise at foot massage?"

"Maybe."

He loved the astringent scent of Douglas fir needles, the perfume of post-rain petrichor oozing from thirsty soil, everything that sprang from the earth. I loved numbers, brain teasers, puzzles. We shook our heads—what strange and probably incompatible passions.

The lure of him was tectonic, but so was the danger. Equal parts. Push-pull. Hot-cold. Love-hate. As we rose to leave, our bare arms grazed for a second, maybe a millisecond. Just enough contact for cells to fizz, an acute physical incursion. The onset of an addiction. A place that required revisiting. Even the uncertainty was arousing. But I wasn't ready to yield, still disbelieving that this oh-so-eligible *Body Specialist* could truly be attracted to me.

It was a slow creep to the inevitable. Five meetings for coffee. Two river walks. Talk about our work, the weather, what we did the previous weekend—a hike for him, a movie for me. Talk strikingly devoid of references to our families. Day #25 he invited me to his house for dinner. Crab cakes, asparagus, polenta, and salad. He was as fastidious in the kitchen as he had been when he tended to my feet in the wilderness, and I'd never had such a luscious meal in my life.

After we ate, he hummed tunelessly as he pulled the blinds in the living room of his orderly bungalow, closing out the summer twilight. He laid a blanket over the carpet and lit several salt lights that emitted dim orange-yellow light. He encouraged me to sit on the blanket while he went to the kitchen and returned with the same bottle of olive oil he had used for cooking. He sat beside me, cross-legged, and laid the oil on the blanket and raised his fern-green polo shirt to peel it off, finding my eyes again, his face softening, the undulant musculature of his chest breathtaking in the warm light.

"You?" he said softly, gesturing toward my clothing. He kept his insistence in check, didn't press, only suggested. I was weak with desire, and paralyzed by self-consciousness. Because I was wearing an uncharacteristic dress (an attempt to impress), there was no gradual way to expose myself. Placing my naked self beside his Adonis body seemed unthinkable.

"No need for embarrassment," he whispered. "Your body is a turn-on."

My organs suppurated. I lifted the skirt of my dress gracelessly, exposing underpants and bare belly, then remembered the zipper. He moved in to assist, soon was casting my dress into the shadows and filling his hands with oil, not caring that it slopped onto the blanket. He slathered me, unhooking my bra to toss it away too, then cradling breasts, stroking belly and buttocks, shoulders and neck, face, his hands omnipresent, roving, reveling, dispelling awkwardness, creating a new galaxy for us in which I began to swab him too, chest, belly, groin. Underwear magically gone, we lay on the blanket now, slithering over and around each other, frolicking worshipping porpoises. Slap, suck, slick, salt-light gold. Groans rose to fill the room, primal arias.

You get the picture. We let go. I'd had reasonably good sex before, but nothing like that. I sensed the same was true for him. It was sex far beyond a mere bodily exchange, so it became a new language and suggested the presence of a world I'd never known existed. Before I left, overcome by the sense I'd been irreparably altered and needing to be alone to think things over, he held my waist, brought his face close to mine.

"I thought it might be like that. I began to imagine it when I was massaging your foot. The way you groaned—it did something to me. It's hard to explain. I guess I've never heard anyone expressing pleasure so honestly."

"That's why you kept pressing?"

He nods. "A rare thing, you."

I was a rare thing. I couldn't get over it. It wasn't possible, not for the ignored middle daughter, sandwiched between two talented sisters who loved being the center of attention: Sue a debate team champion all through high school, so articulate and persuasively logical she was destined to become the litigator she is today; Sally who excelled at the violin and played in the Junior Boston Symphony, and ended up teaching private lessons though she could have been a professional performing musician had she chosen to be. In that context I had always been content to occupy the sidelines, the conciliator with whom no one had to compete.

Now I'd been noticed, admired, desired. Now I was rare. *Rare.* Do you have any idea how that feels?

5

On the first official day of the trial I reported for duty hungover and exhausted, a headache parked at both temples, so I was relieved to be told what to do by the court staff, as I wouldn't have been able to generate any sensible action on my own.

There were fourteen of us, twelve jurors and two alternates. The judge's assistant Lenore, the power-hungry pantsuit woman from the day before, rules-stickler and burgeoning petty tyrant, lined us up just so and only reluctantly allowed one of the other jurors to use the restroom. She distributed our badges and led us through the courthouse maze, up and down and around, others in the hallway regarding us warily as if we were untouchables, until we arrived at what was called the "jury room." Dominated by a long rectangular table with twelve chairs, a few extra seats around the room's periphery, a smaller table with coffee and hot water, it was a surprisingly undistinguished location for important decision-making. The bathroom was almost penal, a cubicle with sink and toilet carved from a corner of the room and separated by a thin plywood door that allowed for no aural privacy. "Make yourselves comfortable," Lenore instructed us. "We'll summon you soon."

I chose a seat on the room's periphery as far from Drew as possible, the long table a bulwark between us. Being on the jury with him may or may not have been illegal, but it didn't seem right; worse, it placed me in a personal firestorm. His presence was dredging up memories I didn't want to revisit. Not only the unpleasant demise of our relationship, that was the least of it—there were other worse nemeses. My father was there, barking irrelevant instructions, and in his wake that insouciant teenage duo, Jeff and Dan. I still wanted to obliterate those two.

I immersed myself in my phone, checking email, mostly junk, the news which was the usual horror show, and Facebook which I despise but occasionally visit to lurk around its edges. I was waiting for myself to take some action to fix what was out of whack, when something dawned on me: I had stopped actively loving or hating Drew years ago, telling myself I was neutral, but now I could see that the hate and love were still alive in me, side by side, dormant but not dead. What did love plus hate amount to now, eight years past their active phases?

An intervention was needed. I could and should ask someone—our chaperone Lenore or one of several stony-faced, seemingly inter-changeable bailiffs—to notify the judge that there were grounds for my release. But I couldn't get myself to move; passivity encased me like hardening magma. I didn't understand it; I'd been known to be lazy, but I wasn't passive. Even my hangover didn't account for it.

Drew kept to his side of the room. It was impossible to tell what he was thinking. I fixed a slant eye on him as he chatted with three wom-en: the wholesome young blonde, a woman with waist-length gray hair the texture of straw, and an attractive Latina in impeccable business attire. Their conversation was friendly and energetic, governed by Drew. A grayer Drew than I'd known—he had turned fifty-two in May, I'd turned forty-nine in March—and beardless, but still in most ways identical to the man I'd married. Elsewhere in the room other jurors were introducing themselves to each other, but no one approached me.

Lenore led us into the courtroom, a march with all the joy of a walk to the gallows. We proceeded in strict order according to our assigned seats in the jury box: alternates first, #14 and #13, as they sat in two seats behind the rest of us; then the back row: #7, #6, #5, #4, #3 (me, not my favorite number), #2, and #1; then the front row: #12, #11, #10 (Drew), #9, #8. Drew was five places behind me in the marching line, so I was already in my seat by the time he took his in front of me, almost the same place he'd sat during voir dire but a little to my left, so I could see the side of his face when he gazed straight ahead. I was glad he wasn't behind me—I wanted to be the one doing the looking. Before he sat, he glanced back at me briefly and smiled and I didn't avoid his gaze this time. To anyone observing, the look we exchanged was probably understood as the brief regard of disinterested strangers. For me, there was no denying the needles of communication darting between us, but I was unable to read him as I used to and felt more awkward than angry. Nothing felt right.

"All rise."

The judge exploded through the door from her chambers and scuttled up to her perch, reminiscent of a beach crab, low to the ground and predatory. When she was settled, Lenore announced the court was going on record. A display of red digital numbers fired up beneath the judge's bench, frantic and inexorable and impossible to ignore—at least for me, a numbers person—counting down the hours, the minutes, the seconds, as if to remind each one of us our time was roaring to its end. I felt myself being swallowed into another shaft of time in which experience would balloon and slow, where the sameness of the room and the cast of characters in it would be at odds with the drama of the events narrated, where the weeks of the trial and the subsequent days of deliberation would also seem to fill years, crammed with a swill of feelings, revisited and relived, phantoms from past lives appearing unbidden, and geysers of new parallel feelings bubbling up in our bellies, including the terror that we might someday be on trial ourselves, the frightening realization that no human life is safe or unique.

You've felt this way too?

"The defendant before you . . ." the prosecutor, Ms. McCarthy, began. She wore a standard-issue professional woman's gray suit, a white collared shirt beneath the jacket, brown shoes with clunky two-inch heels, not a touch of fashion flair or personal style. While she addressed the jury directly, she kept her distance from us, as if not wanting to be seen as too intrusive or pandering. She gestured to Jessie who maintained her dignified posture.

"Jessie Snell is a powerful woman. She was born on the Alaska frontier in a home heated by wood, miles from the closest town." (*I was right,* I thought.) "She learned early how to take care of herself. She is older by four years than her deceased husband Eric Hotchkiss, and, as a trust and wills attorney, she made far more money than he did. In their relationship, she held all the cards."

The defendant was *an attorney*?!

"Her husband Eric worked as an EMT and was known for his gentleness. He desperately wanted to have a baby, but the defendant was dead set against having a child. She was controlling, refusing to take birth control pills and often refusing to have sex at all, consenting only when he agreed to use a condom. Emasculated, he sought solace in an affair. When the defendant learned of the affair from a private detective on the day of the murder, she was infuriated. That afternoon she went to the home of the Eric's lover, Lily, and threatened her. Then Jessie returned to work. At home that evening, she did not confront Eric immediately. She waited until they were at a party together a few blocks from their home. There, in public, she announced to the gathered group that Eric was having an affair. He was humiliated and they quarreled. She left and he followed. At home, inebriated and angry at one another, they continued to fight. Eric was repentant. He begged to be forgiven, assured her that the affair meant nothing, that she was the one he loved. He said he would terminate the affair immediately. How do we know this? The defendant has reported this conversation herself."

I searched Jessie's sealed stoic face, found no signs of corroboration or denial.

"After this conversation they had sex. This was not rape as the defense would have you believe, this was consensual sex, a husband and wife making love in an attempt to repair things. Forensics will show you there was no sign of a struggle during sex. After the sex, however, the defendant became angry again, furious her husband had not used a condom. She was so irate she called 911 and said she'd been raped. You will hear a recording in which she says to the 911 operator: *I'm gonna kill him.* That right there says it all—she had the *intent to kill.*"

Jessie's shoulders rose with a sudden irregular intake of breath. Was I the only one who noticed?

"And guess what, folks? Minutes later she *did* kill him, having already announced her intention, knowing full well what she was doing.

She hit him hard on the head with an unopened wine bottle. He collapsed, hitting the edge of the coffee table as he fell. He lay on the floor unconscious, his brain hemorrhaging. Then, as he lay there, already dead, she *cut his penis with a shard of broken glass.*" McCarthy paused, allowing distasteful images to fill our brains.

"This was not, as the defense will have you believe, an act of self-defense. She was the aggressor here, the one who was pushing and hitting. Forensics will show you the defensive bruises on his forearms, scratches on his face, his skin cells beneath the defendant's fingernails. The defense will try to excuse her actions by telling you that she suffered from Post-Traumatic Stress Disorder, which impeded her ability to think clearly. But this is a woman who has always prevailed in situations of stress. This is a woman who may be her *best* when under stress. This is a woman who ran the Iditarod, 1,000 miles alone with her dogs through blinding snow and blistering cold. She didn't succumb to PTSD then and she didn't the night of the murder. The defendant before you is not a shrinking violet, not someone who falls apart. She's a smart, calculating woman who is accustomed to thriving in a man's world, and who has always had to be in control. She killed her husband, Eric Hotchkiss, not by accident, but because he spurned her, and she felt she'd lost control of him. *Jessie Snell wanted him dead.*"

She bit off the final word *dead* and stood rooted in place, letting her story sink in around the courtroom. *Wanted him dead. Dead, dead, dead.* The words ricocheted off the acoustic tiles and traveled visibly over the musculature of all the faces in the room. Even the judge's face seemed to quiver. Perhaps she, too, was envisioning the cut penis. Stunned as I was, I was having trouble suppressing a nervous laugh. In front of me, Drew remained unresponsive; I imagined he—and all the men present—had to feel squeamish.

Counselor McCarthy sat. Jessie's posture was no longer regal. Her angular shoulders curved forward as if she'd taken a bullet to the chest. Ms. McCarthy's tone and volume may have been carefully modulated, but her words were invective, cruel as any bullet or dart, intended to destroy and diminish and present themselves as the only acceptable narrative. How could anyone, from now on, see Jessie as not guilty? I resolved in that moment to give her the benefit of the doubt.

My pulse raced, a rare occurrence for me. Was it last night's wine? Or was it this confrontation with murder and a savaged penis? The other jurors did not seem to be responding in any particular way. How was it possible not to feel riled? Jessie was writing on a notepad. She ripped off a sheet and slipped it to Vitale who read what she'd written and nodded.

The defense's opening argument was supposed to come next, but Vitale approached the bench and mumbled something to the judge and Lenore called for a break. A break now? Why? Did it have to do with Jessie's note? No one told us. Knowledge here, I was beginning to understand, was a game of control. The facts would be doled out one by one, carefully and abstemiously. *Hold your questions, we'll get there in time.* We were not supposed to be overeager. We were not supposed to think too much. *Mute your intelligence; don't make connections yet.* Such a sham, this supposition of control. You can't tell people not to think when, as I've said, thinking is exactly what we human beings are designed to do.

We filed out, back to the windowless jury room which smelled stale, sickening really. I've never been hypersensitive to toxins—they're one of the many unavoidable perils of being alive—but in that close room it was impossible not to notice. Fire retardants? Insect repellants? Asbestos? The building dated back to the last century, and it didn't look as if it had undergone much upgrading.

I wended my way to the coffee table, jumbled thoughts stuck on Jessie, on how successfully the prosecutor's words had already defeated her. This woman who had run the Iditarod and cut a man's penis, whatever that meant. Had she cut it *all the way off* like Lorena Bobbitt?

In a room this small, Drew was unavoidable. I felt him watching me as I opened the tap on the coffee urn. He came up behind me, muscling in to help himself to hot water for tea. We stood shoulder to shoulder, busying ourselves getting drinks. Heat roared off him. My entire pelt puckered in an attempt to fend off his encroachment.

I'd mistakenly served myself decaf. I began again with a fresh cup and had to wait for one of the other jurors—all still strangers, this one a sixty-something housewife type—to finish before I could access the regular coffee. Drew remained beside me, sifting through the basket of teabags, taking his time. Remarkably, I was not the least bit skittish. I felt solid and immovable like that song about the tree standing by the water: *I shall not be moved.* I wasn't going anywhere. I was taking a page out of Jessie's book, the stalwart Jessie of yesterday, not the vanquished Jessie of today.

Cup full, I searched for cream. It was in Drew's hand. He was keeping it from me—no, he was offering it to me. Nothing a stranger wouldn't do, but of course he wasn't a stranger. I took it with a brief nod of thanks, still without regarding him. Then, reconsidering, I looked up.

"Thank you," I said. I smiled toothlessly, unsure what I wanted to communicate.

"Of course," he said.

If he could be stoic, I could be too. I wasn't going anywhere. Right then and there I abandoned the idea of alerting Lenore, or one of the bailiffs, or the judge. I'd been selected for this jury and I would stay and do my duty and find out the truth about Jessie. Drew could make his own choice and, if he chose to stay, we would be cordial with each other, and our past liaison would remain sealed between us. We were both rational grown-ups.

6

What has more bearing, the argument you hear first, or the one you hear last? You remember better what you heard last, but isn't the first thing more indelibly etched on the brain? There must be studies.

We had heard Jessie described as a murderer. We had seen her slump as if she accepted that description of herself. How were we to be convinced by the defense attorney that this was not true? The guy was dead. She'd cut his penis. I was determined to remain open, but I worried about how the other jurors might be reacting.

Counselor Vitale stood close to the jury box, bearing down. In dramatic caesura, he scanned us, lingering on each person, nodding a little.

"I can see on your faces that you've all lived complicated lives. You know that people are not exclusively one thing or another, that we all change according to circumstance. And we're certainly not 100 percent good or 100 percent bad." There was a touch of the Bronx in his voice, a street argot he'd learned to keep in check. "You have your extremes, of course—Charles Manson on one end of the scale, Mother Theresa on the other—but those are exceptions. Most of us are somewhere in the middle, muddling through as best we can.

"I'm not here to tell you that my client is Mother Theresa. It's undeniable she played a role in the death of her husband. But what role is that exactly? Before the law, nuances matter. Intentions matter. My client is not a heartless killer as the prosecution would have you believe. She did not want her husband dead. Far from it. She loved her husband, and when she discovered he was having an affair she wanted to work things out. On the morning of the day in question she learned from a private detective about Eric's affair. She went by Eric's lover's house and confirmed that, yes indeed, Eric and Lily had been sleeping together for three months. But when she returned home from work that day, Eric was not there, and when he returned home at 7:00 p.m., it was clear he had been drinking, and he quickly departed again for the party down the street, so there was no time to talk. After an hour or so, uncertain what to do with herself, she went to the party too. No longer able to contain herself, she confronted him about his affair.

"Let's look more closely at these two individuals. Jessie Snell is not the one who called the shots in this marriage. Yes, she is older than her husband by four years and she made more money than he did. But Eric Hotchkiss's assets were more consequential.

"For one thing, there was his physical size. He was 6'4" and he weighed upwards of 250 pounds. He was all muscle, known for being able to lift his EMT patients easily. Jessie, as you can see, is also muscular, but she, at 5'5", is almost a foot shorter than Eric was, and she's less than half his weight. Physically, he could do with her what he wanted. Furthermore, he had a history of violence—she had good reason to be afraid of him. He had recently been suspended from his work because he had punched out his partner.

"I'd like to direct your attention to a more important source of power Eric possessed—the class advantage. Yes, Jessie is a high-wage earner, very successful in her career in wills and estates law, but Eric came from old money back East. New York. Manhattan, to be specific. He had a sizable bank account and a trust fund to the tune of millions awaiting him when he turned thirty. This held enormous sway over Jessie who, as you have heard, grew up on the Alaskan frontier in a family that could barely make ends meet. Everything she had in the world, she made for herself. Everything he had was given to him. He used this background to control her."

Like an actor milking his monologue, Vitale strolled from one side of the jury box to the other, surprisingly nimble for a man of such mass.

"There's another critical thing you need to know about this dyad. Jessie did not want children. From the get-go she said this—it was a condition of their marriage. She knew how easily kids can be damaged, and she knew this because she herself had been damaged as a young person. Her father was an alcoholic who abused her sexually from the time she was thirteen until she left home at the age of seventeen. She never told her husband about this abuse, though she has suffered from the effects of PTSD all her life. She did not like to take pills of any kind because they affected her badly, so she urged Eric to have a vasectomy. But he refused. He harbored the belief that she would relent and agree to have his children. Meanwhile, he had agreed to use condoms.

"Let us turn our attention to the night in question. When the couple returned home after the party, Eric was furious that she had outed him about his affair. The verbal argument escalated into pushing and shoving. She admits to shoving him, but then he pushed her back with such force that she fell, landing on one hand and fracturing her wrist. The pain was paralyzing. And as she lay there on the living room floor in shock, he began sweet-talking her, apologizing and saying he would stop the affair. Then, he took advantage of her compromised state and, as she lay there in pain, he undressed himself, took off her pants, and entered her without a condom. This was not, my friends, consensual sex. This was rape.

"When Jessie realized what had happened, she ran to the study, locked the door and called 911. On that call you can hear him yelling in the background, calling her a bitch and a cunt. When he realized the door was locked he broke it down—you can hear that crash on the phone call too. She dropped the phone and ducked out to the living room. He followed, grabbed her broken wrist. She screamed in pain and bit his hand. Then he grabbed her hair, which she wore that night loose and long.

"This, my friends, is important. Having her hair touched was a trigger for Jessie, because that was exactly what her father used to do to force her to have sex with him—he would grab her hair, holding her in place. That night, in pain from her broken wrist, and Eric holding her hair, she was terrified. Eric had the power not only to rape her, but the power to kill her as well. So she reached for the closest thing at hand, the wine bottle, and she used it to hit him.

"In that moment Jessie was not the strong Iditarod driver, she was a little girl, defenseless, desperate, needing to do whatever she could to escape. She had no idea Eric would fall and hit his head on the coffee table, a blow that knocked him unconscious and eventually caused his death. She thought he would revive and rape her again—or kill her. In her state of confusion—a fugue state, a symptom of PTSD, characterized by irrational thinking—she cut the member that had been the lifelong source of her pain. There was no long-term malice here, no intent to kill. She loved this man, but her past had blighted her, and she would not, no matter what, agree to have children.

"That night Jessie Snell was afraid for her life, and she did what she had to do to survive. The death that resulted in that living room was an act of self-defense, a justifiable homicide."

So, there we were. Loving couple? Of course they weren't. A woman with murderous intent? That, too, seemed doubtful. A woman with *no* intent to harm her husband? Equally impossible to believe. I couldn't help thinking about all the stuff those cherry-picking lawyers had neglected to say.

How the heat must have crept everywhere that summer night, lodging under the skin of Jessie and Eric like blood-sucking parasites, fomenting decibels of rage they'd never seen in themselves, and making it impossible, through the haze of their inebriation, to see each other clearly.

And what about the socio-economic differences between them? Maybe a mere glitch at the beginning, something they were sure they could overcome in the early days of their love but, after three years of marriage, those differences had become a virus that replicated with the slightest of prompts, so misunderstandings morphed into hatred, not on display all the time, but often enough that anyone who knew them wouldn't have been surprised if they'd parted ways. Nor would it have surprised their acquaintances if *she,* instead of he, had ended up dead.

Words are informative sometimes, sure, but that's rarely all they are. More often they enable human beings to deceive and prevaricate, to control others, to dupe people into purchasing things, to vote in certain ways, to believe in wacky dogmas. I was a PhD candidate in English before I quit and became captivated by numbers; I'd seen how literature reveres language with the most possible meanings—double entendres and subtext—not the clarion language that signifies a single thing. Think of the simple phrase *I love you,* how often it means *I wish I loved you,* or *I used to love you,* or even, *I hate you.*

But I'm preaching to the choir. You know this as well as I do. Words carefully arranged can prove anything. So, I heard those opening statements as nothing more than articulate legalese, stories dressed up to appeal to our basest emotions, offered up to us by a sanctimonious woman with a stick up her ass and a wannabe stand-up comic suffering from hyperhidrosis.

No, I'm not overreacting. Exaggeration is the purview of my attention-seeking sisters. I'm the one who has always been called upon to weigh in rationally.

7

It took several years for my suspicion of words to grow into full-grown rebellion. From childhood I'd always been an avid reader, so when I got to college becoming an English major seemed like the path of least resistance. As an undergraduate at Boston University, English courses were a game to me, a fun challenge. You pick up literary jargon as if learning a foreign language, you figure out how to lace your papers with quotes, you become expert at properly citing your sources. I enjoyed it, though I never took it seriously. We weren't doing anything significant, nothing that would benefit the world, but it passed the time and got me through graduation. At the end of four years the least stressful next choice was to apply to graduate school in English. At the time it seemed like the path to a vocation—I had no idea how meager and unreliable that vocation would turn out to be, but the illusion of a vocation brought me west, to enroll in a PhD program.

At the graduate level there was a distinct shift in emphasis. The professors were obsessed with critical theory. No one seemed to care anymore about the original texts. It was as if the books I'd always loved reading—the Modernists like Faulkner and Woolf and Joyce—had become mere backdrops for showcasing theory. During my first year as a grad student I mostly played along. I was raised, as most women are, to be compliant and, while I've always harbored a certain inborn defiance, I mostly keep it in check. But I found myself sitting in class feeling irked by the endless pointless wheel-spinning among my classmates, the nit-picking and one-upmanship about ideas that held no weight in the world and no interest to anyone beyond academia. Who cared about Butler's belief in embodied cognition, or Kristeva's French feminism, or Barthes's semiotics, or Lacan's theory of the split subject? *Not I*, said the Little Red Hen. I sat in most of my classes flinching.

The situation was made worse by the advisor I'd been assigned to, Professor Chadwick Bigelow. He was a man in his mid-forties who wore a soul patch and always sported something purple—a shirt, a tie, a baseball cap, even shoes, once—as if this was evidence of his great daring. But this quirk of style could not conceal a fundamental conservatism and overall anxiety. He was a Chaucer scholar who had spent most of his professional life reading and rereading Chaucer, and writing books and articles that floated new and esoteric theories about Chaucer's relevance to world history and pestilence and migration and climate change. Reading his work led you to the belief that Chaucer was the lynchpin for understanding the entire cosmos. He was known for his performative lectures in which he would recite memorized sections of *The Canterbury Tales* and impersonate the characters, as if he was preparing himself for a one-man show on Broadway. "You should see him as the Wife of Bath," one of my classmates had said, rolling her eyes.

In our meetings it was hard to imagine him as an acclaimed performer, as he was often irritable and always disinterested in anything I had to say, though I rarely said much. He usually seemed eager to conclude our meetings as quickly as he could. Occasionally he would quiz me about what I had or hadn't read of the canon, exposing my gaps as if they were willful transgressions and lecturing me about the future professional consequences of such gaps. How could I possibly proclaim myself a Modernist if I hadn't read *all* of Joyce, even *Finnegan's Wake*?! When his mood was good he boasted about his latest publications without an ounce of shame. It was my unstated job to act impressed—I remember nodding a lot—and to say I planned to read whatever he'd written, though I never did. I endured those torturous meetings because they were mandatory.

Sometimes I would see him in the hallways currying favor with his colleagues, a performance that was an unsettling amalgam of bluster and obsequiousness, and it would remind me that he, an associate professor, was still hoping for promotion to full professorship.

I honestly felt a little sorry for Bigelow, at his advanced age being so worried about his status, but at the end of that first year my pity dissolved. All the grad students taught freshman composition our first year, but thereafter we were free to apply for a few available slots for teaching the introductory literature class, which was a lot more fun. I thought I had a good shot at getting one of those positions, but I would need Bigelow's recommendation. In our spring meeting, Bigelow wore a purple necktie that he stroked as he addressed me.

"I'm not going to be able to recommend you for the lit position," he said.

"Why not? I've done really well in all my classes and my teaching evaluations are good."

"Yes, but—" He pursed his lips and shook his head as if declaring me a lost cause. "It's an attitude issue. You don't seem avid like some of the other students. I daresay you occasionally appear disdainful." He paused. "And I'm not the only one who sees this."

They'd been discussing me? "Who else?" I said.

"I'm not at liberty to say."

I knew it was unlikely I'd be able to convince him of my qualifications, so I said nothing. A month after that meeting I learned that the three jobs had gone to two men, neither one a bright light, and a pretty blonde ass-licker.

I returned the second year determined to forge ahead, but a crack had opened, and my doubt and dissatisfaction poured into it. Writing those jargon-filled papers was no longer an amusing game. No one seemed to care about clean, clear sentences. The whole academic enterprise began to feel like a sham, a way to announce your smarts and keep the general public at arm's length. I dropped out of the program, unpedigreed, after fall term.

I had already been helping friends with their taxes, and I realized that tax work could become a good source of income. I put out the word and people came. Later I got a CPA certificate that made it easier to peddle my skills, but at first I was uncredentialed and people still came. It surprised me to learn how many people are afraid of numbers.

I have always found them comforting because they're simply themselves, low on pretense.

My sisters and most of my friends thought it was odd that I chose to become an accountant. So boring, they said. Drew thought so too.

No one knows about the secret lives of accountants. Our profession doesn't spark the imagination. No one tries to picture our days, romanticizing us, wishing they could *be* us. As a group we are thought to be boring, and nothing will close off a conversation with a stranger as abruptly as telling them you're an accountant. It makes people yawn, or turn away, or both. Occasionally you get the *that's interesting* response, but no one really means it.

Here's what I know. Each number has a unique timbre. Some shiver with harmonics. The even numbers are major, the odd numbers minor. Some accountants, including me, have a mild version of synesthesia that links colors with numbers. The white of a 1. The green of a 7. The blue of an 8. Most of us have a favorite number. Not that we'd advertise this—it's mostly a private thing. You wouldn't want your taxes done by someone obsessed with the number 3.

Some numbers tunnel into your memory bank and stay there, refusing to move. The birthdays of old elementary school classmates, the number of nights you slept with a certain insignificant man. The date, 9-3, in early high school when you began to truly, permanently hate your father.

My favorite number is 8, a palindrome of a number, symmetrical and beautifully divisible. You can settle into an 8, stay there for a while then take a stroll, looping happily back to where you began. Eight is a cool blue, a resonant middle C. Push an 8 onto its side and it becomes ∞, infinity. This is one of the joys of what I do, taking custody of all those beautifully-endowed symbols and manipulating them, not only to deliver meaning, but also utility.

But that is only *part* of what I do. The other part is interfacing with my clients, who arrive at my office bearing stacks of paper. Some are paragons of organization, with everything paper-clipped and labeled and assigned to folders. W-2s, bank statements, investment records, spreadsheets showing deductions—everything so ordered my work is practically done. Others are car wrecks, dumping bags full of random papers on my desk, scraps covered with hair and coffee stains, irrelevant bank statements, receipts from purchases that can't be deducted, records from the wrong year. No worries, I sort it out, that's my job. In that corner of my life I'm exceedingly organized.

But here's the thing. Everyone, male or female, disorganized or not, is in some state of high emotion when they come to me. It may not be discernible to the casual observer, but I see it as soon as they take the seat across from me and begin to dig for their papers, laying them anxiously along the edge of my desk. They eye me skittishly, or with stony stares, depending on their personalities. They see me as their judge. Perhaps they have made too little money and they feel inadequate. Perhaps they have spent too much money they didn't have. Maybe they made a great deal of money but gave too little to charity. Maybe they're worried about an astronomical tax bill. Maybe they're embarrassed by their poor record-keeping. I am the only one who knows these things—I must know in order to serve them—so they hand me a broad omniscience that reduces them in my presence. *Am I okay?* they seem to ask. *Will I be okay in the future? Am I good enough?*

It is oft-discussed that money is a more taboo topic in our culture than sex. Possibly in all cultures. You can be pretty darn sure my clients aren't discussing their finances with their friends and neighbors—when did you last share a beer with friends and discuss these things?

When I start crunching the numbers, the tap-tap of my calculator indicates the job has been handed over to me, and they begin to relax and talk. Because my focus is on the labor at hand and my gaze is averted, they don't seem to understand how closely I'm listening. Perhaps they feel free to confide in me because they're sure I'll forget—but no, I hear and absorb and remember everything.

The guy, nervous as hell, who doesn't want his wife to know the investments he's made have tanked.

A woman who's furious she didn't get the raise she was promised.

Another man who was laid off and spent two of his three months of unemployment vacationing in Hawaii, blowing through his savings, and now he's full of remorse, can't believe what he's done.

A woman whose mother died unexpectedly, leaving her a small sum of money, but the daughter hates that money—she only wants her mother alive again.

A single father whose son is failing to launch himself and, though the father knows he should stop giving his son money, he can't bring himself to stop.

They want my advice, my blessing, my forgiveness. I become not only judge, but therapist and priest. Some of them weep, not conspicuously, but I see, while pretending not to. The bowl of candy and tissues on my desk are there to console them. They help themselves freely, some squirreling extra candy into pockets and purses. I square away the numbers while they suck and masticate and blow their noses. When I'm done, I offer them ballpark estimates and tell them when they can expect to pick up their completed returns. I say very little about anything else, but nevertheless they leave my office cleansed, as if they've been through a kind of exorcism. Their problems remain, but they've shared their secrets, which is, in itself, a kind of relief.

I told all of this to Drew, and he described a parallel experience with the clients who came to him, wanting him to "fix" their bodies. They wanted him to lay hands on a painful body part and make the pain go away instantly. He did employ a certain amount of manual manipulation in his practice, but to heal fully and deeply, the patient had to do some work herself. She had to be dutiful in the exercises he prescribed, not just for a couple of weeks, but often for months on end. It was the sad part of his work, he said, that so many people dropped the ball, unwilling to put in the effort. The exercises were hard and boring and they took time. More often than not people stopped coming to him after a few sessions—they probably went to their doctors for prescriptions, he said, a quicker route to painlessness, but not to overall health.

It was the handful of patients who did follow through on the exercises, week after week, month after month, who made his work rewarding. It wasn't always the ballet dancer or the marathon runner who persisted. Sometimes it was the truck driver who had neck and shoulder issues, or the supermarket clerk whose knees and feet were sore from hours of standing at the register. Grit, he said, was not something you could see from the outside.

Drew could talk about his work endlessly (one of the many things he liked to hold forth about). He discussed fascia and tendons and ligaments and bones, but muscles were his true love. The attention he paid to them reminded me of an art curator—or perhaps a collector of agates, or maybe a master of baseball trivia. In short, aficionado cum fanatic. He would describe how muscles worked in groups, demonstrating with particular motions or poses and telling me which muscles were activated in performing them. A reaching arm. A leg lifted. A back bending forward to pick up a box. Sometimes he jogged slowly around the living room, pointing out the specific muscles of his legs and abdomen at work. He particularly enjoyed discussing the muscles people ignored, the ones that *should* be used instead of the ones that *were* being used—often that was the source of pain, he said. Posture and ergonomics should be a part of the elementary school curriculum, according to him; most adults would be a lot happier if they'd been taught early to move in proper alignment.

Sometimes he urged me to stroll around the living room myself, and he would analyze my gait. I was using my quads too much, he said, when I should be using my hip muscles, the gluteus maximus and the piriformis. I needed to activate the adductors of my inner thighs and spread the weight more evenly across my feet. But I'd been walking in my own way for close to thirty years by then—how was I supposed to change? For a few days I would try to keep his advice in mind, walking everywhere deliberately and awkwardly, until I found the whole project untenable, and I'd lapse back into my old habits like the worst of his patients.

You're amused? I was too. Often it was hard not to laugh when he got into one of his muscle lectures. He appeared a tad crazy as he flexed and relaxed his biceps or stood on one leg, extending the other straight out, remaining there for minutes on end as he described the interactions of flexors and extensors. He was an undeniably beautiful physical specimen—and he knew it.

But I digress.

I speak of words and your first thought is sex? Haven't you heard enough about my sex life? I don't see what bearing it has.

Okay, okay. Yes, the sex remained good for most of our thirteen years together. That isn't so unusual, is it? We developed certain habits, I guess you'd say.

A few days after the first time we had sex, we were having gin and tonics in his backyard, bathed in rose twilight, the backdrop for many of the best times in our relationship. We would be having sex soon, but now we were savoring the fullness and promise of *before*, the anticipation and innuendo; every blade of moving grass and passing fly signified something crucial, a mystery about to reveal itself to us alone. We chuckled at everything. Chuckling as breathing. Chuckling as the grammar of satisfaction. Our bodies were readying themselves, emitting the necessary fluids, tissues swelling with blood. Even if we didn't touch each other at all, the sheer force of our imagining brains could have made us come.

My arm was balanced on the chair's arm rest. He reached out and laid his forefinger on my pinky nail. Just that, no more, and my system flushed with energized blood.

"Dem bones, dem bones, dem dry bones . . ." Half singing, half chanting, he rose and crouched by my chair, gazing at my arm which he took into both hands. I let it go limp.

"The phalanges connected to the meta-car-pal . . . the metacarpal connected to the car-pal . . . the carpal connected to the ra-dius . . ."

His fingers traveled up my arm, lightly articulating my anatomy, electrocuting me as if I was a skeleton coming back to life.

"The radius connected to the hu-mer-us . . . The humerus connected to the cla-vi-cle . . . Below the clavicle you got that ster-num . . . Across the sternum you got the—" he paused, sighed, "booooob flesh." He closed his eyes and sighed again, then, eyes still closed, "Now hear the word of the Lord."

He took my hand and led me to the living room where he pulled the blinds and laid out the blanket as he'd done before. I'd never been such a willing follower.

"I'm Bony and you're Boobs. Bony wants to come between Boobs' breasts."

There he brought to life our new personas, Bony and Boobs. My extra flesh was a source of explosive forbidden pleasure for him, not surprising for a man who had come of age in a religious family that eschewed pleasure of all kinds. He immersed himself in my orifices, journeyed the lengths and depths of my curves and fissures, drank in my smells, kneading and groaning and trying, with his supreme talent of self-control, not to come too soon.

Perhaps this is the time to tell you that Drew shaved much of his body. Initially I took his hairlessness to be a natural condition, but once, during sex, I detected stubble on his legs. It took me a while to bring my observation to his attention, as I wasn't sure how he would react, but then, in a moment of post-sex languor, I summoned the hutzpah.

"Do you really shave your whole body?" I should not have used the world *really,* but it slipped out.

He pointed to his beard, smiling a little but clearly embarrassed.

"But your legs? Your chest? Your arms?"

"It allows my patients to see the musculature more clearly."

"Oh," I said, flummoxed, wondering if that was really his reason.

"You shave your legs, don't you?"

"Yes, but I'm—" I couldn't bring myself to say *a woman.* It seemed so passé to believe that should make a difference. Why shouldn't he shave if he wanted to? "I don't mean to criticize. It's fine. I mean, it does make for smooth sex."

Once he believed I didn't judge him, he gave me a demonstration. He stood in the shower and raised one leg to a ninety-degree angle, placing his foot against the shower wall. Then he drew a straight razor from his ankle clear up to his crotch, creating a discernible path through the scant stubble, neat as a mown lawn. He was breathing slowly and deeply as if engaged in a meditative spiritual practice. After working on both legs, he moved on to his chest and arms, deploying

the straight razor with impressive dexterity over the contours of muscle. He was deft even when he used his left hand, and I never once saw
evidence of a single nick.

So, there you have it—conclude what you will.

The sessions I've described laid the foundation of our sex life, the
ligature of our entire relationship, and they were repeated hundreds,
no, *thousands* of times in our thirteen years together. At first, delighted as I was by his desire for me, I was also puzzled by it, but I gradually
came to understand how my body released him. He, who had not an
ounce of adipose tissue, whose fit smooth body was a source of pride,
could explore and exploit my breasts and buttocks and belly, reveling
in my extra flesh without having to wear it on his own body. And, as
the name Boobs suggests, he thought of me as his mother too, not all
the time but often during sex. When he donned his Bony persona and
laid his head between my breasts, painting me with his viscous brown
eyes, he became a child in need of succor, and I gave him succor freely.

He assembled a storehouse of props. In addition to all kinds of oils—
olive oil, but also coconut, avocado, jojoba—there were dildos, metal
balls for my vagina, lacy bras with holes for the nipples, pantyhose he
wore himself so I could caress him through the sheer nylon then cut a
hole to suck him off, finger in his anus. The oil flowed freely everywhere
on both of us, no body part was off limits. Sometimes he hummed as
he explored me, sometimes, Body Specialist that he was, he whispered
the names of muscles and bones. *Latissimus dorsi, teres major, vastus
medialis.* As if they were the names of sacred objects, or ancient cities, or
astounding little-known queens.

8

Milling around the jury room on the second official day of the trial—still impossibly aware of Drew but resolute in ignoring him—it occurred to me that I had to do something I didn't normally do: befriend the other jurors. We were colleagues after all. Team members, comrades, confederates, whatever you chose to call us, we would have to work together. Technically we'd already begun to work together, though so far it had only consisted of parallel listening.

Coffee in hand, I sidled up to a group of four women. I introduced myself with a quip about the terrible weather we were having and what a relief it was to come inside to a room without windows. They regarded me strangely—the weather, though promising to become hot as the day advanced, was sunny and clear, in other words, notably nice. It dawned on them slowly, smiles appearing on their faces one by one like rising dominos, that I was making a joke.

There was Chrystal, who sat to my right in the jury box, a soigné Latina with anxious brown eyes; Shanti Moonbeam (a name she said she'd taken in her twenties), an aging hippie, wearing a loose hemp tunic over loose hemp pants, with gray hair that ran clear to her waist, soft-spoken, but not the least bit shy; Joanne, one of the alternates, a solid sixty-something woman who described herself as a housewife; and Anna, the wholesome college student, an Environmental Studies major, who was much too eager to please. They drew me in, pleased I was no longer making myself an outsider, and they pointed out the other two women they'd met the day before: Karen, perilously thin, hair trimmed so short she almost looked bald, who sat in a chair against the wall, immersed in a paperback, a nurse, they said, very shy; and Neal, a woman whose largesse put mine into perspective, who was working on her laptop, an executive at the local power company, Chrystal said, raising her eyebrows as if cowed by Neal's importance.

They knew less about the men. Tom, the other alternate, was an electrician and "very nice," Joanne said. They had all met hyper-talkative Kevin, a mid-forties Walmart manager who routinely positioned himself at the center of the room and impressed me as a blowhard.

"And Drew," Anna said, pointing discretely. "He's great."

"Yes," Shanti agreed. "He's wonderful. I have a good feeling. I think we're a terrific group."

"Is anyone else scared?" Joanne whispered. "I don't know if I'm ready for this."

"I didn't expect anything so—serious," Chrystal said.

A sudden affection for these women bloomed.

It took two more break periods for me to identify the remaining men: Sean, a reserved Asian American programmer in his thirties; Dev, a beret-wearing linguistics grad student who appeared to think highly of himself and wore a perpetual, off-putting, Jack Nicholson grin; and Cory, a young sanitation worker who scarcely said a word and had latched onto Walmart Kevin, following him around like a sidekick.

Then there was Ray, who sat to my left in the jury box. He was a logger, or former logger, according to Shanti (who retained a remarkably clear memory of what people had said during voir dire when my attention was drifting). All I knew of Ray was that he emitted a caustic body odor which, sitting next to him, was impossible to escape. (Chrystal had noticed it too.) I tried to draw him out, but he only divulged his name and the rural town from which he hailed. He occupied the same corner of the jury room on all our breaks, sitting in the same chair nursing black coffee, forearms on his knees, gaze on the carpet, periodically glancing up and shaking his head as if we all offended him.

The Arresting Officer, the prosecution's first witness and first on the crime scene, was called to the stand. He was a young guy with a buzz cut and a soupçon of cockiness. McCarthy asked him to narrate what he'd seen when he arrived at the apartment on Lawrence Street on the "night in question."

The defendant answered the door, he said. She was distraught, crying, cradling her swollen wrist, clearly in pain and speaking rapidly. She wasn't holding back—even without prompting she was keen on telling him everything. It was like she wanted to get something off her chest, he said.

She and her husband had been fighting. Her husband pushed her hard, and she fell back and landed on her wrist. She suspected it might be broken. Looking at the puffy wrist, he thought she was probably right. It looked nasty. After she fell, she remained on the floor, disoriented, in pain, trying to get her bearings, and as she lay there, distracted and maybe in shock, her husband removed her pants and entered her without a condom. She would have tried to stop him if she'd known what he was doing, she said, but she was out of it. They'd had a deal apparently. According to her they always used condoms. When she realized what had happened, that he'd entered her without a condom, she was furious. It was rape, pure and simple, she said. She snapped to attention, rushed to the home office, and locked the door. She called 911 to report the rape. Her husband overheard her and, shouting, he broke down the door. She dropped the phone, ducked back into the living room. He lunged. She thought he was going to assault her again, maybe kill her.

After that, the Officer said, she couldn't remember exactly what happened. *Did you hit him?* he asked. She hesitated. *Maybe I did. Yes, I did. I hit him with a wine bottle.* She pointed to the shattered glass scattered around the victim. He examined the body. She hovered nearby. When he announced the victim was dead she acted surprised. He then noticed the penis. It had been sliced near the scrotum, and there was a shard of glass on the floor beside his thigh.

"I asked her: *Did you do this? Did you cut him?* And she was, like, in a daze. She said: *No, I don't think . . .* She paused and looked at me, pretty confused. Then she asked, *Did I? Do you think I did that?* It was like she thought maybe she had, but she couldn't remember for sure."

The Officer's delivery was even, almost monotone, as if none of what he'd seen that night mattered to him one way or another. A distraught woman who said she'd been raped. A naked dead man. Another day, another dollar. Only the cut penis seemed to affect him, because it was something he hadn't seen before, and after he mentioned it he paused and raised his eyebrows in unredacted commentary, but otherwise he reported these events as if they were everyday occurrences. Was that what it meant to be a beat cop, accepting as the norm that people were always living in close range of violence and death?

I tried to think back to moments in my own life when I might have forgotten what I'd done. I remembered a period of time when my younger sister Sally sleepwalked. Once she got up in the middle of the night and played a Mozart sonata on her violin, and the next morning she had no recollection of what she'd done. Another time she got herself a bowl of cereal, brought it back to bed, and awoke amidst a paste of cornflakes and milk without knowing why.

Don't we all forget certain things we do habitually, like locking the house, or brushing our teeth, or taking our vitamins? Cutting a penis, however, might be hard to forget.

The Officer had brought a recording with him—Jessie's call to 911. I did not want to hear that call—I knew it would be a strong gale, likely to flatten me. It might topple formidable Jessie too. She would have to listen along with the rest of us and relive the pivotal night when her life veered off course. Bracing myself, I sucked breath audibly, prompting a glare from Ray.

Her voice blasted through static, strafing the courtroom. *I've been raped.* A voice inflated with rage, with Doppler shifts in frequency as if we were all moving past each other.

Jessie's chin rose as if led by a string. Her eyes rested on the acoustic ceiling tiles, their dizzying assemblage of dots.

Okay, hon, hang in there. Where're you at? I need your address. Is he still there?

Yeah, he's here. I swear I'm gonna kill him.

Static. A background of blaring phones and raised voices. A man yelling—Eric?—*Bitch! Cunt!* Thunderous knocking followed by a crash.

Jessie's eyes were closed. Ms. McCarthy stepped toward the jury box and regarded us in her keeper-of-the-order way. *You all heard that?* her expression said.

My mind had taken on a Velcro quality. Details were sticking and I couldn't detach them. The sound of Eric's voice yelling *Bitch! Cunt!* Such ugly words, always spoken in a spume of rage. I was also stuck on the idea of knocking down a door. There had been no mention of his using a tool—had he used his hands to do that? I'd never tried to break down a locked door, but I was quite sure I couldn't do it.

We were shown an overhead shot of a beefy man lying naked on a dark green carpet, the corner of a wooden coffee table visible just above his head. On first glance, he could have almost been a man asleep, youthful and clean-shaven, face slack, arms and hands relaxing a few inches from his torso, legs slightly splayed. But the body looked powerful, even in death, with a barrel chest and weedy dark hair sprouting between prominent breast plates. Gradually I took in blood and wine pooling behind the head, the unusual coloration of the crotch.

For at least a minute we scrutinized the image of this naked stranger. This dead man. This well-born Eric Hotchkiss. Chrystal interlaced her hands. Ray's breathing morphed into a low growl. Drew's upper traps rose a couple of millimeters. Jessie stared down at the table. A journalist in the spectators' benches scribbled on his pad. Another spectator, a prim woman of late middle age, rummaged in her purse for a handkerchief.

A closer shot. Purple contusions on the left side of his face and head and ear where the wine bottle hit two or three times. Another shot of the broken skin at the base of his skull where, in falling, he had collided with the coffee table's corner. A brain scan photo revealing massive hemorrhaging.

The collective hush.

"And these contusions on the side of his head from the wine bottle's blow could have caused the hemorrhaging that was the cause of death?" McCarthy asked.

"Yes," said the Medical Examiner.

Then Vitale in cross-examination: "But the brain hemorrhaging could have been caused by the victim's head hitting the coffee table?"

Medical Examiner: "Yes."

Vitale: "So we cannot conclude definitively that the blow to the head was the cause of death?"

Medical Examiner: "That is correct."

Another close-up. Confusing at first. A rainbow of pink, purple, red, hints of blue. Human flesh. A penis, a scrotum, a bit of thigh. The scrotum was brown and textured as a fungi-covered rotting log, the penis flopped off to the right, curling in on itself as if to hibernate. It was crescent-shaped like a lobster tail, and bifurcated by a wiggly line near the scrotum, where it had been cut with the glass shard. The flesh yawned open, but there was only a trace of pinkish blood.

Everyone in the courtroom reacted in some way. Eyes narrowed, lips pursed, hands crept to shield crotches. Counselor Vitale cleared his throat—he didn't like this, but he'd seen it before. The prim woman in the spectators' benches stared into her lap. The journalist kept scribbling. Jessie's head hung at an odd angle, exposing her bony nape.

A break was called. Joanne, the housewife, steered herself to the toilet cubicle and vomited. We all heard and tried not to grimace. She emerged pale and shaking, found Lenore and begged to be excused. Everyone could hear their conversation which took place in the center of the room. She wasn't necessary here, she pleaded, she was only an alternate. We tried not to stare; we felt bad for Joanne. Lenore escorted her away, ostensibly to see the judge.

When court was called into session again, Joanne was back in her regular seat.

The Sexual Assault Nurse Examiner was short as a munchkin, with frizzy hair, a low voice, and a purposeful air. She had come there, it seemed, as a Guardian of the Good. She described, blow-by-blow, her

routine in any rape exam. First the victim is asked to narrate the attack. Then she removes her clothes to be offered as evidence. Then her
body is examined for external bruising. Nothing is done forcibly, the
nurse stressed, permission is asked at each point along the way. Photos are taken. Then myriad swabs and samples. Head and pubic hair.
Swabs from the vagina, the oral cavity, the anus and perineum. Blood
and urine samples. Skin cells from beneath the fingernails. All these
samples are sent to a lab for analysis.

The key points in Jessie's case: There were no signs of external bruising around the thighs or buttocks. There were no internal vaginal tears.
Yes, semen was present in the vagina.

Was this information supposed to tell us that Eric was a gentle
rapist?

I'd be remiss if I neglected to mention another thing Drew and I shared,
an element that cemented us almost as much as the sex. We both
thought the world was a cesspool and most people in it were thinly-
disguised assholes; insincere, crass, uncivil, avaricious, scared-as-shit
assholes. Drew, having grown up in a family in which swearing was a
sacrilege, loved saying that word *asshole* in the privacy of our home.
He would draw out the hiss, reveling in the linguistic insubordination.

We got together just over twenty years ago when things in the public
space were not half as bad as things are now, but even back then this was
our favorite subject. We would loll around after sex, absently touching
each other's bodies—he loved to play with my hair—relaying to each
other the most recent examples of bad behavior we'd witnessed that
gave credence to our thesis that people were fundamentally no good
and the world was in steep decline, our country in the lead, government
agencies populated by avaricious, morally corrupt ignoramuses who
were giving license to numerous other morally corrupt ignoramuses
to do whatever they wanted. We gloated over the incidents of incivility
and rudeness we'd witnessed: the people who blithely ignored stop
signs and sped through red lights, often those entitled young men I've
referred to; the people who honked at the old and infirm in crosswalks;
those who muscled to the front of a supermarket line pretending not

to see you when you'd been there waiting patiently all along. We saw incivility and rudeness wherever we looked. The world was going to hell.

We usually exempted our friends from these harsh judgments, but sometimes we saw evidence in them too of this *me-first, me-only* cult.

Such conversations made us feel smug about ourselves, yet we also worried aloud about whether we, too, might be unwittingly tainted by this ruthless, narcissistic cultural moment. *Tell me if I ever do anything like that*, we routinely said to each other. Drew, due to his religious upbringing, worried more than I did about the possibility of becoming a "bad" person. I gave lip service to the concern, but worried less actively about it, knowing that long ago I'd been tainted.

9

Really?
   Okay, okay, if you must . . .

When I was in sixth grade I came home from school one day to find my mother sobbing in the kitchen. My father, an attorney—yes, yet another attorney in this sorry tale!—had been arrested, charged with insider trading, embezzlement, and money laundering, words I had to look up to discover they were felonies. To this day I don't know a lot about his transgressions, beyond the fact that he was bilking some of the biggest clients in his firm. Our mother didn't want us to know the details, and I've never researched it. To what end? To corroborate that he was a bad man, something I already knew? He had always spent long hours at work, and I felt I hardly knew him—what I did know I wasn't fond of.

It took less than a week for most of my classmates to learn of the arrest. Most sixth-graders know little about discretion or kindness, and both girls and boys had no compunction about asking me what had happened, usually very loudly and publicly, their voices full of scorn. They weren't interested in real answers, only in humiliating me to assert their own stature. *Did your father commit a* crime? *Is he a gangster? Is he going to* jail? *Maybe that's why you* smell. *Hah-hah!* I turned away from these questions—I understood their malign intent and hardly knew the answers myself.

I became a social liability and lost most of my friends post-haste. Only one remained loyal to me, Ellen, and that was because she had a speech impediment and didn't have many friends herself, despite being a talented student and very funny. It was an unspoken pact between me and Ellen that we never discussed my father.

My older sister Sue, in eighth grade at the time, also became a social pariah. But things improved for her a few months later when she transferred to a different school for high school, and her new classmates had no idea what had happened. Our younger sister, Sally, in third grade, was enough younger that she remained mostly untouched by the stigma.

My father holed up in his attic study as he awaited trial; then, when he took a plea deal, he was sentenced to three years in a state penitentiary, one of those places with ultra-thick cement walls topped by barbed wire. My sisters and I visited him there only once, a bleak occasion I'd rather not describe, sitting in orange plastic chairs surrounded by noisy squabbling families, him quizzing us as if we were the offenders. Our mother visited every week for a while, then every month, then not at all. Two years into his incarceration they divorced.

Things got bad for me in early high school when he was released from prison. He'd been disbarred by then and had trouble finding work and was short on funds. He lived in a halfway house for a while, a run-down place in Woburn where he looked down on his fellow residents. When he finally found employment as a car salesman in a depressed town near the New Hampshire border—our mother rolled her eyes as she reported the car salesman thing—he moved into an equally run-down second floor apartment. I never saw those places, but we heard about them from Mother. She had no interest in seeing him, but sometimes he called, and she took pity on him and they would meet for coffee. She was keenly aware he was still our father—would always be our father—but none of us knew what that meant going forward. He told her he wanted to see us. We weren't *required* to see him, she said, it was our decision; he had no legal right to see us, but we probably *should*. We weren't hot on the idea. We were teenagers by then— well, Sue and I were—and we were busily shunning all the adults and all the *shoulds* in our lives.

He started showing up at the house, unannounced. The first time was a Saturday morning when Sue was out at debate team practice, but Sally and I and our mother were there. I had slept late and was still in my pajamas, eating a bowl of Cheerios at the kitchen table, still only half awake. From where I sat I could see Mother talking to him through the screen door. "You should have called," she said.

"I called. You didn't pick up. What was I supposed to do?" he protested. "They're my kids too."

She let him in, and he followed her to the kitchen. Seeing him was a shock. He didn't look like the man we used to live with. He wore a rumpled gray suit jacket over brown polyester pants, a pink tie, clothes he would have reviled in his pre-prison life. It looked as if he was striving for formality but had come up instead with eccentric. Was this what prison did to your taste? Then I realized—he had no money, he must have gone to Goodwill.

"Hi," I said, pretending this was an everyday occurrence, though I was deeply embarrassed to be seen in my threadbare pajamas and embarrassed by his attire too.

"Come on, get up. Give your old father a hug."

"I'm eating," I said, shoveling cereal into my mouth more quickly than I was able to swallow it.

"Sybil," Mother said.

"For fuck's sake," I said.

"Sybil," she repeated.

He was standing beside me and I rose and put my hands in the vicinity of his shoulders, keeping our torsos apart, feeling his arms like cudgels on my back. Withdrawing abruptly, I sat.

He pretended to be satisfied and took a seat beside me. "You're sleeping too late," he said. "It's not good to sleep so much."

I raised an eyebrow at him. He had no idea how much or little I slept.

"Of all my girls you've always been the laziest. You've got to go out there early to get the worm."

Oh right, I thought, the worm that landed you in jail?

"Where are the others?" he said.

"Sue is at debate," Mother said. "Sally is upstairs." She went to the foot of the stairs. "Sally, your father is here!"

Moments later Sally appeared, violin case slung over her shoulder. His arms were already spread for a hug and Sally, not yet a naysaying teenager, succumbed without resistance.

"How ya doin', Sal?"

"Good. But I have practice now. My violin teacher started a string quartet and I'm playing first violin."

"Good girl. First violin! You go and have fun. I'll see you soon. I'm around now."

I rushed after Sally and hissed at her on the front stoop. "You can't leave me with him!"

"I have to go. It'll be okay."

"No, it won't."

She took off on her bike, and I had no choice but to go inside and endure.

"You should be more like your sisters," he said, "getting out there and conquering the world."

"I'll work on it."

Our mother made it a rule thereafter: no surprise visits. He agreed, but only if we would make plans to see him elsewhere. We felt trapped, so we complied, but we never met him alone. There were always at least two of us, safety in numbers, and we never saw him more than every couple of months. It was usually me and Sally who met with him, since Sue, being older, was already absurdly busy. Sally didn't care where our meetings took place, but I was determined not to meet him where anyone I knew might see us. To Sally those visits were boring—to me they were deeply humiliating.

We often met at a diner in Watertown—I knew no one in Watertown and we could get there easily on the bus. He always wore some kind of rumpled suit jacket that seemed to me to announce he was down and out, along with a fedora that was too small for his large head, a ridiculous affectation, as if he was auditioning for some depression-era movie. He had a game he would play with Sally, the only one of us who could still play unselfconsciously. He would put the fedora on her head and quickly replace it each time she took it off. On-off-on-off.

They both thought this game was hilarious—or at least they pretended. I could tell he really thought of himself as a charmer. At the time I was disgusted, though now I see how sad it was.

He always arrived early and had already ordered for us: burgers and milkshakes. "Whatever you want," he said, but it always turned out to be whatever *he* wanted for us. Sally didn't care, but I never ate a thing. "How did you get to be so plump when you never eat anything?" he kept asking me. I was the target of all his correctives.

At every one of those meetings he began by "setting the record straight." He wanted to persuade us that he was innocent, that he'd been set up by an associate. Some money went missing, but he wasn't to blame; his associate was responsible and that associate, he said, got off scot-free.

"The justice system—well, let's just say we should be calling it the *in-justice system*. That's why I've always told you girls not to trust anyone . . . But enough about that, let me tell you what I've learned about cars."

Cars? That was the last thing we cared about. He had his eye on a silver Porsche, he said. In a couple of years, he'd have the savings. As for us, when we came around to getting cars, we should get reliable German cars, none of those "Jap cars" so popular around the Boston area. "I know, I'm not supposed to say Jap, but I'm an old-school guy. In the old days we said Jap."

Sometimes he glanced around the diner before he spoke, and I worried his paranoia was going to make him do something crazy. The conversation often focused on what kind of people we were turning out to be. "I mostly like what I see," he would say, "but there's room for improvement. That's the hallmark of O'Malleys—we improve ourselves." And he would tell the story about being chewed out by his high school history teacher when he was a sophomore. The teacher told him, in front of the whole class, that he was bright but lazy.

"That teacher—Mr. Dellenbach was his name—can you believe I still remember his name?—went on and on for fifteen minutes, making an example of me. Was it embarrassing? You bet it was, but it turned out to be the best day of my life. After that I turned myself around. No more baseball cards. No more Saturday afternoons with my friends. I got motivated. I worked hard and didn't stop. What do they call it now—grit. I learned to use my grit. Got into law school and everything.

"Sybil, you could use a little more grit, a little more ambition. Follow the example of your sisters. Next time we get together I want to see you've made some headway. Okay? Right? Are we on the same page?" He held up a fist for me to bump and, when I didn't reciprocate, Sally offered hers. I was a mediator, but not when it came to our father.

As my high school graduation was approaching, I worried he would come. I hoped he would be unaware of it, but I was wrong, he knew the exact date and time and place, and he wanted Mother to get him a ticket. I told her no, I *did not want him there*, embarrassing me in front of my classmates. I told her if he was going to come, I wouldn't be there. But I had to go, she said, because—and she wasn't supposed to tell me this—I was going to be getting an award for all-around academic excellence. If I didn't show, *she* would be embarrassed.

"But why does *he* have to go?"

"Because he's proud of you. He loves you."

I didn't buy it, but I agreed he could come if he didn't sit with us.

The occasion took place outside on the playing fields, spectators in the bleachers; it was horribly hot and the sound system crackled and squeaked, making a mockery of the familiar graduation march. It took forever for everyone to file in, for the speeches and the handing out of diplomas. I had to cross the stage twice, first for my award, then for my diploma, and I advanced in my black robe like a blindered horse, only capable of looking straight ahead.

I had no idea where my father was sitting, if in fact he had even showed, but afterwards he sought me out for one of his appropriating hugs to announce to the world I was *his daughter*. I had joined my mother and sisters then, and I endured his hug as stoically as I could, deciding not to make waves. Then I hissed to Mother that she had to send him away. Amazingly, he complied, and as he sauntered off I saw he looked better than usual, almost dapper in his navy suit and red tie, as if, at least for one day, he had erased all traces of his past.

We like to believe we can escape the molding of our original families, that we can shed any inevitabilities associated with DNA, but come on, who are we kidding? The past can't be erased for any of us. I still carry my father's legacy everywhere, the shame of being his daughter; a man who, even after incarceration, refused to own up to the damage he'd done. When I was a high school student he seemed particularly dumb to me, despite a respectable IQ. I couldn't stand the way he made himself an authority on things about which he knew so little. I couldn't stand that he wasn't self-reflective enough to be ashamed. Later, I would see shades of that same shamelessness in Jeff and Dan, but I'm getting ahead of myself.

For the record, Drew knew nothing about my father. What quicker way to scare a man off?

10

After the Medical Examiner's testimony, I became obsessed with Jessie. Already she seemed to be at such a disadvantage. Her hardscrabble background, as with the rest of us, could not be erased and it made her suspect—or so the prosecution wanted us to believe. I couldn't imagine what it felt like for her to sit in that courtroom all day for the sole purpose of being judged by strangers. She existed there as a Rorschach test, awaiting our projections. I stared hard, trying to use my eyes to excavate her thoughts. Her gaze was usually on the testifying witness or downturned to the table in front of her, occasionally straight ahead to a distant horizon, as if to obliterate the entire room. Some days she was so dispirited she hardly glanced up. Then, I noticed my own body slouching to match her abject posture, shoulders hunching, ribs and belly sucked inward, arms limp.

Once, she turned toward the jury box and found me staring. I felt singled out, caught. We held eye contact for a lifetime of seconds, thirty at least, maybe more. It was as if she and I were alone in a vast aerodrome, approaching each other step by step. Her bewitching blue eyes kept me under their spell until she had wrested full control and she was the one evaluating me.

Home alone after that memorable testimony, I sat outside in the light-spangled dark, nursing a second glass of wine, thinking of Jessie. What did it feel like to cut human flesh? What concentration it must have taken to cut that wobbly organ with a shard of glass. How damaged— or angry—a person would have to be to do such a thing.

The chickens next door, usually quiet at night, awakened in squawking, flapping bluster. The lights went on, a screen door opened, and my neighbor Brenda came outside to investigate. *Get out, you asshole*, she yelled. A raccoon? A fox? A rat? I was too lazy to get up and ask across the fence. Eventually she went back inside and turned out the lights and the chickens calmed down.

A rat problem had erupted in the neighborhood. Brenda, a single mother in her forties who fancied herself an urban farmer, had chickens in her backyard. She fed them kitchen scraps, and at night wild animals would arrive, drawn by the scent of food as well as the scent of the chickens themselves. She had regular visits from raccoons and foxes who she mostly foiled with traps and elaborate fencing. To look at her coops you wouldn't have believed anything could possibly get in. But rats are smart—they say at the end of the world it will only be rats and viruses, both highly adaptable—and those rats started digging holes under her fence, devouring the scraps, and once massacring the chickens themselves. One morning she dragged me over to see that scene. Dead chickens everywhere, perfectly healthy-looking birds slumped on their sides as if a toxic cloud had hit them. I half expected they were playing a joke and on cue would rise up dancing. Some of the chickens had died simply from fear, she said. After that she purchased another boxful of chicks that grew with astonishing speed. The rats, having proliferated as rats do, were out in full force by then, not just in her yard but in all of our yards. It didn't make for peaceful sleeping.

I could be sitting in my Adirondack chair in my backyard, trying to relax in the evening and, without fail, just as I began to feel a touch of peace I would hear the telltale scuttling, and I would see a pair—or pairs—of malevolent little eyes glinting, sprung from the shadows by my outdoor light. Some of my other neighbors were suing, but I wasn't getting involved. I had enough on my plate.

So, I was sitting there that night thinking about Jessie and dead naked Eric and replaying the events of that fateful night when I heard the rats rustling around by the back fence. My wine glass was empty. I didn't feel drunk, but I must have been because I smashed the glass hard on the arm of my chair. The broken shards scattered and caught bits of streetlight so they fell like shimmering hailstones.

I lifted one of the shards that had landed in my lap. Curious, my forefinger traced the slim sharp danger of its broken edge. As if in a dream, I dragged the point across the mound at the base of my left thumb. The flesh parted willingly, without pain. Blood, black in the low light, was slow to fill the fissure. I watched calmly, mesmerized, my perspective shuttling between cutter and cuttee. After a while mounting wetness jolted me from my daze.

Bandaged, but still abuzz, I lay awake for a long time.

When I finally succumbed to sleep I dreamt of her. The assaulted Alaskan-born skin, textured and tawny as the stucco of a sun-baked Mexican wall. The hair a tumbling, golden-brown crown of defiance. The eyes, ocean-azure with a touch of viridian, always quivering a little, even when locked in a stare. At night, in my bedroom, they glowed with phosphorescence. A beckoning. A portal in.

A world concussed with sunlight. Sled blades scraping the crusty snow. We are a blitzkrieg, my dogs and I, smashing through the silent blue light with our clanging ropes and chains, the huff of our breath. Cold is a contagion laying waste to nostrils and throat, a machete to larynx and lungs. The slats of the brittle wood sled slap the ground, shudder through feet and legs. Tassels of mucus dangle, congeal, freeze on the upper lip.

We plunge through it all, deafening, singular, thinking of Libby Riddles, the first woman to win the Iditarod, of Susan Butcher charged by a moose, her dogs killed, the worst luck. Beyond the noise of us, the hush of true wilderness, devoid of humans, white and phantasmal. Creatures watch, but keep their distance.

Easy does it, Goldie, Scooter. Pell-mell along a river gorge, sparse trees, shadows stippling the white path, a conversation between light and dark. Branches lash us, here and there a root leaps up from the snow, a chthonic hand from the dead. But the dogs are nimble and, true to their species, dogged. Sidestepping when necessary. Scooping up air. Diving into the clarion cold. Tireless. Over snow bridges with open water on both sides. Past ziggurats of ice.

You pray. Other women have done this. You will be among them.

We break into a long legato of straightaway, an open plain, the sky an ardent blue, clouds wispy as cobwebs. An occasional bird paddles the air. In the distance mountains preside like monarchs, pompous and certain, impervious. Why should they care?

Go, go, go. Doing great, guys. Take it easy. The clouds thicken into schools of fish, darken into tessellated brain-like clumps. A light smirr turns to snow. Wind hoots down the ravines, harvests the snow, spins it. Seen through eye slits, half-blind, the world shrinks.

You stop under a copse of scrawny Sitka spruce, blink hard to get your bearings, water your dogs, survey the wrangling snow and wind which are bringing on early twilight and a new level of cold. Your dogs drink as if inhaling the water. You replace some of their fraying booties, inspecting their paws, murmuring to them, overcome with adoration for their hot, loyal bodies, the perfect embodiment of love. You try to ignore the insentient blocks your entombed feet have become. Your cheeks, having lost all mobility, droop from the jaw bone like sessile sea creatures. You cannot allow your thoughts to linger, ever, on fire, hot soup, the body's brokenness. This is a crucible you have invited.

Your dogs whine, ready to move again. You crouch over them, feed them each a treat. *Good dog, Rafe. That's the way, Sophie. You're nailing it, all of you.* Burying your face in their coats, you feel the pulsing organs beneath, lungs three times more efficient than those of Olympians.

Looking up, you see the snow receding. Only a few lazy flakes remain. Then, nothing. Stillness. The setting sun languishes for a moment on the horizon, an exploded oxblood yolk. A color you may never see again. Breathless, reverent, you try to memorize that extravagant color, then you press on, the dogs rocketing forth with unfathomable energy, nuclear, beyond the simple computation of caloric intake.

Twilight deepens to a Prussian blue. The sled glides more quietly now. Trees and mountains draw inward, genuflecting as if in prayer. As darkness matures, it sutures you in safety and danger. You work against held breath—breathing is paramount.

In a few hours, the next checkpoint, almost halfway, five hundred miles will remain. You will sign in, declare a rest. Your dogs will devour food and water, sniff their surroundings, whine, bark, collapse into death-like sleep but for the muscle memories stored in their twitching paws. Sleep for you will come and go, a liminal zone, a penumbra, not the deep sleep your body needs. Motion churns on, the basso continuo of your days. Were you to stop, you'd never start again.

You shove away thoughts of rest, turn on your headlamp, blinding but necessary, adjust the angle of its blazing beam so all you see is the red tip of your sled and your team of twelve. Channeling your dogs' ancient wisdom, you plunge ahead with them into darkness.

11

A mother who regularly slaps her children. A former classmate who is unsufferable. A president who spends four years prioritizing the white and the rich. Once these people are dead, their life narratives are rewritten. Their faults are recast to color them as would-be saints and first-class citizens, at the very least people who overcame terrible odds. The mother who slapped her kids did so in the name of love. The unbearable friend was only grating due to a crippling lack of confidence. The president who prioritized the rich dreamed in private of a more equitable world. How reliably humans beatify our dead.

In that courtroom we watched two diverging attempts to reconstruct the persona of Eric Hotchkiss. The prosecution wanted us to believe that he had been a gentle teddy bear of a man, concerned about his EMT patients, eager to become a father. The defense sketched a darker picture, of course, of a controlling man with an impulsive streak and a proclivity for violence.

Eric's story was first outlined by his best friend Brad Eaton, an Eric booster, a voice speaking to the unassailability of the dead. He settled into the witness chair as if he was already a celebrity. Twenty-nine years old, the same age as Eric would have been. A former football player, neck thick as a water main. Shiny cheeks. A smug smile. He had studied business and gone into banking. You could almost smell the cologne wafting from under his polyester suit jacket. Brad and Eric had begun college together, and though Eric had dropped out after two years, the two had remained friends. *Best buds, you know? Brew bros.* Brad's choice of words, not mine. Ms. McCarthy drew out the details concerning the length and breadth of their friendship, what activities they'd shared together, first classes, then later attending football games, going on ski trips, going out for beers after work. Once Brad had even accompanied Eric on a visit to see his family in New York.

I was riveted by Brad's receding hairline. The vast swath of his gleaming forehead and pate reflected the overhead light almost blindingly, as if intentionally orchestrated to showcase his premature wisdom. Anyone with such a gleaming scalp had to be trustworthy.

Eric's story, as reported by Brad, went roughly like this. He had come West to flee the steroidal expectations of his aristocratic family back East where all his relatives were respected and wealthy professionals—doctors, lawyers, judges, a few professors. Eric, the youngest of four brothers, was the proverbial black sheep; dyslexia and ADHD had made it difficult for him to get through school. He liked sports, but not the sports prized by his family—tennis and golf—preferring the rougher, working-class sports like football and hockey. His family disapproved of every choice he made.

He arrived in town after high school and enrolled in the state university, believing it wouldn't be as challenging as its East Coast cousins, but after a year and a half he was bored and couldn't keep up. He dropped out, kicked around for a year tending bar, before getting certified as an EMT. He secured a job. It was the best thing he had ever done. He was proud of himself. He loved the work, felt he'd found his calling.

Responding to calls from 911, he finessed people from under fallen trees, prised them from crushed cars, recovered and iced their severed digits; he staunched blood, jumpstarted hearts, suctioned airways, warmed newborns in his incubator. His vehicle was a mobile miracle of modern medicine: defibrillator, suction unit, infusion pump, syringe drivers, oxygen cylinders, bandages, medications, drip bags, spinal board, cervical collar. Equipment he was skilled at deploying to prolong the life of even his most desperate victims. He was known for whispering to his patients to reassure them they'd get through.

He met Jessie at Starbucks. She was assembling a tray of four coffees for her coworkers and he first noticed her agility as she pirouetted around the counter, fetching cream and sweeteners. He admired her lively forearms, then her long neck, and eventually he found himself glimpsing her high cheekbones. He was fixed in place, staring shamelessly. When she turned he found himself directly in her sightlines. Her indignation turned to laughter. *Excuse me,* she said. *Those eyes,* he thought, *my God!* They shimmered like holograms, passing from blue to green and back, looking the way a certain pair of his mother's jade earrings used to look under the light. Her eyes excited him the way, as a child, Easter baskets had excited him, or surprise balls, objects that contained many layers to be unwrapped.

Yeah, sure, I'm paraphrasing, but you get the picture.

From that moment on Eric was smitten. Brad heard the blow-by-blow of each of their dates. Eric liked that Jessie was so different from himself and from all the other girls he'd dated. Four years older than he and from a legendary frontier state he'd never visited, she seemed to know who she was. She was physically strong, whip-smart, tough, a survivor. He knew immediately that she was complicated. He could learn things from her.

The classic romance, right? You seek to complete yourself with someone whose difference entrances you. You can't believe such a person exists; you need to know what makes them tick. You hook your horse to their wagon, understanding the perfection of your match is in direct relationship to its unlikelihood.

"In all the years you knew Eric did you ever see him display any violent tendencies?" McCarthy asked of Brad.

"Heck no. He was the gentlest guy I knew."

"Do you know that Eric was put on probation for an incident at work in which he punched his coworker?"

"Sure. Eric told me all about it. It wasn't his fault. He was just trying to do his job and Rick got in his face. Maybe Eric overreacted a little, but only because Rick was insisting on doing something he wasn't good at. They were intubating a kid and Eric had much more experience. But Rick wouldn't back off so Eric had no choice but to force him. I'm telling you, that says nothing about who he usually was. Believe me, he certainly wouldn't rape anyone."

A thin, ponytailed blonde took the stand. She turned out to be Brad's wife, Brittany. The two couples often socialized together, and all four were present at the party on *the night in question*.

"Yeah, it was the first party of the season," she said. "June 29."

The scene was clear. One of those raunchy youthful summer parties in a backyard strung with Kewpie dolls and red pepper lights. A guy flipping burgers and hot dogs on a rickety charcoal barbeque. Two packed coolers of beer. A long folding table, paper tablecloth, bags of chips and Oreos and Chips Ahoy, cardboard cartons of deli coleslaw, tubs of oozing ice cream. The women/girls were dressed in warm weather finery: ultra-short skirts and dresses, tank tops, sports bras, bikini tops. The guys wore shorts and tees. Flasks and joints circulated, gossip too. Flamboyant smooches and sudden shrieks assured everyone: This is *Fun*!

A formidable gaggle—no, a *pride*—of women, including Brittany and Jessie, clustered near the firepit, faces a sheeny sweat-brightened orange, heads tilting toward one another. Jessie was among them. They spoke of pregnancy, as young women sometimes do. Would they or wouldn't they? If so, when? It was speculative more than urgent, soothing even. What fun to imagine their future selves with offspring—babies!—while reveling in the drunken abandon of a summer night. Jessie was notably silent but no one was prepared for her sudden *Fuck no!*

What's wrong? Brittany asked, reaching out to calm her. *Don't be upset. It's okay.*

It's not okay, Jessie said. *Never. I'm not getting pregnant. Ever. Got it? It's on the public record as of right now. Especially not with* him. She was yelling by then and pointing to Eric, getting really worked up. "It was pretty weird," Brittany said.

Eric hurried over and took Jessie's shoulder in his firm grip. Ever-nimble and fleet, she ducked away, concealed herself by the fence in the yard's shadows. Then, to everyone's surprise she popped out again and took center stage, silencing the thirty to forty guests and corralling their attention.

Okay, if you're all so interested—that fuck *is having an affair!* She stood there for a moment, fierce and defiant and sure of herself, a machete slashing the party's atmosphere. Then she left. Moments later he did too.

"What was your reaction to this?"

"I was shocked. I think everyone was kind of shocked."

"Was this unusual? How did they usually act with each other?"

"I don't know. They were married. They acted married."

"And that means . . . ?"

"You know, sometimes they argued. But not real arguments, more like kidding around."

"Can you recall any of those moments of kidding around?"

A long pause. A couple of darting glances toward Jessie. "Well, like I said, Jessie could be a little checked-out sometimes, and that would bother Eric. So, he'd go, like, *Earth-to-Jessie, Earth-to-Jessie.* Trying to bring her back, you know?"

Moments later, Vitale in cross.

"Did Eric ever say things to Jessie you thought were mean?"

Brittany shrugged, recoiled, scowled at the judge who, after a chunk of silence, ordered her to answer. "Maybe," Brittany said.

"Did he ever ridicule Jessie about her background?"

"Maybe."

"Alright then, let's review some specifics. Do you recall him saying: *You know my wife is in a class all by herself. She's the only person I know who's eaten squirrel?*"

"I guess."

"You guess?"

"Yeah, he said that."

"On another occasion do you recall him saying, in a conversation about Alaska: *It might be beautiful, but you wouldn't want to grow up there. You could end up with bad teeth like Jessie. When I met her, she had missing teeth because she'd never once in her life been to a dentist.* Do you remember Eric saying that?"

"Yeah. But he didn't say it meanly. He was laughing and we all knew he was kidding."

"How did Jessie respond to such comments?"

"She'd just stand there, not saying anything, kind of staring him down. She has a way of staring that's—I don't know, I guess you'd say scary. Almost crazy." Brittany's eyes again flicked to Jessie so quickly it appeared involuntary. You could see the friendship dissolving right there in the courtroom.

Meet Eric. A considerate man. One must always feel sorry for the dead.

12

I glanced at Chrystal who smiled back at me. I surveyed the other jurors. No one was reacting to the lie being foisted on us. Did they agree with the prosecution that Eric Hotchkiss, a man who mocked his wife, was a *nice man*?

Jessie caught my eye, as she'd been doing more and more of late. I shook my head to say, *I get it.*

Incidents came flooding back to me.

Me, standing at the kitchen counter making sandwiches for a picnic, bread and cheese and turkey and lettuce and tomato all laid out for easy assembly. Drew, in the kitchen doorway, wincing. "You've washed your hands?"

I stare at him with the same withering look I used to give my father. "I'm a grown woman, not a five-year-old."

He sighs and leaves.

Me emerging from the bathroom, showered and dressed for the dinner we're about to attend at the home of some friends, mainly his friends. "You plan to wear that?" he says, nodding toward my go-to outfit of black.

"What's wrong with it?"

He shrugs. "It makes you look like an undertaker."

A small dinner party at our house. My friend Val is there, along with two other couples. I am trying to outline the fundamentals of

Keynesian economics, a subject I admittedly have no business trying to explain.

Drew taps my shoulder. "Are you done yet?" He turns to the others. "Sometimes she likes to think she's an academic. The East Coast thing—always a touch of superiority."

Do I shut up? Of course. Do I point out his rudeness? No. *Why not?* you ask. Because it would have ruined the evening, and because I hate conflict, especially among friends.

Another dinner party at the home of people I barely know. They're hiking types who were friends with Drew long before I met him. Wine has been drunk and apparently it has gotten to him.

"Sybil and I will be hiking in the Himalayas soon," Drew says. A sound emerges from him, a low protracted humming that lasts for a socially awkward period of time as the other couple, both fit types like Drew, try to conceal their surprise. It is left to me to explain that no, we won't be hiking in the Himalayas, he was only making a joke.

As you can see, I remember each and every one of these apparently trivial incidents. Over thirteen years there were many. As I report them to you now I understand how I appear to have been a pushover, but I wasn't really, only a survivor. The bond between me and Drew was contingent on accepting this occasionally arrogant side of him, and being my father's daughter had equipped me well for that. Years earlier I'd become an expert at shrugging off derision. The path of least resistance. Furthermore, I understood why Drew needed to assert himself in these ridiculous ways. We had visited his family at their cattle ranch on the high plateau of Eastern Oregon many times, and what I learned there was clarifying. Our first visit was particularly memorable.

Drew's four older brothers—a twenty-five-year gap between him and his eldest brother—had gathered from their adjacent ranches with their wives. Daniel, Adam, Abraham, and Abel. I couldn't hear those Biblical names without wondering whether Drew, with his non-Biblical name, had been destined, from birth, to leave the family fold.

A long wooden table accommodated all twelve of us, and halfway through the meal I realized they'd been summoned for the purpose of assessing me. The brothers were all in their late forties or fifties, old enough to be our parents (Drew and I were in our early thirties at that time). Alma, the matriarch, a bow-legged woman in her seventies, weathered and trim from an outdoor life of ranching, let nothing escape her. She chided Daniel for his dirty fingernails, told Abel he was eating too fast, questioned Adam about why his daughter was going to college in Florida when there were plenty of fine places to go in-state. There wasn't the slightest hint of gentleness in her observations and inquiries. She intended to find out what was going on and fix whatever wasn't to her liking. She served up the food from her place at the head of the table, deciding on the appropriate portions for each person, making sure Bethany, one of the overweight wives, didn't get potatoes, prompting me to wonder if I, too, would not be served potatoes (I was, though I took note of Alma's hesitation).

Everyone seemed to accept Alma's rule without resistance. The brothers spoke laconically, mostly in response to Alma's questions. They were replicas of one another, taller and quieter than Drew, their gazes oblique and slit-eyed, as if they were constantly on the lookout for a flaw, a predator, an exit. Away from the table they were always in motion like Drew, but they moved more slowly, as if speed might dampen their vigilance.

Bill, Alma's resigned uxorious husband, sat beside her, complying mutely with her directives to fetch items from the kitchen. Plates served, Alma said grace, praising God, blessing her grandchildren, decrying the state of the world. No one seemed bothered by the TV blaring in another room, tuned to an Evangelical station.

As people began eating, Alma turned her attention to me. From whence did I hail? What had brought me West? What kind of work did I do? What religion did I practice? I saw no point in lying and laughed as I told her I was an "infidel." She worked her cracked, Vaseline-smeared lips like silly putty in response to my answers. Beside me Drew drank his full glass of water nonstop, and I understood how being there infantilized him. Though he had made a defiant life for himself in another place, he had never stood up for himself in the midst of his family.

I'd never witnessed a family under such unitary control. Alma called all the shots. With her pinched mouth and silver bun she was American Gothic from the neck up; the jeans and cowboy boots suggested Annie Oakley from the neck down. Religion coursed up and down her spine like a scepter. Drew had no name for this religion, he could only say that it prescribed a number of rules for right living. No cursing. Regular and thorough handwashing. No public displays of emotion. No laughing, no eating to excess, no drinking alcohol, no dancing or singing or having sex for reasons other than procreation.

Meeting the family explained so much about Drew. He'd accepted his black sheep status and made himself into everything they were not. No wonder he insisted on living with such gusto, immersing himself in fellowship and hilarity and the gratifications of the flesh (my flesh) as well as fine food and wine. Nor was it a surprise that those very indulgences took their toll. He had myriad ways of punishing himself. He would fast for several days (once, worryingly, for an entire ten days), or eat only rice for a month, or spend the better part of a day running, or dedicate himself to silence for a full weekend. Sometimes I could see what prompted those bouts of self-flagellation—perhaps he'd eaten dessert two days in a row, or he'd drunk too much at a party, or he'd told an unsavory joke. Sometimes it seemed like a response to our sex delivering unacceptable levels of pleasure. Other times I had no idea why he punished himself, only that there was some inscrutable internal prompt. He'd come to live his life on the seesaw of feast and famine.

There's one more thing. As a child he'd had ADHD—yes, just like Eric Hotchkiss, though there the resemblance ends. Drew's condition went undiagnosed and untreated, and it made him a terrible student and ashamed at home. He was jealous of me for having been a reasonably good student, not ambitious but smart enough to get by easily. When he confided these things to me, how could I not feel sorry for him? I wanted to accept all of him, cut him some slack as his family never had. So, when he would say things like *Here's Sasquatch tracking mud through the living room again*, I would smile and shrug. I'm not saying these things made me happy—his comments often stung—but I kept a lid on my anger and waited for it to pass.

I wasn't dumb. No one, including me, understood why he and I were together in the first place, but I understood the balance of power between us—he held most of the cards. Overall it was a good life that accommodated our differences easily. We had everything I wanted, and so much more than I'd ever expected.

Then, two things happened. One evening, a few years into our relationship, we were lolling around after a satisfying bout of sex. As usual he had been burying himself in the flesh of my boobs and buttocks, ecstatic and downright worshipful. But now he took hold of my love handles and kneaded them, so for a second I wondered if he was about to initiate another round of lovemaking. I want to add here that I was not obese, as it might sound, only somewhat overweight: plump, zaftig, curvy, full-figured, choose your word. He began to squeeze more insistently, harder and harder until it hurt.

"Ouch." I slithered away from him. "What're you doing?"

"You'd be a lot happier, you know, if you lost some weight."

You can't imagine. Well, maybe you can. I was *verklempt*. That expression, by the way, comes from the German word that means "pinched or squeezed." I was, in that moment, both literally and figuratively pinched and squeezed—and truly furious. He couldn't have it both ways, extolling my flesh and also deriding it.

I rose from the blanketed floor where we were lying. I went to the bathroom and locked the door. After twenty minutes he started begging me to come out, apologizing, possibly crying. I couldn't quite tell, but I didn't relent. I stayed there for a full hour, lying in the dry bathtub, listening to his knocks and pleas. When I finally emerged, I didn't speak for several hours, taking a page from his book. I immersed myself in one of those impossible round red puzzles and deployed my anger to make astonishing headway with it. He paced from room to room keeping his eye on me, expecting some explosion perhaps. I knew I had the upper hand for a change, and I experimented with what it felt like, the delight of manipulation.

The second thing, possibly more destructive in the end, was our ongoing disagreement about kids. It didn't arise until we'd been together at least five years. When we got married, we agreed on a no-kids union. We'd both felt stultified by our own families and had no need to replicate such arrangements. On my side it was my mother's experience that had become the groundwork for my skepticism about children. After our father was arrested and imprisoned, our lives changed. Our mother, a high school English teacher, had to move us to a smaller house on the working-class side of town where it was easier to support us on her salary alone. She was often tired and ill-tempered. I used to say she was mean. My judgment has softened, but even back then I saw how motherhood burdened her. I concluded that becoming a mother always signaled the abrupt end of life's satisfactions. That idea was underscored by watching some of the least mature girls in my high school become pregnant as teenagers. Dina Angelo and Maureen O'Mara were both mothers by our senior year. They had to drop out—they hadn't been strong students to begin with—and, as far as I knew, that was the end of their education. I felt for them a mixture of pity and scorn, and by the time I got to college it was clear to me that I had no desire to marry or bear children. I took steps I thought would ensure that outcome: adopting a uniform of black jeans and black shirts, hiding my hair under hats, consciously styling myself as butch and being fine with being regarded that way, though I wasn't a lesbian. Before Drew, I'd had liaisons with men, mostly brief affairs and never with anyone I wanted to commit to. I was a relationship and motherhood skeptic, having seen what coupling and childbearing had done to my mother.

I couldn't have anticipated what began to happen a few years after Drew and I married. As I approached my mid-thirties I would find myself at the supermarket or a coffee shop stilled by the sight of a tiny human creature. Sometimes it was a breeze-blown tuft of silky hair that caught my attention. Sometimes it was a pudgy starfish hand reaching for something. Sometimes the mauve, bud-like lips or the fledgling skin, soft and translucent as agates, or the eyes that laughed in my direction. I loved the attitudes of those babies as they relaxed in slings or strollers or backpacks, so content in their passivity, so trusting of the adults who cared for them. I would often skulk down the supermarket aisles behind mothers, trying to look nonchalant as I angled for a closer look, lusting to touch those creatures, awed by them as one is by a masterpiece of art, moved to near tears by the perfection in which life begins.

Beyond the babies themselves, there was what happened when the infants interacted with their adults. A look exchanged or a quick touch and they were cocooned together, the air between them coalescing into a bower that sealed them off, protecting them and excluding others. I wanted to exist in such a bower myself, safe and uniquely adored, a different kind of adoration than I shared with Drew.

Baby lust. It was entirely Pavlovian. Hormones swished through me, appropriating heart and head and loins all at once, completely beyond my control. I understood I was only a creature after all, subjugated by my glands and chemistry, the biology that becomes instinct. I could not will those feelings away, or pretend they were not there, and I began lobbying Drew. He was startled. What about our contract, he wanted to know. Hadn't we agreed not to have kids? *Things change*, I said, *now I want a baby.* But babies grow into *kids*, he reminded me, and neither of us wanted a kid. *I think I do*, I said.

After a while, he became annoyed when I raised the subject. *How many times do we have to go over this? Kids are not in my future. We already agreed on this.*

A pattern developed. I would initiate the conversation and he would excuse himself, withdrawing in the way he did. He might go on a long run, or stay late at work, or make plans to dine out with someone else, or come to bed long after I was asleep, making reparative sex out of the question.

Over time I began to see that he was probably right about himself—he would probably not be a very good father. His own father was spineless, completely subservient to his mother. It was unlikely Drew would want to adopt a parenting style like either one of them. What would the alternative be? He didn't trust himself to find it.

One Saturday morning in late fall, he left the house dressed in out-door garb, leading me to believe he was going on a hike. A few hours later he reappeared, earlier than I'd expected. He quickly busied him-self in the backyard, neatening the vegetable beds to prep them for winter. The air trembled with his agitation. It was obvious something was amiss. I ventured out to where he was crouched, stabbing at a re-calcitrant weed with one of his diggers.

"What's up?" I said.

He kept his focus downward. "I had a vasectomy." *Ka-thunk, ka-thunk.*

"You what?"

"You heard me." *Ka-thunk. Ka-thunk. Kathunk.*

I went back inside, afraid of what I might do if I lingered in his presence. After that, silence surrounded the topic, a gaping fault line.

13

It's hard to say who occupied more of my thinking in those early days of the trial. In the jury room I was fixated on Drew, trying to find some balance in my attitude toward him, but balance eluded me. One minute I hated him as if we'd just broken up; other times I could feel the sight of his body working its charms on me against my will. How was it possible I could still find him attractive? It bothered me that he did not appear to be altered by my presence. He chatted with the other jurors calmly, as if he was scarcely aware I was there. Even now I hate to admit this, but I felt a continuing ownership of him. I wanted to tell the young woman Anna and hippie-woman Shanti to back off and stop their flirting. Sometimes I imagined blurting the private things I knew about him as a way of claiming him. As for whether some other woman had claimed him in my absence, I still had no idea. He wore no wedding ring, but that meant nothing.

A few times he approached me for a stilted faux conversation in which we both pretended to be strangers. Once he asked me what kind of work I did, and I told him I was a "Numbers Specialist," a reference to how he had once called himself a "Body Specialist." I hated the pretense of those conversations, but he seemed to enjoy their challenge.

As soon as we entered the courtroom, however, my attention shifted to Jessie. A tattoo decorated the back of her left wrist, an unsurprising generational mark. She sometimes tugged her sleeve to cover it, but frequently she forgot so those of us who cared to look did. From the jury box, it wasn't easy to discern what the tattoo was beyond swirls of dark blue ink. Some days it appeared to be a fantastical creature, other days a mere abstraction. But even the most abstract of tattoos always holds some meaning, if not for the casual observer, at least for the tattooed. One clear-eyed day, my surfeit of looking paid off: *Lucky,* the tattoo said in elaborate cursive. Suddenly it couldn't be clearer. Did she really think of herself as lucky? Or did she hope she would become lucky? She'd been lucky in her escape from her family, but the outcome of her marriage to Eric didn't seem so lucky.

I couldn't stop staring, not only at the tattoo, but at Jessie's entire body, a body honed by life in a wilderness cabin in a severe climate, a body that had chopped wood and built fires and schooled its own brain and run the Iditarod, a body that had endured unwanted paternal attentions, and eventually, finally, with unspeakable relief, had escaped, retooled itself as a legal whiz, married and made some kind of life, happy or not. I imagined the happiness she'd known was fleeting and mercurial, the kind of limited happiness so many of us are acquainted with, but she had resisted bitterness as well as she could. She and I had bad fathers in common, and controlling husbands, and we'd both escaped from our painful origins, but the rest of her life was unfathomable to me. In my view she had grit enough for a thousand women, and were she to know me she would certainly abhor my sloth; still, I was certain we would be friends, given the chance. We might go into business together, she doing the wills and estates, me doing the taxes. That probably sounds silly from our current vantage point, but these were the things I thought about.

Over the days of watching her, she became my avatar, my younger sister some days, my daughter on others, and when her adroit azure eyes swept past me, they always returned to linger. She was investigating the entire jury, gathering what she could to evaluate her chances for freedom and, though she spent time assessing each of us, it seemed as if she returned most often to me, placing her appeal at my feet. A channel opened between us, a conduit that widened each day and gushed with messages of need and longing, encrypted to the others. She must have sensed my admiration and hoped I would vote to acquit. Maybe I'd persuade the others. Not that I'd made up my mind—I had not—but she must have understood that, no matter what the trial uncovered, I might be hesitant to curtail her freedom.

Her eyes were the lynchpin. They had the same magnetism of Shawna's eyes, but Jessie's were more adhesive. Once they caught me, I couldn't break free. Entering the complex filaments of her irises was like stepping over the threshold of a labyrinth and discovering an array of narrow brambly paths, no choice clear, no obvious route through without treachery, and yet somewhere there was a right choice that would lead to an Edenic room, walls of robin's egg blue and filled with light and floral scents and plush cushions and a table spread with delicacies, a hidden paradise she kept afloat in her mind as the place to which she was headed. With the luck she'd fashioned from grit, she would arrive there. With her help, maybe I could too.

I couldn't wait to hear her testify. I imagined her voice, not the panicky voice we had heard on the 911 call, but another one, husky and authoritative, reassuring us all that she should be absolved.

It's hard to say precisely when I began to take an interest in the prim woman who sat in the third row on the right, the side of the gallery closest to the jury box. She had the wary aura of one who was visiting from another country, dressed in an outfit that was neat and expensive and oblivious to contemporary fashion, a throwback to the mid-century, last millennium. Minus the pillbox hat. When she first came to my attention her outfit was a short lavender jacket and matching A-line skirt. Low black pumps with pantyhose, despite the heat. A string of pearls hung at her neckline; a white designer handbag was tucked under one elbow, close to her body as if she expected to be pickpocketed, though she had the entire row to herself.

At some point it came to me that she must be Eric Hotchkiss's mother.

She was there every day, becoming a fixture, as much a part of the courtroom as the judge and the attorneys and the omnipresent bailiffs. Some days she was the only spectator present. Her face was unusually long and, though her body and face barely moved at all, her contempt for the entire operation was palpable. Disdain for her violent daughter -in-law, disdain for the protocol of the law and its glacial search for justice, disdain for the fact that she, a wealthy aristocrat, had to walk the same hallways where addicts and drug dealers and rapists came to plead their cases, tainting the air that was hers to breathe. You could see she believed she was better than everyone, even the jurors. We were all sorry people, living in a throwaway town in a nothing state, no doubt descendants of ruffians and ne'er-do-wells, at the very least people who hadn't been able to cut it on the right coast. She couldn't stand that she'd been forced to come here seeking retribution for her offspring.

I studied her often and saw a glint in her roving eyes that suggested she might have a preference for old-school methods—a duel perhaps, a brandished lance or sword or dagger—something to bring a quick end to this interminable process, some immediate restoration of the family name.

I never, in the three weeks of the trial, saw Jessie and this woman acknowledge one another. They were mother-in-law and daughter-in-law, linked through the dead man Eric. Did this woman feel sorry for Jessie and hope for her acquittal? Or was she furious at Jessie for being the agent of her son's death? I watched them both closely, looking for clues. Finding none, I filled in details myself.

I pictured Jessie visiting the New York apartment where Eric grew up. The Upper East Side probably. One of those places where the elevator opens directly into the living space. Room after opulent room decorated with antiques, art, Persian carpets. Everything expensive and tasteful. Views overlooking a vast swath of Central Park. Jessie would have been nervous about etiquette. Where was it permissible to walk? Where should she sit? The family gatherings were peppered with cultural references she knew nothing about, making her feel like an ignoramus, despite her smarts. Their questions, polite enough, felt booby-trapped. "Tell us about Alaska. Tell us about your family."

These were tests she would never pass. What could she say? How would she describe the four rooms of living space in which the six of her family members inhabited? How could she possibly talk about her rowdy brothers or her father, who was so smart he saw the world with painful acuity? Driven to escape, he moved his family from the "civilization" of the Lower 48 he despised to the remote Alaskan wilderness. Once there he still felt the need to blunt his world view with drink.

After imbibing a little alcohol he became darkly funny, but too much alcohol and he became mean. He cornered Jessie for sex whenever he could, wouldn't leave her alone. How could she say any of that to these refined people in these curated rooms of the New York upper class?

She clung to Eric on those visits, and he, perhaps for his own self-preservation, shielded her from too much scrutiny. But Eric's mother was hard to avoid. On every one of those visits she insisted on having Jessie all to herself at least once, taking her out to lunch or shopping, usually both, trying to have a woman-to-woman talk that would help her understand her son's odd choice of a wife.

What struck her was Jessie's stiffness, her aura of indifference. She rarely smiled or laughed or shared confidences. How could you feel intimate with a woman like that? How could her son have come to love such a woman?

She tried, oh she tried.

She wanted to buy something nice for Jessie at Bergdorf-Goodman's, something elegant and sexy. With a body like that—long and lean and athletic, just enough in the hip and breast department—well, she could wear anything. But the girl had no apparent desire for the things at Bergdorf's. She didn't even have opinions about fashion, about clothing or shoes or jewelry. Eric's mother had never met a woman with so little frivolity. Jessie shrank from the sales clerks so Eric's mother had to do the talking.

They finally bought a sweater, a beautiful ocean-blue cashmere V-neck, that matched Jessie's eyes perfectly. It was stunning, and Eric's mother was proud of herself for unearthing it. A shopping coup. Eric would appreciate it, if Jessie didn't. Back at the apartment she slipped Eric a sapphire necklace from her own jewelry box for him to give to Jessie once they got home. It would be more special that way, more intimate.

She never once saw Jessie wearing the sweater or the necklace. And she never heard word one of thanks. It didn't have to be a handwritten thank you note, but at least an email, for God's sake. She now wondered if she would ever get that necklace back. A trivial thought to be having at a juncture like this, but there was so much time to think. The necklace, from Tiffany's, diamonds interspersed with the sapphires, was worth at least seventy-five grand. She never hated her daughter-in-law, but there were certainly signs from the start that things weren't right.

14

By Friday of the first week we'd heard three days of testimony, all for the prosecution. It was like being back in school. The way we were marched single file from the courtroom to the jury room and back as if we were young children; hours of waiting followed by hours of listening while being afraid if you let your attention wander you'd miss something critical, yet still your attention sometimes found an escape. And the endless sitting. Even for someone as sedentary as I, it was challenging. I imagined Drew, a movement maniac, was probably going crazy.

At the end of that Friday, back at home, I wasn't sure what I would do with myself during the long blank weekend that stretched ahead. I was loath to get together with Val, not trusting myself to keep silent about the trial. The judge had harped on this just before dismissing us. "It is very tempting to talk to friends and family about what has happened here," said. "You must be on guard."

I made myself a tuna fish sandwich and took it to the living room couch. I set my computer on the coffee table and browsed the internet as I ate. One click led to another. I knew I was violating the judge's orders, but in the solitary privacy of my own home I couldn't see what harm it would do. I'd been out of town at the time the "murder" had taken place. Other jury members had seen the news reports in the local paper, they'd said so in voir dire. Shouldn't I be entitled to fill myself in?

It was easy, with a few key words, to locate Jessie Snell and Eric Hotchkiss. Neither one of them had a huge cyber footprint, but there were glimpses of them. I came across a police report about a fatality at their Lawrence Street address in June of the prior year; another report from two days later said Jessie Snell had been taken into custody. There was an obituary for Eric Hotchkiss. There was an announcement of their wedding five years earlier. The reports were brief and not very satisfying. I found pictures of Jessie Snell from when she was hired by the law firm where she worked. She was photographed against a blurry blue backdrop that could have been anywhere. She wore a suit and a slight patina of makeup and her hair was coiffed into a smooth "do" that made her look blandly corporate. Even in that insipid picture she exuded intensity.

Probing deeper into the past I found pictures of a younger Jessie at the finish line of the Iditarod, one of her dogs licking her face, the rest of the team circling her, the grin on her weather-reddened face suggesting she'd witnessed something almost sublime. Another smaller picture showed her at the start of the race with some of her competitors, all male. I wondered if any of those men knew her well, could ever have imagined where she'd end up. In all of the photos of her I searched for her "Lucky" tattoo, but in the Iditarod shots a jacket and gloves concealed her wrist and in the corporate shot her forearms and wrist were beyond the frame.

Shots of Eric were more scarce, though I found him in a group photo at his graduation from the boys prep school he'd attended. It was impossible to glean anything from it—in fact all the classmates resembled each other so much it took me a while to identify which one was him. He was somewhat taller and beefier than the others, but they all exuded the same attitude of self-importance.

A tapping on the living room window startled me. I looked up to see Drew pressing his face against the glass. I slammed my computer shut. Outside he couldn't possibly have seen what was on my screen, but the mere proximity of him underscored my violation. Alone, what I was doing hadn't seemed so bad.

I went to the door, opened it halfway. "What're you doing here?"

"Paying you a friendly visit."

The past muscled its way into the present like one of those pop-up books Shawna loved. It came alive in my body, and it snaked through the house though this was a different house than the one we'd shared. We weren't the same people after a decade's worth of miles traveled, conversations engaged in, cells shed. What of our souls? Even that seemed up for debate.

"As far as I know, we're not friends."

"Ease up, Sybil." He said this gently, but the words irked me nonetheless.

We stared at each other for at least twenty silent seconds. This was the first time I'd looked directly at him since the trial had begun. Shaving the beard had changed him. Thick and dark, his facial hair had always suggested an ancestral virility. Without it, his chin was more pointed than I'd thought it was, his cheeks more chiseled, imparting the contemplative mien of an artist or philosopher.

He turned to one side, distracted by the sound of one of Brenda's teenage sons entering their house next door.

"I thought we were supposed to be strangers," I said.

"In the jury room, yes, but don't you find it a little odd? Not to mention stressful."

"Hah. You think it's stressful?"

"Don't you? Come on, I know you do—it's written all over your face. I thought if we talked a bit, caught up, it might be easier. What are you doing now? Can I come in?"

"No." I glanced back at my computer to ascertain it was closed.

"After all these years you can't still be mad."

"I'm not mad."

"O-kay." He drew the word out like a malleable piece of taffy. "I see that—I see you're not mad."

He slung his weight into one hip as he'd always told me not to do. Then his attitude shifted and he eyed me curiously. "Hey, are you alright? You seem so nervous. You're making that face."

"What face?" I palmed my cheek.

He shook his head as if to tell me I was a lost cause. "Never mind." He spun on one foot like a tap dancer, ever-lithe, then sped down the steps to his car and took off.

How well I remembered such behavior, his sudden mood shifts, his retreats into punishing silence, the habit he had of slipping away, ungraspable, a smear of emotion in his wake.

Ten years into our marriage. In early August we visited my older sister Sue in New York. I don't know what we were thinking—summer is a terrible time to visit New York, the heat and humidity so claustrophobic one has no trouble imagining the end of the world—but we had always loved visiting Sue, and we loved small doses of New York too, so there we were.

Sue and I could not be more different. She is slim and driven and hyperactive, partner in a big Manhattan law firm, undeniably an Important Person. I am devoted to Sue and we laugh about our differences. Sue's husband Larry is an attorney too, but he works in the DA's office and is more laid back. Their one son, Charlie, went to a boarding school in New England back then, and during the summers he was always enrolled in some "enrichment program," so he was rarely around.

Sue loved Drew, as all women do. Sue and Drew, yeah, it sounds like a Dr. Seuss story, I know. Drew loved Sue too. She was, to him, a curiosity, so different from his outdoorsy Oregon friends. I liked to see my sister and my husband flirting. It allowed me to be withdrawn and central at the same time.

Despite being high-strung, Sue was always an excellent hostess. She would take time off from work, make elegant meals, and show us around town. Wanting to assure our comfort, she was sometimes a tad fussy about sheets and towels, about what we wanted to eat and when we wanted to rise in the morning, but her generosity was always unimpeachable.

I suggested we go to the Museum of Natural History, but Drew wanted to walk in Central Park.

"It's too hot," I objected. "Doesn't air conditioning sound appealing?"

"Heck no!" He broke into song. "Mine eyes have seen the horror of the New York summer heat/ It roils down all the avenues and churns through every street/ It sucks our precious fluids 'til we beg for a re-prieve/ But WE GO MARCHING ON!"

Drew and Sue walked in the park, and I went alone to the museum. As I expected the air was deliciously cool and, because it was early, there weren't many visitors. The museum had changed since I was a child. The scale was bigger now, inviting visitors to look up and around, instead of gazing myopically down into glass cases. I couldn't find the mummies anywhere.

I wandered toward the Hall of the Universe where there was a model of the solar system to scale. The exhibit told me there are more than a hundred billion galaxies, composed of orbiting stars, swirling gas and dust. Incessant motion, explosions, squalls of hot atmospheric gases and wind. How was it possible that we could walk in a straight line amidst so much tumult? The din, the heat. The Earth itself moving at an approximate rate of 1,000 miles per hour. Celestial was far from gentle.

A sculptural model of a black hole showed matter streaming into it. Black holes were so massive, so powerful, the exhibit said, nothing could escape them; they were gravity's triumph over light. Around the black hole's opening, riotous gases churned. Penetrate that miasma and you would arrive at the infamous event horizon, the point of no return. Should you pass that point you would be sucked to the center, a place of infinite density, the singularity. I wanted to hover at the edge of a black hole, peer into its center. Was there any other way to know infinite density? There is far too much one must take for granted to live reasonably in this world.

I met Drew and Sue by the Willamette meteorite, fifteen and a half tons of iron and nickel, traces of cobalt and phosphorus, even some iridium. It was the largest meteorite ever found in the US, discovered in our own state of Oregon, on loan to the museum from the Grand Ronde tribe. The meteorite was smooth and brown, full of convolutions and cavities, as if supersized termites had gone to work on it.

I approached Drew and Sue from behind and placed a hand on both their shoulders. They parted to let me in between them. "Good walk?"

"The things you see," Sue said. "It never gets old. There was a woman with a two-scoop ice cream cone and one of the scoops fell into the grass and she picks it up, scrapes off the grass, smashes it back on her cone, and keeps licking! I was disgusted—so was Drew. But he thought *you* might do the same thing. Would you?"

"Probably. Why not?"

"Even if dogs might have peed in that grass? Or humans?" Sue said.

"Three-second rule."

"That's disgusting."

"Keeps my immunities strong."

Sue shook her head. Drew had not said a word. He stared at the meteorite, zombie-like.

"You're not amused, Drew?" I said.

A twitch beneath his beard. A lip half retracted. Sue shot me an ambiguous look. There was no mistaking the moment's taint, the tumble past the event horizon.

The silent walk home from the museum was agony, Drew walking ahead of me and Sue, Sue making incoherent faces in my direction. Back at the apartment I escaped to the guest room and sat on the bed, my heart like an entire percussion section as I waited for Drew to join me. He stood above me, chin protruding, squinting down.

"I guess she told you?"

His whisper was scarier than any yelling would have been. "I've known you, what, more than ten years? The pivotal event of your life, Sybil. I thought we told each other everything. She couldn't believe I didn't know."

"It didn't impinge on *us*—there was no need to bring it up."

"*Didn't impinge?* My God, it's impinging right now. By the way, in case you didn't know, Sue told Larry from the get-go, before they were married."

"I'm not Sue."

"That's pretty clear."

Okay, that wasn't good. I probably should have said something earlier. The thing is: I wasn't hiding my father's malfeasance from him. I just wasn't saying it.

But really, aren't lies the bedrock of most relationships? Not intentional lies but omissions, central facts about ourselves we've shunted into the wings, their presence a thrumming background noise we convince ourselves is trivial. Aren't we drawn to partners who allow those omissions to remain in the shadows? Only when they come to light do they morph into something we call a lie.

So yes, my father's criminality was such an omission. But my mother and sisters and I had cut ties with him. We'd shed his name, and he'd become a nobody to us, an occasional thorn in our sides.

"He's half of your DNA," Drew said when we were back at home, and his anger had cooled somewhat, though he still spoke with the clinical distance I imagined he used with his patients. "You can't just cut him out of your history. That makes him even more influential."

I disagreed. Maybe Drew was envious that I'd been able to rewrite my own history successfully, which was exactly what he wished to do with his own family but could not.

15

Saturday morning, after another terrible sleep, I took my coffee to the backyard, for more privacy, along with my computer. I had no particular plan except the overarching project of trying to relax. The fence was low enough that I could see the heads of Brenda's two boys, River and Larch, bobbing on the other side. Young teenagers, thirteen and fourteen, they were playing with some kind of dodgeball, squealing and shouting each time the ball hit one of them. It wasn't exactly peaceful, but I was trying to make the best of it, converting their shouts to white noise.

I discovered an email from Drew. He hadn't emailed for years, but neither of our addresses had changed. *Sorry I surprised you yesterday, but I meant no harm. I hope you're okay. I still care about you. D.* Oh, for God's sake—I didn't for a minute believe that he cared.

Just then Brenda's head appeared above the fence. "We're going to the farmer's market—want to come with us?"

I had nothing else to do. Why not? I needed to get some vegetables anyway. So off we went, me riding shotgun beside Brenda, River and Larch in the back seat poking each other and hooting until Brenda ordered them to stop.

Brenda had a frazzled aura about her, attention flitting here and there as if she's playing whack-a-mole and things are flying out of her control. It isn't a feeling entirely unfamiliar to me, though I think I don't show it on the outside as she does. Perhaps it comes with being a single mother. She also had internalized a certain left-of-center mandate about how to live in a conscious, humanitarian way, hence her urban farming, her volunteer involvements with green groups and efforts to help the homeless, along with her mission to raise feminist boys. I don't mean to mock her—it's all laudable—but the breadth of her involvements makes her a little crazy and it's hard to imagine, thin as she's spread, how effective she can be. As we drove downtown she tried to convince me to come to a meeting, being held the following week, about the city's climate change policies.

"I'm kind of busy," I said. "The trial and all."

She was too kind to point out that she knew, having a front row seat on my life, how unbusy she'd observed me to be.

In the back seat the boys were having a contest to see who could burp out the longest sentence. "I'm—too—busy—" one of them burped, followed by an explosion of laughter from both.

"Enough," Brenda said as sharply as she could, but what she said carried little weight with them.

We parked and walked to the green where the farmers market took place, not far from the courthouse where I'd been spending my recent days. The streets were mobbed with people bearing empty grocery bags, heading exactly where we were heading. The boys, still antic, took up too much sidewalk space with their sudden sidestepping and out-flung arms.

"Boys, boys, settle down," Brenda said. "You're annoying people. And Sybil isn't used to being around untamed animals like you."

"They're fine," I said, but she was right—they unsettled me.

"I'm trying," she apologized. "But you never have the control you think you're going to have."

We ignored the craft booths and crossed the street to the produce section. The sidewalk was narrowed by farmers displaying their offerings on either side of us, tables overflowing with seasonal vegetables grown on organic farms within a fifty-mile radius of the city. Peas, beans, half a dozen varieties of lettuce, chard, arugula, asparagus, mushrooms, peppers, berries, everything so much more appealing than their supermarket counterparts—and organically grown to boot.

Drew and I used to go to this market over a decade earlier, one of the few things we enjoyed doing together. We would make a list, arrive early, get only what we'd come for, and leave before the crowds

came. Had it been my choice I would have lingered, done some impulse buying based on how things looked, then browsed in the craft
area, but since Drew was the primary cook, he called the shots in
regard to food purchases.

There were many more booths and tables now, a number of
them displaying identical produce so it was impossible to choose
between one vendor and another. There were also many more
patrons: young families and university students and retired couples,
most walking in groups, strolling and pausing unexpectedly and
sometimes standing still in the middle of the flow to answer a text.
There were many more young children now too—or so it seemed to
me—babies stuffed into Snuglis and strollers, some toddling along
unsteadily on their own, and masses of school-age kids fanning out
from their parental units like maypole streamers. All of them so
perfect, so cherished, even the screaming ones. There was no need
for me to think about them. They weren't my responsibility, and
they were easily erased from my sightlines. But I remained aware—
consciousness absorbs more than what is directly in the sightlines.

It would have been hard to navigate the crowd on my own, but
it was especially difficult to navigate while staying tethered to
Brenda and her boys. Brenda was easily distracted by everything,
pausing on a dime, chatting with acquaintances and vendors, and
the boys either lagged behind us or sped ahead.

Then Brenda herself disappeared and the boys came to me.
"Where's Mom?" one of them asked (River or Larch, I still wasn't
sure which was which). I had no idea where Brenda had gone.
"Let's wait here where she can find us."

We hovered by a table piled high with various kinds of
outlandishly shaped wild mushrooms. The boys were entranced
for a while, poking and prodding the gnarled brown flesh.

"Ew. Look at this! Gross!"

"No touching," the vendor warned, shooting a look at me as if
the boys were mine.

"I'm not—" I began.

The boys, already bored with mushrooms, had spun their attention to an adjacent table filled with peppered jellies for tasting, and in doing so they knocked over a basket of the mushrooms which sailed off the table and landed on the sidewalk, directly in the path of pedestrians.

"Christ Almighty!" said the vendor, hurrying out from behind his table to rescue what he could. I tried to help him, but he waved me away. "Just clear those boys out!"

I corralled River and Larch and succeeded in guiding them away from the mushroom booth, and for a moment they seemed chastened, but then they spotted a man in a kilt. They began speculating about whether he was going commando, which prompted hysterical whole-body laughter. So much for raising enlightened boys, I thought.

"Stop here!" I commanded when we arrived at a place where there was a bit more sidewalk space. I placed a hand on one of their shoulders—River? Larch? He looked at me as if I was a child molester. "Stop!" I repeated as he recoiled.

While I stood there, an impotent proctor for those unpredictable boys, Shanti walked by, arm in arm with a man about her age who, distinguished and conventional-looking as he was, did not match her hippie look at all. She grinned at me, then noticed the boys and perhaps my panic. Raising her palm in greeting, she moved discreetly on. As soon as she was gone, I found myself wishing she'd stopped to talk, which might have diluted the animus I was developing toward the boys.

Was I becoming a person who hated children? I'd loved children, had once yearned for them. But boys like this—well, if I had a trigger, they were it. Their feral natures. Their unrestrained bodies. Their mob mentality. Their shamelessness. The pure id of them.

Thankfully, Brenda came hurrying up to us before I did or said anything I'd regret.

"I'm so sorry. I saw someone I haven't seen in *ages* and we had to catch up."

I told her it would be easier for me to do my shopping solo. I would walk home.

"Really? It's a long way."

"It'll be good for me."

My arms were killing me after walking those three or four miles home lugging two full bags of produce, but I decided it must be penance for hating those boys as irrationally as I did.

16

Her name was Lily, a pathetic slip of a thing, a mere girl, laughable as a rival to Jessie, and so young she almost made me weep: the vulnerability of young girls, the way the world devours them and spits them out. Jessie kept her gaze on the table, as if her rival still held power. I felt terrible for both of them, their sexual and emotional lives peeled open like that, exposed so neither one was likely to come through untarnished.

Rivals, I knew, are seldom what you imagine them to be. Watching Lily on the witness stand, biting her lower lip and picking at her fingernails, it was hard not to question whether she was worth the *sturm und drang* Eric had summoned into his life. She might have been pretty in a photograph, but in the flesh she was much too cowering to be attractive. A sad, powerless young girl caught in the crosshairs of a more important drama, mere collateral damage.

McCarthy began her questioning as if she was Lily's mother or therapist, her tone soft and reassuring. At first Lily responded reluctantly, her answers clipped. But with each subsequent question she waxed more confident and eventually exhibited a kind of feistiness. For all her apparent insignificance, she wasn't going to be pushed around.

She and Eric had taken a class together while he was still in college, Business 101, a lecture class. They would sit next to each other in the last row, chatting and texting, both bored. After the class they lost touch. Then, three months before the *night in question*, they ran into each other again. He came in for coffee where she worked as a barista (apparently Eric saw coffee shops as a place to pick up women). They made a plan to go for a drink, then started hanging out. She went to work early and was often free in the afternoons. When he was suspended he had lots of time on his hands and they spent much of it together. They usually met at her place. They would drink a couple of beers, have sex, watch a movie. She knew he was married, yes, but that was his deal, not hers. In fact, she felt she was helping him out because he had problems in his marriage and needed to talk about them.

"What kind of problems?" McCarthy asked.

"Oh, you know, his wife was cold and never wanted sex, and she didn't want a baby either. She wanted him to get a vasectomy, but there was no way he was doing that. He really wanted a baby and was sure she'd change her mind. I've seen tons of people change their minds. Plus he worried she was getting old and by the time she changed her mind she might not be able to get pregnant."

A man yearning to be a father, how it moves a jury. But how does taking a lover, even an insignificant lover, support the idea that Eric was a nice man? Is manipulation ever nice, even if it is sometimes effective? You had to feel a little sorry for Lily, but my sympathy for her only went so far. Why didn't she *wake up* and feel some anger at having been used, feel some anger at *still* being used?

McCarthy paused, a deliberate cessation of forward movement like one of those moments in movies where there's a backing off from the tension, allowing you to catch your breath and speculate about what comes next, before the story resumes its pell-mell pace, going for broke.

"Did you ever meet the defendant?" McCarthy resumed.

"Yes. I. Did."

"Will you tell us about that encounter?"

It was early afternoon and Lily was at home in her ground-level apartment when she heard an unexpected knock on the door. A delivery from Amazon, she thought. But no, she opened the door on a woman she didn't recognize.

"*You're Lily?* the woman said. And I said yes. And then she starts yelling—no, more like hissing. And she said, *Stay the fuck away from my husband!* That's when I knew who she was."

"She was the defendant?"

"Yes, Jessie."

"And what happened then?"

"So, she's getting in my face, really mad and kind of losing it, and coming in close so I thought she might hit me. And then she says: *If you don't stay away from my husband, you're gonna suffer. Believe me, I'm a lawyer.* And then she holds up some pictures of me and Eric that some private detective had taken. She'd had us followed!"

"Were you scared?"

"Heck yeah! I was terrified. The way she was coming at me and hissing like an animal. Like I say, I really thought she was going to hit me and then she threatens me like that! It was . . . I don't know, it was bad."

"What happened next?"

"I just slammed the door on her. I looked at her through the peephole in the door. She hung out on the doorstep for a while, like maybe only a minute, but it felt like a long time. Then she drove off. Everything Eric had said about her was totally true—she was a real bitch."

Vitale: "You say the defendant threated you. After she left did you call the police?"

"No."

"So you were really scared, but you weren't scared enough to call the police?"

"I didn't think they would come."

"Is it possible you didn't think they would come because you didn't think it was a serious threat?"

"No, I thought it was serious, but—"

"No more questions, Your Honor."

Jessie's head was bowed and I wanted to enfold her and be the mother that McCarthy was pretending to be with Lily. Jessie's whole body was a testimonial to her life struggles. Anguish issued from her face and torso and arms as palpably as sap oozes from a tree. Sticky and redolent. I'd never seen such a physical manifestation of wounding on another human being. It was especially mapped on her face. She'd taught herself to do deadpan fairly effectively, but to anyone observing closely there were telling cracks in her façade: twitches, winces, blinking, barely perceptible headshakes. I'd learned her facial language. *I see you, Jessie,* I radioed from my perch. *I would have been angry too.*

I see you know the myriad ways things can fall apart. You have a keen eye for danger and have learned to anticipate collapse before it happens. Financial ruin. Addiction. Loss of will. Over the years you've become a smart student of entropy.

You know to keep moving as a way to outwit these threats. Working at the law, you protect your clients against predators who might come to seize their assets, drawing up impenetrable trusts, airtight wills, legal documents that cannot be abrogated. It's a game of deploying precise language, as well as understanding how often human beings possess dark and scheming hearts.

Days go by when you do not recognize yourself as you've become. Married to a rich younger man from back East. A fancy office. Clients who trust you with their affairs. Who would have imagined any of this? You've become sheathed in the apparatus of a stranger's life, the kernel of your authentic self concealed under multiple layers. At the hair salon where you go to maintain a professional look, Brianna fusses over you, filling the silence with talk of her children. You never look into her mirror which would tell you of the multiple ways you've betrayed your true self, becoming a person you wouldn't have chosen to be if you'd slowed down and paid more attention. But here you are. Like one of those Russian dolls that splits in half and opens to reveal a smaller version of itself which also splits and opens on yet a smaller version that also opens. On and on until you get to the doll at the center, tiny and least elaborately painted, but the only one that is whole. In that one resides the original girl who once, for a short while, trusted the world.

You think of your dogs so often, longing for them, imagining a life ahead of you with more dogs in it. How can anyone not love dogs? Dogs make a person real. You would have laid down your life for those dogs. Never have you felt such keen love. Your dogs taught you this love, its give and take. The people who claim that the Iditarod dogs are exploited are full of shit. You and your dogs were in it together. You can't survive that race without extreme passion for your dogs. Extreme devotion. It is a love that surpasses any you've ever seen between humans. Love propels both sides—the dogs love as much as the people do.

As your dogs slept after a day of racing, you would put your ear to their hearts to witness the furious pumping begin to subside. Miracles of cardiac fitness those hearts, hearts that would put human ultra-marathoners to shame. They knew how to rest too, giving themselves over to sleep without worry about what might befall them. You always tried to learn this from them—run hard, then rest hard too—but you never managed to master the resting part. So often you've wished to *be* a dog, running and resting and loving without all the claptrap humans attach to such things.

One of your dogs, Goldie, died two thirds of the way through the Iditarod. Her gait became lopsided and she began to stumble. You thought she was dehydrated, so you stopped to give her water and food. Back on the trail she didn't improve. You pulled into the next station and lingered for several hours, talking to the vet, who agreed Goldie shouldn't continue but was optimistic about her recovery.

You thought of quitting the race. How could you possibly stay tough when you were worried about Goldie? The dogs were affected too—dropping out would be respectful to them as well. But they were the ones who insisted on not giving up. They whined and leaped and nudged you with their impatience. You stood in front of them. *Shall we keep going?* you asked. They told you *yes* in so many ways. With their bright eyes and the wagging plumes of their tails, their paws scratching the snow, some of them barking. *Yes!* And so you went on, suppressing the nagging sense that Goldie might be dying. You tried to be present and enthusiastic, because that was how your dogs needed you to be. You and your dogs finished. By then Goldie was already dead of a congenital heart condition you never knew she had.

Sometimes you found yourself measuring your love for Eric against the love you had for your dogs. The dogs always won, but you concealed that thought, believing others might think it was abnormal. If people in the courtroom want to think that this wisp of a girl Lily drove you to desperation, let them, but they would be wrong—you've known far worse heartache.

There was a painting in your in-laws' apartment at the end of a hallway outside the room where you and your husband stayed. An abstract face split down the middle, forehead to chin, the two sides matching in shape but out of alignment. A fault line of the face, the aftermath of a skull quake. *It's faux Picasso,* your husband told you. *A copy from some no-name artist. I don't even know why we have it—it's not very valuable. The pieces in the living room are much more valuable. The Chagall. The Mondrian.*

Value was the farthest thing from your mind. The mere idea that paint on canvas could have enormous monetary value had always struck you as laughable. It was the image itself that made an impression. A split face. You'd seen the faces of stroke victims that sagged on one side, but never a clean split like this. Logs split, families split, fortunes split. Now a face.

After the race you collected Goldie's body. It was nothing like the Goldie you knew. Her life force had evaporated, been absorbed into the atmosphere like smoke. Where had all that energy gone? To the stars, perhaps, or maybe to another dog? All that zest for running had to have gone somewhere. You clipped a tuft of Goldie's thick pure-white coat and stored it in a Ziploc bag. You had Goldie cremated by a vet and kept the ashes in the box the vet returned to you.

You tried to tell Eric about this, what it meant to witness Goldie failing, then knowing she was dying as you finished the race. How guilty you felt for not being present at her death. You tried to explain how Goldie's absence was, for a while, like the darkening of the entire electrical grid.

Harsh, he said. He'd never had a pet.

It was unconditional love, you said. But that sounded wrong, too human-psychological. You couldn't explain the powerful thing that existed between you and your dogs, abstract, but also squarely situated in an energy exchange between bodies.

That's why I want a child, he said.

Again, words failed. You were sure a child would not be the same.

It suddenly came to me. Jessie's "Lucky" tattoo referred to her dogs. She was lucky to have known such deep love for her dogs.

"Juror #3! Step down!" The judge's voice was penetrating and harsh. It took me a minute to remember I was Juror #3. In my reverie, I had missed something.

I approached the bench as the other jurors filed out for lunch recess. The bailiff had led Jessie away too, so the only people remaining were the two attorneys gathering their things, the judge, and me.

The bench was higher and more imperial than it appeared from the jury box. The judge lowered her glasses to regard me. "Ms. White-Brown, what do you think you're doing?" Her face wore a no-admittance look, but I fought its diminishing intent and made myself return her query with equal force.

"Excuse me?" I said.

"What do you mean by staring at the defendant as you've been doing. Holding eye contact with her?"

I thought I'd been passing under the radar, but instantly I understood how naïve I'd been. Of course the judge would notice. She was presiding. It was *her* courtroom. It took me a moment to formulate a response.

"I'm trying to understand the defendant, Your Honor. I thought that was my job as a juror."

"You and the defendant are staring each other down. You don't need to stare to understand."

"She's always staring back at me."

"Leave the defendant out of this. You are not to engage in any more of these stare-downs. If you persist, I'll have to dismiss you. Do you understand?"

"Yes, Your Honor."

She paused, squinting as if to check me for ulterior motives. For a moment I worried she might have some way of knowing I'd Googled things. Or maybe she knew about my father. Then her face softened ever so slightly.

"What kind of a name is White-Brown anyway?" She shook her head, amusement poking through her disgust.

"Shall I explain?"

"No, no." She fluttered a hand behind her head. "Go have lunch. And no more staring, you understand?"

"Right. No more staring."

17

I had no call to visit his side of the bed, which was always immaculate
compared to my own messy side. But one spring afternoon I was
bitten by an uncharacteristic urge to clean. Even slobs sometimes feel
such a need. I vacuumed the living room, scoured the kitchen and
bathroom, washed the towels and sheets. I remade the bed and pulled
out a lightweight quilt we had stashed away for winter. I gathered the
used dental floss, crumpled tissues, and wax-crusted earplugs from
my bedside table and sponged it clean. I wasn't doing this for him, but
I knew it would please him. Then I moved to his side. His ubiquitous
water glass, a pad of yellow Post-its, a pen. I opened the drawer to store
the Post-its and pen, expecting the drawer to be empty.

It was not empty. There was a book in there. A book of poetry. *Address*, by Elizabeth Willis. I had not heard of Elizabeth Willis. I devour
fiction and nonfiction, but I read poetry only occasionally. Drew never
read poetry. He never read anything. I opened the book to a Post-it-
marked page.

> Take this spoon
> From me, this
> Cudgel, this axe
>
> Take your fear
> From its closet
> Take this shirt
> in need of washing
> this unread book

◆ ◆ ◆

Take my wife
even if I meant
to keep her

There was more but that was all I read. I had no idea what Elizabeth Willis meant with these lines, but I had my own ideas. The mind cannot be imprisoned—it flies where it wants.

Draw yourself a rival, ornately feathered and bejeweled with all the attributes you lack. The perfect *not-you*. Shimmery. Slim and tall and fit and elegant. Gregarious. Replete with social graces. A smart dresser. Admired by all. Not a trace of cynicism in her bones. In my case the person I sketched was not overwrought, not reclusive, certainly not the daughter of a criminal. Okay, maybe I'm being a little hard on myself, but you know what I mean.

It turns out a rival cannot be so easily drawn as one might think—they ambush you. R was an artist, a painter, known locally but not much beyond. Flamboyant abstract oils done on large canvasses. Would it surprise you to hear I'd never liked them?

From a distance, speaking purely about appearance, R was more or less the rival I might have envisioned, if I'd been thinking about rivals (which I was not): tall, slender, blonde, with an oval, buttery-skinned face. But up close the image of perfection fell away. Eerily skeletal, her collarbones protruded, and her pointy elbows and hands were so barren of flesh you could easily imagine crushing them. Her lips, perennially painted a bright red, were thick as banana slugs—collagen-injected?—more inflamed than sensual. And her personality was a far cry from the rival I would have imagined. She was loud and solipsistic and took up more space than Drew, which is saying a lot. She almost made Drew look like a wallflower. And while Drew attracted people naturally, R interposed herself, often interrupting conversations where she wasn't welcome, talking over people until they shut up. It's amazing, in retrospect, that our friends tolerated her. She was the kind of oblivious person who, in a conversation about death, might announce she'd recently stubbed her toe.

Still, people seemed to admire something about her. Her persistence. Her artistic ambition. She had Personage status and people flocked to her art openings. Drew and I were among the hordes who traipsed to those openings. We made the rounds, pretended to consider and admire her work. On our way home we trashed her. Her faux humility. Her cackling laugh. The way she seized our forearms to drag us to meet people we had no interest in meeting, as if we were mere pawns on her chess board. At the end of those evenings we would tumble into bed, laughing at her expense and having better sex than ever.

Yelling was not in our wheelhouse. Once the situation was clear, and Drew had confirmed his involvement with R, and it was equally clear he neither wanted to discuss the relationship nor drop it, I packed up my things while Drew motored around the rooms I was not occupying, occasionally calling out: *Take the rug in there. Don't you want at least one chair? You need some dishes.* I didn't want anything except the few things that had always belonged to me.

No, that's not right. I wanted him to explain what he saw in R, the woman we had so frequently mocked. I wanted him to say it meant nothing, she wasn't his type, he would end it. I wanted him to implore me to stay. Those things were not being offered, and I certainly wasn't going to beg for them. He helped me carry the last of my boxes to the car. It looked like the vehicle of a college student making a quick getaway.

"Can I give you a hug?" he said.

I didn't answer. I stashed myself out of reach in the driver's seat, closed the door with deliberation, and drove off. I saw him in the rearview mirror, still standing on the sidewalk, tiny and abject, waiting for absolution.

My sister Sue, who's undergone scads of therapy, has told me more than once that I have trouble with endings. My answer to that is: *Who doesn't?* Who moves wholeheartedly forward without ruing what has been lost?

As I said, I did not take many of our joint belongings, but I did take three books of poems that were not mine. I found them in his bedside table as I was packing up. The original Elizabeth Willis book, and collections by Pablo Neruda and Mary Oliver. I slipped all three into my suitcase beneath pants and shirts and underwear.

The ways we console ourselves. I'm smarter. Stronger. Faster. Fitter. More creative. More artistic. More beautiful. Funnier. Tougher. Craftier. Better read. Better at business. Better at math. Better with my hands. Sexier. More musical. More spiritual. More obedient. More precise. Neater. More flexible. More defiant. More patriotic. Classier. Better dressed. More cultured.

I expected him to ask for those books. I imagined him texting me: *You took my poems. Bring them back.* I wouldn't bring them back had he asked, but he never asked. After I'd found the first book of poems, I pictured various scenarios. Me on the couch leafing through the book, him watching me, stewing, cornered, unsure what to say. Maybe I would read a line or two aloud. Or maybe I'd say: "What wonderful poems!" Or maybe he would say: "Where did you get that book?" He might say something more confrontational: "What're you doing with that book?!" Though that would reveal too much, so he'd probably opt to say nothing at all, initiating a silent war between us.

None of those scenarios happened. I never sat on the couch reading his book. I left the book in the drawer. I kept my cover. Until I didn't.

After I left, I crashed on my friend Val's couch for a month. I never went out, fearful of running into R or Drew, or both of them together. I didn't want to run into anyone else either, acquaintances who might inquire about how I was doing. I was doing terribly, of course. The world wasn't safe, and in that unsafe world no one had my back.

Val and I snorted over those books of poetry. Not the poetry itself, but poetry as a strategy for wooing, as much a cliché as wooing with etchings. How transparent, we said, how unoriginal. Just like R. How dumb of him to succumb to a woman like that. Or had she succumbed to him? We weren't sure. However it had gone down, he wasn't letting her go.

I wrote postcards. One line per card.

Are you still Bony?

Do you come between R's nonexistent boobs?

I am gray, overcooked meat, no longer rare.

I wasn't stupid enough to send those cards.

Six weeks out he sent me an email masquerading as an apology. *I just felt we had played ourselves out.* There was other stuff in the email, but that was the only line that stuck with me. *Played ourselves out.* Perishables with a shelf life.

I WAS A RARE THING! AND THEN I WASN'T.

Once I had my own apartment, I would often wake in the morning and lie in bed for a long time looking up at a corner of the ceiling where cobwebs were gathering. It wasn't a terribly high ceiling—I could easily have swept them away if I'd wanted. But here is the crux: The will wasn't there. I didn't have a ladder so I would have had to drag myself to the hardware store and invest in a duster long enough to reach that corner. Then I would have to make the time to use my newly purchased duster. In other words, I would have had to care. I would have had to think it mattered. It didn't matter to me, and no one else noticed or cared if my corners were full of cobwebs.

Increasingly, there was very little to care about. I began to wonder why anyone did anything: run a marathon, write a book, run for office, not to mention the ordinary things like dusting, or washing dishes, or getting dressed, or going to work. I could picture a time when my will would be so eroded I would never go out again. Nor would I be able to prevent wild animals from coming inside. Spiders and ants would scuttle in and busy themselves making nests and webs wherever they chose. Birds would fly inside through the vents under the eaves. A few snakes and squirrels, and maybe some neighborhood rats would find an entrance through the dryer hose. Those creatures would take what they needed and leave me alone, and we would live side-by-side without too much friction. The refrigerator would be off limits, of course. And I would prefer it if they didn't poop on the furniture. As for the rest, fine, have at it. Make yourselves a cozy home.

When the will dissipates, doesn't life itself follow? This thought led me to ponder my own breath, the in-and-out of it, how it segued from deep to shallow and back again. I wondered whether my last breath would be the effortful in-breath, or one of those long glorious out-breaths nourishing my organs and extremities one final, ineffectual time.

At some point, I became aware that these ruminations could destroy me. I had to act. The moment had come to move back East.

18

The parade of prosecution witnesses bled endlessly into the second week. McCarthy had obviously done her homework and produced a string of cheerleaders for Eric, but I began to wonder if McCarthy's diligence in gathering fans of Eric might turn out to be her Achilles heel. Did others feel as I felt? I was dying to compare notes with someone. Anyone. Back in the jury room, preparing to go out for lunch, I scanned the room for someone who might defy protocol with me and discuss the case. I deemed most of them to be law-abiding citizens. I'd gone to lunch with Chrystal the first week and we had established a good but superficial rapport. She didn't seem remotely tempted to discuss the trial. I considered approaching Ray, the iconoclast, who sat to my left. He had made himself an outsider and might share his views with me. But I quickly dismissed the thought—he was too much of a curmudgeon.

Shanti approached me and asked me to join her group for lunch. Having seen her discretion at the farmer's market over the weekend, I had a good feeling about her, so I said yes. By the time I realized the group included Drew, we were out on the street and it was too awkward to opt out. That was how I found myself in a café with Drew and four other women: Anna the college student, Joanne the housewife, Chrystal, and Shanti. Drew and his harem.

It was exactly as excruciating as I thought it would be. Drew still had the habit of holding forth and controlling the conversational flow. For some reason this didn't annoy people—they found it endearing, perhaps because he sometimes paused to listen too, and in listening he won people over, pouring his attention onto whoever was speaking, singling them out, his sex appeal laid out before them like a velvet trampoline. I sat in the café that day pushing shreds of iceberg lettuce back and forth across my plate, watching him snow those women, alarmed by how it bothered me. He belonged to me! I didn't want him, but still he was mine, despite the many elapsed years since we'd divorced. We still owned a part of each other's histories. I'm not pretending any of this was logical.

Mostly I didn't say much, but there was one terribly awkward moment when Shanti turned to me. "Hey, Sybil, what did the judge say to you? I don't know if I should be asking but was she mean? Was it awful?"

"Oh!" I said, surprised by her forwardness. "She said I was staring at Jessie. She told me not to stare. It was embarrassing."

"I'm not surprised," Shanti said. "She's pretty intimidating, sitting up there in her black robe."

"Yup," I said then everyone let it drop, understanding we were approaching the edge of illegal.

As we walked back to the courthouse, Drew broke into song, turning and walking backwards so everyone could hear him and see him grinning through the words.

> I've been sitting in the courtroom
> All the livelong day
> I've been sitting in the courtroom
> Much to my dismay
>
> Can't you hear the rigid woman shouting
> Line up, don't be rude!
> Can't you hear both lawyers begging
> Don't cop attitude
>
> Justice will be done
> Justice will be done
> Justice will be done in the U—S—A
> Justice will be done

Justice will be done
Justice will be done for sure.

A couple at a party were fighting
Someone talking shit
Someone's on the hook for mur-ur-der
Does the story fit?

Fee-fi-fiddle-i-o
Fee-fi-fiddle-i-o-o-o-o
Fee-fi-fiddle-i-o
Strumming on the old banjo.

The other women laughed hysterically. What a nice voice he had! What a riot he was! *You never told us you could sing!*

I shot him a look.

"No one told us we couldn't *sing* about the trial," he said in self-defense.

He and Anna took off in the lead, laughing, singing single lines of familiar pop tunes. I fell in with Chrystal, fuming in spite of myself. Too soon I was back in the courtroom staring at Drew's neck again, wishing he'd never told me I was rare.

I had become hyperaware of the judge. She didn't have her eyes on me constantly, but I felt her gaze strobing past me occasionally, and I sensed she didn't like or trust me.

We'd heard rumors that the prosecution was close to resting its case, but we could never be sure of the rumors, where they'd begun and who was spreading them. But the witness we heard that afternoon did turn out to be the last one. It was the Homicide Detective, a guy with an exceptionally long body—he had to be close to seven feet tall—and an exceedingly small head. He spoke in the measured way that can sometimes be a deceptive stand-in for true authority—a lot of pausing that implies deep thought is in progress. We'd heard from him on the first day, so it seemed odd he was testifying again. It didn't take long, however, for the prosecution's strategy to become clear. A long time was spent establishing his credentials—he'd been on the police force for twenty-five years, twenty-two of those years as a detective—and he presided over numerous cases of domestic violence, sexual assault, rape, and murder.

"So in all your experience as a detective, is there anything about this case that struck you as unusual?"

"Yes."

"Can you tell the court what you found to be unusual in this case?"

"I have never in my professional career as a detective seen a male member—a penis—attacked like that."

A chill took hold of the courtroom, despite the room's heat. McCarthy nodded in her slow self-satisfied way. You could almost hear her saying, *Ca-ching! There's my ace in the hole.*

So what now? Was the cut penis evidence of such savagery and malicious intent that little more had to be said? I had reasonable faith in Vitale, but this seemed like a prohibitive hill to climb even with exceptional legal prowess.

Vitale passed on cross examining. *What? Why? No!* I thought at first. But after a second, I knew. There was no way to reposition the bald shocking fact of a cut penis. The Detective would never be bamboozled into saying, *Well, under certain circumstances cutting a penis might be reasonable.*

Also, everyone knows that penises are sacrosanct.

19

That Tuesday evening, the day before the defense would finally have its say, I returned home in a state of terrible restlessness and collapsed in the backyard, unreasonably exhausted. I hoped Brenda didn't pop up for an over-the-fence chat as she'd been doing recently. I needed to rest.

But when I closed my eyes, there was Jessie, rising from the swamp of my exhaustion, beryl eyes protruding from her weathered face, staring directly at me as if there was something I could do for her right then. Moment by moment her expression clarified itself, pleading, aggrieved, hopeful, so many feeling states simultaneously. But their aggregate was: *Don't fail me.* Then, a second image congealed, an ethereal shape from my dreams, owl-eyed Shawna right beside Jessie, their heads listing toward one another, touching, melding like Siamese twins, then morphing into each other, Jessie into Shawna, Shawna into Jessie, both big-eyed, both regarding me intently to see what I planned to do.

How naïve I'd been to think jury duty would be a welcome distraction from the central problems of my life when, instead, it had corralled every trouble I'd ever had and dumped them at my feet, leaving me to watch the theater of Sybil's neurosis playing across my mind's proscenium.

I didn't answer the knocking I heard on the front door, fearing it would be Brenda. I'd let her become too familiar of late, and she was roaring past good-neighbor boundaries. I was not in the market for a new friend. But the social persona is robust and it often expresses itself in a veneer of robotic good behavior, so I finally went to the door with the intent of sending Brenda politely away. It turned out not to be Brenda—it was Drew.

We stared at each other through the fraying screen door. He hugged a plastic grocery bag against his chest—one of those same plastic bags he had always decried—and mounted a smile, brief and feeble.

"Hi." Forlorn, almost sheepish. Some silence hummed back and forth between us, taking on the texture of conversation itself. "So, the judge reamed you?"

"I'll survive."

"Look, I know I was annoying you at lunch. I'm not blind."

"I'll survive."

His upper lip was curling under, always a sign he was wrestling with something. I waited for him to state his reason for being there and noticed for the first time that some of his cocksure quality had dimmed; he appeared more pensive than he'd been in the past.

"Takeout. You like Thai, right?" He lifted the bag from his chest and held it out to me.

He knew full well that Thai had always been a favorite of mine; he had never been fond of it himself, condemning it as too sweet. "Thanks. That's thoughtful. Unnecessary but thoughtful." I felt brittle and formal, my exhaustion dimmed by an adrenaline that dusted my tongue with something metallic. The screen door remained between us.

"You haven't eaten, have you?" he said.

"No."

"Well, are you going to let me in?"

Only at that moment did I realize he hadn't brought the food as a handoff, but something he planned to share with me. "How does R feel about you having dinner with me?" I said, testing the waters.

"R? Oh God, we're not together. We were only together for six months. If that."

"How would I know?"

"Right, of course." Shaking his head to tell me he was an idiot. A charade maybe—I couldn't tell. "So, yes or no—can I come in?"

I pushed open the screen door and let him through. He took a few steps inside, sizing up the barren interior of my living room: couch, coffee table, little else. "Where?"

"The backyard, I guess." I pointed. "Through the kitchen."

I didn't need to tell him where to go—the floor plans of those bungalows are more or less the same. I gathered plates and utensils and napkins as we passed through the kitchen to the back door. We settled in the Adirondack chairs, and he began to lay white boxes on the wooden table, noticing the dust but making no attempt to wipe it away, something he would never have neglected to do in the past. He didn't speak, and neither did I, and everything moved glacially as if this ritual we were performing was entirely new to us and had to be learned, and simultaneously as if we'd been doing it for centuries. We were chimeras composed of shifting teen and elder elements, both of us marked in different ways by age. Inconstancy had become my life of late. And though the ghosts in my head were gone for the time being, overshadowed by the primacy of the moment, I could feel their lingering presence as if they were my puppeteers.

Dishes of rice and chicken with vegetables and pot stickers and salad lay before us, and for a moment they appeared to me like Tarot cards, each replete with a different obscure meaning. The sight of all that food overwhelmed and stilled us both.

"Serving utensils?" he said, catalyzing forward motion again, and I went back inside for serving spoons as well as glasses and a bottle of white wine. Something was desperately needed to ease the strangeness.

He served two plates of food without asking what I wanted, and I opened and poured the wine, and we sat on pause again, plates on our laps, wineglasses on the arms of our chairs, an odd stop-start rhythm having taken firm hold. He surveyed the yard, the weathered slats of the back fence, the rangy crabgrass in need of mowing, the strip along one side of the fence that had once been a cultivated garden but since my habitation there had been vanquished by weeds. He was, certainly, judging me; beneath that charming exterior of his he was always evaluating. I suppose that made him the perfect juror, a person already primed to offer judgment.

He lifted his glass. "Cheers."

"What are we drinking to?"

"Reconnecting?"

"Ah—is that what we're doing?"

He sighed. "Well—"

"Okay. Cheers," I said.

We clicked and sipped and began, tentatively, to eat. It was so much work to be alone in his presence, putting forth the fiction that I was happier and stronger than ever before. I should have sent him away, Thai food and all. Brenda's chickens sent up a sudden collective squawking that startled us and provided welcome relief.

"Chickens?" he said.

"My neighbor fancies herself an urban farmer. It's good in theory, but in practice it's created a rat problem."

I told him about the various wild animals—raccoons and rats—who had been coming after the chickens' food, and how the foxes came after the chickens themselves, but the rats were the worst because they had proliferated, and now they came seeking food in all the neighboring yards too. It was a relief to be discussing something concrete and impersonal, especially something I knew he understood. He had a rat story of his own. He used to tell it so often when we were together that I'd learned to tell it myself.

When he was twelve, the family was having a problem with rats entering the barn at night and devouring the grain. It was decided that someone should stand watch overnight. The rats terrified Drew—their scrabbling feet, their entitled noses, the pointy teeth that had been known to bite and kill babies. His older brothers, knowing how the rats scared Drew, and being the torturers older brothers often are, elected Drew to be the one to stand watch in the barn one cold winter night, armed with a shotgun. He tried to object, but there was no resisting the force of his older brothers. He huddled in a fortress he'd constructed of blankets and straw, dressed like the Michelin Man yet still freezing, his ears receptive as satellites to the whooshing of owl wings, the squeaking of bats, the Jake Brakes of distant trucks, a night dirty with sound. The full moon made a farce of the barn's solidity, its light slipping through holes in the siding and cracks near the eaves, revealing how stupidly easy it was for the rats to enter. Wired as he was, he eventually drifted into sleep. He woke screaming, a rat traversing his chest, its tail squirming over his face, entire battalions of scurrying rats covering the barn's floor. He leapt from his bunker of straw, sidestepping through herds of rats, and fled to the house, sniveling, sobbing, cursing the rats, cursing his brothers, cursing the cruel full moon.

He narrated this story as a comedy that explained how he'd become the person he was, the product of a slew of bullying older brothers, all the confidence he'd accrued built on a trash heap of fear.

"Get a gun," he said to me now, half in jest, knowing that was the last thing I would do.

"A rat is a relatively small target for a neophyte shooter like me."

"Not just for the rats, but for the apocalypse. The day isn't far off when we'll all need to become survivalists and eat the rats and raccoons and foxes from our backyards."

We laughed. The apocalypse had always been a favorite subject of ours, and to laugh felt good, unexpectedly good, an offloading of the evening's tension like air whooshing from a popped balloon, like the heat of a fireplace when you've been horribly chilled, like the satisfaction of ice water on a scorching day. The relief permeated my entire body.

"Why did you leave Boston?"

I hesitated. Yes, I'd relaxed a bit, but I was not going to unzip myself for him. About that I was adamant. The problem was I hadn't yet constructed a concise, protectively glib Boston story. No one but Val had asked me, and with her, of course, I'd told the truth.

I laid down my plate and picked up my wine glass. "Things had changed so much. So many people I'd known there had moved away. And Sally was so busy with her daughters we hardly saw each other. It just didn't feel like my home anymore."

He nodded. "I could never move back to Eastern Oregon either. I wouldn't have any idea how to live there. Or how to live so close to my family. There's so much I wouldn't be able to say to them." He shook his head. "Did you ever think things would get this bad?"

"With us?" I said.

His head swiveled toward me in dismay. "Not us, the world. The ways it's going down the tubes in more ways than we ever thought of."

"Sure. My father's legacy, you know. From an early age I always knew we were doomed in one way or another."

In the ensuing silence I knew I'd said the wrong thing, surprising even myself. I never voluntarily brought up my father. And the subject had always been much too loaded for Drew and me to discuss. We hadn't talked about it since the days immediately after he found out; after that we both conspired to keep the subject off limits. I had no idea if he understood how my father's legacy had trained me to be unsurprised by bad behavior. Had he been thinking of my father, as I was, while we'd been sitting in the courtroom?

"Do you ever think we might still be together if you'd told me about your father from the start?"

I didn't answer.

"I think about that," he said. "I've especially been thinking of it this week."

There was my answer—he *had* been thinking of my father. It shouldn't have surprised me. My father's story had become part of his history in the same way that his rat story, his bullying brothers, and Alma the Iron Lady were all part of mine. You don't obliterate those things when you separate.

"So, it's my fault?"

"I'm not saying that."

"Sure you are. It's an odd thing for you to say when you were the one who dumped me."

"Okay." He reached across the broad arm of his chair and laid the tips of his fingers on my bare forearm. They were cat-tongue rough, but they twinkled over my neural receptors with surprising delicacy. "Let's not go over this—that's not why I came here. I did things. You did things. We were both terrible people. But maybe we're better now."

"Well, so far we haven't murdered anyone."

"Uh." A grunt. A reluctance to acknowledge my reference to the trial.

The oncoming darkness offered a welcome cradle of silence. Having said the word murder aloud, I began thinking about the trial again. I assumed he must be thinking of it too. But apparently his mind was on other things.

"I don't know what I was thinking with R. She repulsed me."

"That's not how I remember it. I remember that you were pretty smitten."

"Only for a very little while."

"I repulsed you too."

"Not true."

"Yes, come on—there was so much you didn't like about me in the end. Don't deny it. You hated what a slob I was. You hated my laziness and all the time I spent on sedentary activities. You said those things to me so many times. Not just to me, but in public."

"God, Sybil, cut me a break. I was young and foolish."

"That gives you a pass?"

"Well, for what it's worth, I've never been fully myself with anyone but you."

I closed my eyes. How was I supposed to receive this?

"I thought you felt the same way I did," he went on, "that even though we were so different we didn't want to change each other. We accepted each other as we were and gave each other space to be the people we needed to be."

I had no idea how to evaluate what he said. Was he saying something he believed? Did he really not remember the numerous times he'd urged me to lose weight?

"Maybe. Maybe not. But then R came along."

He hung his head so his chin thunked his chest. "I am so, so, so, so sorry," he whispered.

A juncture. I could go in for the kill, or let him off the hook. I teetered. I was too tired to fight, and too conflict-aversive anyway. I got up and took the dishes inside. When I came back out, I noticed he'd refilled our wine glasses. The evening had taken on a momentum of its own, and I sat back down, relinquishing myself to whatever came next. The anger I'd been storing all week—at the prosecution, at Drew, at the judge—was ebbing somewhat. It's hard work to sustain anger.

I looked over at him, and he seemed to have shrunk. "Your apology is maybe a decade too late. But I appreciate it." We were even then— both somewhat diminished, both partially exposed. "How has your life been since then?"

He sighed. "It's mostly been the same. I still have my practice. I still hike a lot. Bike. Ski. You know. After R, I had two relationships. One lasted two years, the other lasted a year and a half. The last one ended three years ago and I haven't been with anyone since. I guess I'm a confirmed bachelor by now. That's about all there is to report." He paused to query my face before resuming.

"There's one other thing. A strange thing. Or at least unexpected." He paused, stared down at his plate, and used his fork to corral some stray grains of rice. "About a year ago I started taking a group of developmentally challenged teenagers on hikes once a month in the wilderness. It's been—well—pretty wonderful."

There was Gaylene, he said, the most exuberant member of his teen group who kept him coming back. She liked to hold his hand as they walked, and she addressed the trees and squirrels and slugs as if they were people. She adored being in the wilderness, an entirely new experience for her. She functioned as a leader, her enthusiasm inspiring other members of the group to engage with nature as she did, becoming the heart and soul of their expeditions. He had come to look forward to those monthly hikes more than he ever would have expected. He paused and shook his head, incapable of continuing.

Waves of tenderness and resentment floated over me as I listened to him rhapsodize, trying to picture him holding Gaylene's hand, expressing a paternal urge I'd thought was absent.

"That's a departure for you."

"Sometimes we depart from ourselves."

Departing from self. Strange that he'd given voice to that idea just then, as it was something I'd been thinking about since the trial began. Jessie had, the fateful *night in question*, departed from the upstanding person she had come to be. Her life, henceforth, would have a new trajectory. Thinking about her I'd reviewed my own life, combing for such moments of departure from self, but I couldn't find any. I felt as if I could draw a straight line from the person I'd been as a child to the person who sat in that Adirondack chair that night.

"Do you ever wonder if you could murder someone?" I said. "If you were pushed."

He laughed. "I never wonder that."

"I think any one of us could. Under the right circumstances."

"Should I worry?" He laughed again, as if to fend off my serious inquiry. "You don't really believe that, do you?"

"I do! Look at Jessie. She's a lawyer for God's sake, an upstanding citizen and then things happened she couldn't control and . . ."

"Sybil."

"They're trying to make her look crazy and make Eric look like some big teddy bear of a hero."

"Sybil."

"No. Really. I don't buy it. It's just wrong. She was pushed. She had no choice."

"Okay, Sybil. You have to stop right here. We can't discuss this. They've told us a million times. Save these thoughts for the jury room."

"Oh God, you're such a stickler. What harm does it do? We're both jurors—we'll be talking about it eventually."

"I should go."

Now I was annoyed, just when I'd begun to relax with him again. "Maybe you should."

He leaned forward in his chair and laid his wine glass, still half full, on the table. He ran a hand through his hair then seemed to freeze. "Oh my God," he whispered. "Look—a rat."

I followed his gaze. A rat was nosing around in the shadows by the back fence, ignoring us, his body black and bulbous.

"I told you," I said. "Get out!" My yelling had no effect so I found a broom in the kitchen and ran across the yard, roaring and wielding the broom like a lance, then sweeping it back and forth, almost making contact with the rat's repulsively muscular body until it squeezed itself back under the fence. I collapsed back into my chair, broom beside me.

He chuckled quietly. "You're braver than I am. But you need to shore up that fence."

"It wouldn't do any good. Any animal that's motivated can circumvent a fence. Dig under. Climb over. I am functionally fenceless. Defenced."

My recollection gets murky here. I know there were long stretches of silence. I remember thinking we needed more animal distraction. I remember hearing Brenda's boys coming out to their yard, whispering, the smell of pot wafting over the fence, Drew commenting that despite its legality the smell still startled him. I began thinking about time, the fourth dimension, something I knew too little about. I was wondering what the passage of time had done to each of us. So much had happened to both of us the other knew nothing about. I wished I understood time's wrinkle effect, the idea of parallel lives. At some point I became aware that Drew had risen from his chair.

"Do you mind if I—?" He pointed to my foot.

His meaning coalesced slowly. "Oh, for God's sake, I don't think that's a good idea." Had I summoned this action from him by thinking about parallel lives?

"But you're nodding—you must mean yes."

Did I nod? Maybe. I was overcome with a kind of passivity that I understood might lead to something I'd regret, but what was happening seemed fated. The template was already there, part of my life and his, and it is the nature of templates to recur. He knelt and removed my sandal and took up my foot in both of his warm muscular hands. I could have said *no, this is preposterous*, and he would have honored it. But I didn't say no. I closed my eyes and he began to massage, cradling my foot and kneading it, his fingers moving as if he was performing a sacred ritual, just as it had been all those years ago in the woods. Time played over me like an accordion, back and forth, this single event replicating itself multiple times, at different amplitudes and with new harmonics, louder, softer, but never vanishing entirely, the pulse of human history.

Many people will not understand why I agreed to let him do this. They will say I was foolhardy, even crazy, that I was inviting more heartache. But it was beyond the control of my gray matter. I was an open wound. I needed so much. Attention. Healing. Love. Here was a man who had always believed the body could be an avenue to curing anything. I wanted, more than ever, to believe that too.

He held my foot and I became a beginner again. A rare woman with renewed hope.

20

In court the next day things took forever to get underway, both attorneys conferring sotto voce with the judge, the judge frowning, tugging her chin, Jessie picking at a cuticle, forearms before her on the table, Eric's mother leaning forward as if to sharpen her hearing. We jurors sat quietly in our assigned seats, knowing better than to interact.

In the jury room Drew had ignored me. Was he wishing he had not massaged my feet the night before? Did he remember doing it? Of course he remembered. It wasn't possible I had *imagined* the whole thing, was it? For moments at a time I had no clear idea. Nor did I really know what a foot massage from him might mean in our current context. Once it had been a precursor to sex, but did it always mean that? Couldn't a foot massage be a merely platonic gesture?

The judge's gavel. "The court is in recess until Monday morning. 9:00 a.m."

Really? It was only Wednesday morning, a little after 10:30 a.m. Why three days off? Did it have to do with the trial itself, or with the judge's schedule, or with something altogether different? Back in the jury room we speculated.

"Judge is sick of us," joked Walmart Kevin.

"Maybe someone is going on vacation?" Joanne suggested.

"In the middle of a trial?" Shanti said.

Beret Dev, the know-it-all, shook his head. "I doubt it. It probably has to do with a witness."

Ray and Neal and Karen were already gathering their things.

"Who gives a shit? We're free, right?" Walmart Kevin headed for the door.

Drew approached Lenore whose forearms jutted from her waist, all ten fingers fluttering, as if she was trying to shoo us out. "What's going on? Why three days off?"

She shook her head, one hand taking flight above her head. She wasn't going to tell us anything.

Ray raised an eyebrow in my direction, as if accountable to me. I nodded, surprised he'd singled me out. He returned my nod and took off. Corey followed, then Karen and Neal. The rest of us were still caught there, still stuck in the quicksand of the mysterious dismissal. We glanced around at each other as if it was a social occasion and we couldn't leave without saying goodbye to the host. Anna and Shanti were standing close to Drew. Chrystal and I stood together, as did Sean and Dev, Joanne and Tom. In only a little over a week alliances had developed among us. We had almost galvanized as a group.

I was determined not to look at Drew, determined not to let whatever I did be governed by whatever he was going to do. If someone proposed a group lunch, I would not participate. I allowed myself to be sucked into the swarm of people heading to the door: Chrystal, Sean, Dev, and me, followed by Anna, Shanti, Joanne, Tom, and Drew. We crossed the lobby en masse and descended a staircase, then snaked down the lobby and descended another staircase, still cohering as if bound by a layer of fascia. We passed security and the building spat us onto the plaza, the sunlight blinding. As my eyes adjusted, Drew strode by me, butting my shoulder gently and turning to wink. A slow lowering of one eyelid and an equally slow rising, as if opening a portal long closed. It was neither glib nor dismissive, as far as I could see, but he kept walking with Anna and Shanti, ostensibly for lunch though it was still early for lunch.

The rest of us dispersed, *See you Monday* rippling from person to person. I walked slowly to my car, pondering what had just happened, wondering if I should have joined Drew and Shanti and Anna. But no, I told myself, his wink had told me all I needed to know.

I readied myself, showering and washing my hair, and applying a faintly jasmine-scented oil that imparted a subtle sheen to my skin. I put on a drapey pale green sleeveless sundress that flattered my figure if not my upper arms. I watched myself doing these things, seeing myself in a slow-motion movie, simultaneous actor and spectator, all the while asking: *Is this me?* It was the altered state a person arrives at when she cannot believe she has come to be doing what she's doing.

My speculation was right. He was on my doorstep two hours later—midafternoon—washed and redressed himself, smelling of pine trees, carrying a single white rose and champagne, an offering that had never played any role in our past relationship. I tried to remember what white roses stood for—purity, yes, and maybe apology too?

I'm not going to give you a blow-by-blow—what do you take me for?—but I will say that I discovered that the bicycle analogy holds for sex: You don't forget. I was nervous, at first. I hadn't had sex the entire seven years I'd been in Boston, and I worried he would be repulsed by the marks of age on my forty-nine-year-old body. The skin doesn't adhere as tightly as it once did to underlying muscle and bone. When I reach for something—a mug on a high shelf, a book on a table—I see a pouch of flesh shimmying under my upper arm, moving entirely independent of me, doing things my brain has not instructed it to do. My neck has begun to take on the stringy look I've seen on older women: two parallel tendons popped out like railway ties, accentuated by my weight loss. My cheeks, too, are in the process of remaking themselves, falling like a glacial mudslide to settle around my mouth and jawline, pooling and puckering in less-than-attractive ways. I've never used cosmetics—or nothing more than an occasional swipe of lipstick—and these are not the kinds of changes that can be addressed with cosmetics anyway. Most disturbingly, my larger-than-average breasts have succumbed to gravity, so now, when I'm not wearing a bra they sway near the middle of my ribcage. I know, I know, too much information. At any rate, as we disrobed, I was pleased to see he'd acquired a narrow Hula-Hoop of belly fat himself, and his skin, too, had lost some of its resilience.

We didn't discuss these things. I made a silent pledge not to be stalled by this, to act with as much self-acceptance as I could muster. At some point a woman gets too old to apologize for her body. I can't say exactly what Drew was thinking, but I believe his thoughts were similar to mine, because we both plunged ahead. The crazy pull of him, desire swamping me like a heavy monsoon. No, a monsoon isn't right—I felt as if I'd been slimed, like the scene in *Carrie* where she's covered in pig blood, stunned and disbelieving. I'd thought I was beyond desiring him, that he had become to me like foresworn ice cream—after long enough without it, you lose the craving. And that was true, but what I'd forgotten was that when it's placed before you again the craving flourishes, more irresistible than ever. Maybe you never lost it in the first place.

We were integrating old and new, addressing the urge of the moment along with memories from the past without worrying about the future. We were both aroused—that was quite evident—but we proceeded cautiously, checking things out with each other. *Is this okay? Do you mind if I . . . ?* He had brought a vial of oil with him, scented with some herb I didn't recognize, and we spread it over each other as had been our custom. We had not laid down a sheet or a blanket, so he was careful not to slop oil on the carpet, though it was an old carpet, already stained.

Afterwards, I lay there mute, and he chuckled quietly. His chuckle morphed to a sigh. "Booooobs," he said, quietly elongating the word so it became almost a croon. My heart raced.

"I've missed this so much," he said, noticing for the first time the Band-Aid that covered the cut at the base of my palm where, the week before, in a fugue state (brought on by thinking about the cut penis) I'd sliced myself. He touched it lightly. "How did this happen?"

"Carelessness."

"The world is a dangerous place."

"Populated by terrible people," I said, reciting our old mantra.

The years of our separation thronged around us, so many events and stories we hadn't shared.

He spent Wednesday night with me and we slept late on Thursday morning—something he had never been in the habit of doing before. We made brunch and lingered at the table. Since we'd cleared our schedules for the trial, neither of us had anything pressing to do. I would have loved to discuss my thoughts about Jessie, the prosecution, the judge, but I refrained, not wanting to risk his disapproval, but also because the trial had receded to the back of my consciousness, squeezed from primacy by the unexpected turn of events.

That afternoon we strolled along the river. He adjusted his stride so as not to rush me. We might have been by the Seine, or the Danube, or the river in Prague whose name I forget. All day he remained near me, as if to let me out of his sight would be to lose me altogether again. The years had made him more considerate, more deferential. *Do you want to keep walking or turn around?* He kept gazing at me and reaching for my arm in an apparent state of amazement. *I never dreamed this would happen again,* he kept saying. *I can't believe how lucky we are. I feel like an amputated limb has been restored to me.* I, having never been given to effusive emotional expressions, said very little, though I do remember smiling a lot and working hard against expectations for the future.

How could I not warm to such attention? How could I not adore being rare again?

He stayed on Thursday night and again we slept late and went for a meandering walk in the woods that afternoon. Early Friday evening he went back to his place for fresh clothes, and I wondered if he would return. He had promised me he would, though I wasn't sure how much to trust him. But sure enough, after an hour and a half he was back in clean clothes with a bag of groceries.

It was a glorious unexpected vacation. We stayed up late every night, wallowing in the cocoon of my bed, which we dubbed *The Garden of Earthly Delights*, a place of unparalleled hedonism with its plethora of pillows, along with the oils and sex toys he'd brought with him. We played with each other's bodies as we used to, though more ruminatively than before, and when we'd sated ourselves we slept hard, as if drugged. We eschewed all routine, foraging for food, bringing plates of crackers and cheese, apples and carrots, nuts and dried apricots to bed, along with coffee or wine. But hunger was mostly far from our minds.

After sex we told each other things. Certain things. A toe in the water. The sex effect: breaking down the defenses, opening the floodgates, making you want to share more than you should. He told me his mother, Alma the Iron Lady, had died four years earlier, and her death had released in him an unexpected rage. That made perfect sense to me. He had not expressed rage towards her when we were together, only guilt. I suppose his leaving me must have had something to do with his mother, but I didn't mention that, didn't particularly want to explore it myself. At first, I was somewhat guarded; I told him more about what it had felt like to be back in Boston, a stranger in my own birthplace, to see how much distance had grown between me and my younger sister Sally.

He had scheduled appointments on Saturday afternoon with two of his needy clients who had been upset that he was gone for the trial. He told me this apologetically, not wanting to interrupt our idyll. "You wouldn't feel like coming with me?" he said. "You could take a walk while I work?"

I nodded, 100 percent agreeable, smirking a little at how our clingy behavior seemed so adolescent. Neither one of us wanted to leave the other, even for a few hours. So we drove to his office, and while he saw his patient I ambled around downtown in a kind of disbelieving enthralled daze. I had the profound feeling of having crossed back to safety, of returning to the self I'd once been. How lucky I was. What serendipity this trial had been.

The sidewalks were relatively empty, not unusual for a summer weekend when many residents were engaged in outdoor activities at the river, or on the coast, or in the mountains. The street people were just coming to life with their dogs, lighting up the first joints of the day, considering their next moves. Clouds of weed wafted over me, imparting a contact high. I wandered past slick new restaurants and cannabis shops, co-existing alongside shabby niche businesses—a lingerie shop, a clock shop—that had mysteriously survived for decades, and I regarded it all with a fondness I didn't usually feel. The rose-colored glasses of sex and of being part of an intimate twosome.

Being downtown, not far from the courthouse, and away from Drew's immediate presence, brought thoughts of Jessie back to mind. I wondered where she was waiting out these days of recess. A cell somewhere? At home? Shouldn't I know? Wherever she was, it was doubtful she was enjoying the delay as Drew and I were. If only I could reassure her that things would turn out in her favor. Reconnecting with Drew had underscored to me that successful outcomes were possible, maybe even likely. Jessie had to know that too—why else had she tattooed *Lucky* on her wrist?

I have no idea how much intention was involved in delivering me to the front door of Empress Tattoo on the periphery of downtown. I had walked there of my own accord, but I didn't remember *deciding* to go there. I stared at the Day-Glo graffiti art on its facade, feeling yet again the hand of fate that had taken me there.

The buzz of instruments issued from behind a curtain. The air was redolent with a heavy composite of patchouli, weed, anesthetic. Several twenty- and thirty-somethings bent over a glass case displaying piercing options. I was an alien there, middle-aged and not visibly stylish. But the green-haired young woman behind the counter greeted me without surprise, and when I announced my intention she pointed me to the books of tattoo designs. If I wanted "custom" it would cost more, she warned.

I already knew what I wanted, but I flipped through the books out of curiosity. Pages of the expected serpents and snakes and dragons. Pages of trees and flowers, flags, peace symbols, musical notes. There were faces and body parts, even breasts and penises. If you want a specific tattoo, chances are, someone has already designed it. Eyeing the other customers, I noticed I was the only one there without a companion. I wondered if I'd go through with this. I knew I would.

The inner wrist, where I could see it, I told Mindy, my tattoo artist, a speedy nonstop talker. I settled into her reclining chair, eye pillow blocking the light, while she described the array of designs she'd done over the years, the vibrating points of her "pen" bearing down relentlessly, a blur of pain that did not confine itself to my wrist, but took over my whole arm and torso, radiating to my back and neck and scalp. For a few minutes I could hardly think, then the pain eased and with the easing came a kind of exhilaration that buoyed me, as if I were detached from the world and sailing though space in a hot balloon.

The vibrating ceased. The pain ebbed. I pulled off the eye pillow. Mindy was still swabbing antibiotic ointment, but she paused for a moment, grinning, lifting her cloth and raising my arm to show me her work. **Lucky**. Almost like Jessie's, but the font was less fanciful, more straightforward. Exactly what I wanted.

By the time I was bandaged and out of the chair and loaded down with detailed instructions on how to care for my "wound," I was already late to meet Drew. I jogged back through the streets, more elated than ever. *On my way,* I texted. I was twenty minutes late, winded and sweating, when I found him waiting in front of his building.

"I was beginning to worry." He spotted the bandage. "What happened? Are you alright?"

I lifted the bandage and held forth my wrist for inspection.

"Oh my God!"

"I couldn't resist." I saw the concern seeping over his face. "You get it, right? Why I did it?"

"I guess so. But that thing—it's *permanent.*"

"I know. I want it to be permanent."

"Even though luck comes and goes?"

"It'll remind me luck is always there, waiting in the wings."

He laughed and shook his head. "If you say so."

I didn't mention Jessie's tattoo, nor did he. It seemed possible he hadn't noticed it.

For all his dismay at the impulsive way I'd "maimed" my body, he took wonderful care of me that night. He insisted on cleaning the tattoo and changing the dressing himself, and when we had sex he was careful to steer clear of my left arm.

After the sex and the talking, we lay in semi-darkness gazing at the shadowy outlines of each other, wondering who we were, what we were doing. The tattoo seemed to have stirred something in him, but when I asked him what he was thinking he wouldn't admit to being bothered.

The next morning, Sunday, we woke a little after nine. After sex we lolled in bed with coffee, savoring that rare delicious state of being simultaneously under-rested and more alert than usual. The trial's recess had stopped time and granted us the most perfect hiatus. I was acutely aware it was the last day of our reprieve before the trial resumed. I pushed that thought away, savoring my luck.

Then, the imminence of change prompted me to talk.

PART TWO

21

Not long after I'd moved back to Boston—having fled Oregon following the divorce—I was in Logan Airport on my way to New York for a long weekend with an old friend. A photo lassoed my attention, daring me to stop, even as I raced to my gate, dragging my too-heavy wheelie, already late for my flight. It was her eyes, opaquely dark and anime-large, their guileless pleading, their scary openness, set in a tawny oval face. She wore an old-fashioned sashed pink dress, a "party dress" as my sisters and I would have called it, and her glossy black hair was drawn into two braids fastened at the bottom with white ribbons. Against the photographer's backdrop of blurred bucolic greenery, she resembled a child from another century. Seven, I guessed, though I was wrong—she was ten at the time of that photo. Even later, at the onset of adolescence, her eyes remained like that, porous and inviting though she had so many reasons to be wary.

The airport hordes veered around me as I stood staring. Those displays of foster children hoping for adoption had never snagged my attention before, not beyond passing cynical comments about what the photographers must have done to make the children appear desirable, but now I was overcome, in some kind of love. I searched for a number to call and found it by the side of the display before hastening off to my flight.

When Shawna first came to live with me we were practically strangers. We had seen each other a total of three times, all in Edna the social worker's Roxbury office, which was small and dusty and cluttered with stacks of unfiled paperwork that put me in mind of Bartleby. Shawna's three-dimensionality shocked me. She looked exactly as she'd looked in the photograph, but there was a palpable selfhood I'd failed to imagine. She was not a child, but a *person*, I thought, feeling suddenly unprepared for the interview. Though she was just shy of eleven by then, she looked at least three years younger.

When I arrived at the office Shawna was hiding behind Edna's chair, only a flare of blue dress letting me know she was there. In a sudden burst she sprinted to the other side of the small room, elbowing a stack of papers that fluttered to the carpet, then crouching against a file cabinet and giggling at Edna. I wanted to laugh along with her but didn't think that was the adult thing to do. Edna, without any evidence of alarm, gathered the papers and restored them to their pile. Clearly used to such unpredictability, she settled back into her rolling chair, a solid oasis of calm. Shawna's giggling eased and the office went quiet but for the carping of traffic. Shawna stood still, an elfin statue, netting observations of me and reeling them in, then shutting herself off, staring at the carpet as if to say *enough*.

"This is Sybil," Edna said after a while. "Sybil, this is Shawna."

"Hey there, Shawna." As gently as I could I fed her questions, trying not to put her on the spot. *Have you enjoyed your winter vacation? Are you looking forward to summer? Do you like to swim?* Nothing yielded a response so I offered a few things about myself: how I love going to the beach, eating ice cream, going to the river and watching the boats. Edna chimed in until she and I were a duet sharing our favorite summer experiences, hoping Shawna might join us. She did not. She eased herself around the periphery of the room, cleaving to the furniture like a monkey needing a branch, finally arriving at Edna's chair where she rested her torso and cheek on Edna's lap, eyes directed at me. I couldn't decipher her look—maybe a dare? I envied Edna and felt foolish for trying to force myself on Shawna, for trying to make her like me. What arrogance on my part to think I could sail easily into her heart after so many adults had failed her. Edna had given me the broad strokes of her background. Taken at the age of four from her drug-addicted parents in the Portuguese community of Fall River, she was first placed with her mother's mother who contracted fatal cancer a year later. Shawna was then placed in a foster home, the first of three. The woman who ran the first foster home became ill with Lou Gehrig's disease, the second foster family ran into financial problems, the third was also on its way to disbanding.

For a day or so after that first meeting, I thought of bowing out, but thoughts of Shawna herself prevented me: Her impishness testified to a feisty spirit beneath her doll-like exterior. A week later I returned to our second meeting.

Shawna sat on the carpet not far from my feet, bent over a pad of paper and bearing down so hard with her crayon that she seemed to be arguing with the paper itself. Red cried up from the shape on the page. She flipped to a new page, carefully restored the red crayon to the box and selected a black crayon, again attacking a pristine page. Her care, almost tenderness, with the crayons was a stark contrast to the fury of her drawing. After sailing through several pages in this bellicose manner, she focused on one page and, as if she'd exorcised something from her system, she drew with slower more intentional strokes, using several colors. Every once in a while, she glanced up at me, but she never spoke, not a single word. When it was time for us to part, I asked if I could see her drawing. Considering, she gazed at the pad dangling from one hand, then held it up to me. She had filled the page with roiling color that wasn't the least bit random. Three similar shapes, like long crenulated Japanese lanterns, dominated the picture, in shades of red, pink, and orange. Around them were fleecy clouds of green and pink, and I began to pick out what might have been eyes and mouths amidst the green, though I could have been imagining it. I was impressed by the drawing's sophistication, the underlying talent, though it was abstract and I didn't fully understand it. I was trying to formulate a response when she ripped the paper in half with obvious glee and began to crumple both halves. Before more could be said, the driver arrived to take her back to Fall River.

In our third meeting she was drawing again and, perhaps because I was no longer a complete stranger, she began to speak. She spoke quickly and breathily, as a talking butterfly might speak. The words elided, so comprehending required my full attention. She liked kitties, she said. Would I let her have a kitten? I didn't see why not. She said she'd seen a kitten who jumped from a window and flew down to the street. He liked flying but he died. She ceased her drawing for a moment and held her arms wide and squeaked a little, a stand-in for the flying, dying kitten. "Oh," I said, eyeing Edna for cues. "Oh," feeling lame. During the last couple of minutes of that visit she agreed to sit on my lap. The sharp bones of her buttocks—*ischium,* thank you Drew— poked my thighs, her wing bones—*scapula*—jutted into my breasts, compressing my heart with fear-laced elation.

She was scheduled to arrive in June. We would have the summer together before she would have to start school. I was living in Somerville, where I'd moved upon my return from Oregon and where I plied my trade as an accountant from home, getting most of my referrals from former acquaintances. The apartment was a second-floor, two-bedroom on a tree-lined street, with a living room alcove I used as an office. The extra bedroom I called the guest room, but for the year I'd been back in the Boston area it had gone unused. In that year I'd begun to question the wisdom of my return. I'd thought I was moving not just away from the site of my divorce, but to a place I thought of as "home." I quickly realized I had no idea what home was. Was it a place? I'd always identified with Massachusetts, but not necessarily with the suburb where I grew up and not really with the city of Boston where I'd lived only as a college student. I found myself misremembering buildings and streets around Boston and Cambridge I thought I knew well. None of the landmarks I visited—the Rude Bridge in Concord, the Swan Boats in the Boston Public Garden, Fanueil Hall—had the effect of grounding me. In only a decade and a half the entire metropolitan area seemed to have lost its grittiness and even much of its history, becoming slick and homogenous as any twenty-first century American city.

Was home people? A few old friends remained, scattered here and there around Greater Boston, but most of them I'd fallen out of touch with. As for my family, they'd dispersed. My mother had died a few years earlier, just shy of her seventieth birthday, succumbing to a cancer I imagined was, if not stress-induced, certainly stress-exacerbated. My father, a few years after his release from prison when my sisters and I had left home, had retreated to somewhere in Northern New England. No one was quite sure where and no one cared to know. We were consciously trying to remove the taint of him from our memories. Sue was in New York by then, had been for a long time, so the only family member who remained in the area was my younger sister Sally. She lived in an upscale suburb west of Boston with her husband and two teenage daughters. I had thought we would become close again as we had been as kids, but the year had revealed her to be extremely occupied with her daughters, and we had trouble finding time to see one another. So I had not returned to any place or any people who made me feel I'd arrived home.

As soon as I knew Shawna was coming to live with me—when I'd passed the required background checks, endured the interviews and home visits, provided the masses of paperwork, and finally been approved to adopt her—I began fixing up her room. She wasn't able to tell me what she wanted. She'd never had her own room. Most of her life she hadn't even had her own family. Edna said an art table would be good, so that was the first thing I obtained, a low table and chair and a shelf full of supplies: pencils, paper, water colors, crayons, even some acrylic paints. I equipped the queen-size bed with a puffy pink quilt, a mountain of soft, variously-sized pillows and several stuffed animals, the plush Gund brand. I bought puzzles, Lego sets, a harmonica, some bongo drums and a triangle, and an abacus as I've always been partial to them. I inflated one of those large yoga balls for her to bounce on, placed a beanbag chair beside a bookshelf full of children's books I'd always loved. I tried to think of everything that might possibly interest her—knowing full well I was being excessive.

She came to me on a Saturday in mid-June, on a day when the overheated air molecules churned around the apartment, audible as tumbling stones, a humid heat that announced the imminence of a clobbering summer. Edna was driving Shawna up from Fall River and had said she expected they would arrive in the early afternoon, one-ish. She'd call if they were delayed.

Have I mentioned that I always know the time within a minute or two? I'm always calculating how many years, months, days, and minutes I might have left until death descends. In the bulk food aisle I instinctively scoop a perfect half pound of roasted almonds. I routinely guess my heartrate accurately. I have a habit of scanning crowds to estimate their size. You learned to do that in elementary school, didn't you? Maybe middle school. You take a sample area and multiply it out. But you probably don't do that as a matter of course as I do. Numbers, you see, anchor a person like me. They provide a scaffolding for the flighty scarves of the mind.

They would arrive at 1:00.

From then on, Shawna and I would be a 2-some.

I had 5 stuffed animals for her.

She was 11. I was 44. If I had given birth to her I would have been 33. I was 33 years older than she. When she was 33, I would be 66. When she was 44, my age, I would be 77.

Being a phlegmatic person, my anxiety rarely manifests itself physically, but that day I jittered from room to room, double-checking things, charting my future with Shawna, her future with me, wondering if she would go to college, what kind of work she would find, if she would have a family, musing about these things but never losing a sense of the minutes ticking over and through me. At 9:00 I made 2 tuna fish sandwiches in the already stifling heat. I put them on plates and covered them with plastic wrap and put them in the fridge. I checked the bathroom for the 2 toothbrushes, the 2 plastic drinking cups, blue and pink, and I laid them out like place settings. On the rack where I'd hung a set of pink towels that would be hers, I made a magic marker sign that said: SHAWNA'S TOWELS. At 11:08 I realized I'd forgotten ice cream. I needed ice cream—it was one of the few things she had explicitly said she liked. I knew I had time to dash out and back before they came, but I hated to leave. Yes, no, yes. I made it to the grocery store and back in 17 minutes. 4 flavors of ice cream: vanilla, chocolate, cookie dough, and peppermint stick.

There was nothing more I could do. I sat in the living room attempting to read. I called Edna's cell, but it went to voicemail and I didn't leave a message. I wasn't worried that something had happened to them—I was worried about the rest of my life, about me and Shawna being right for each other. Is there an analogy for what I was going through, the myriad pathways of speculation I was traveling? Perhaps it was like an arranged marriage—I had committed to a lifelong relationship and there was no backing out. My heart rate surged from its usual resting rate of 73 to 86, then 97, though I was only sitting and reading, not-reading. It spiked to 106 by the time the bell rang at 2:17.

There they were, stalwart Edna and little Shawna, neat as ever in what looked like a christening dress. Edna had been to my place before as part of the pre-adoption approval process, but it was Shawna's first time seeing where she would live. As soon as she stepped over the threshold, she froze. "Hello there," I said.

She looked to be on the verge of tears, and she seemed to have shrunk in the two weeks since I'd last seen her. There was a sizable pimple on her chin. I considered bending to embrace her, but thought better of it. Three counts on the in-breath, three counts on the out—the best I could do.

Edna, giving Shawna some space to adjust, chit-chatted with me about the horrendous traffic, the weather, the usual phatic chatter that puts human beings at ease, while Shawna scanned the living room, only her eyes moving, taking it all in, thinking God knows what. Eventually I suggested we look at Shawna's room. Edna agreed and they traipsed behind me. Edna exclaimed about everything. She loved the colors, loved the stuffed animals, loved the art table. She circled the room, lifting and admiring things, bouncing her rump gamely on the yoga ball. Shawna stood in the doorway, skinny brown arms dangling at her sides, hands fisted like mini tetherballs, only those eyes in motion.

"Do you like it?" Edna asked and Shawna nodded ever so slightly.

Edna said she had to go. She rattled her keys and my panicking heart rattled in kind. "I'll come by for visits," she said. "You both take care." She shook my hand and bent for a quick hug with Shawna. As she was turning the knob on the front door, Shawna charged her from behind, arms circling Edna's ample buttocks. Edna bent to Shawna again. "You're going to be just fine, Shawna-honey. You and Sybil are going to have a grand time together."

Shawna's eyes were closed now and she continued to cling, but Edna had no trouble peeling her away. Glancing back at me—*We'll be in touch*—she Houdini'd out the door.

There we were, Shawna and me, now a family.

22

Shawna and I never went outside that first day, though it was still early. We sat on the floor of her bedroom—all the fans going but it was still hot—and one by one I brought out the things I'd bought for her, beginning with the puzzles and Lego sets. She shook her head at each offering. I couldn't tell if she was not interested, or if she couldn't imagine they belonged to her. Even the art supplies didn't seem to tempt her. In my eagerness to please, I babbled.

I selected some of the books I'd shelved, stories I'd loved when I was a child: *The Secret Garden,* the Laura Ingalls Wilder books, *Harriet the Spy.* I knew Shawna wasn't a skilled reader—her attendance at school had been spotty and she would be placed in remedial classes—so I narrated a little of each story in hopes of sparking an interest, but she kept a tight lock on her preferences.

A spore of panic came alive in my gut. The heat bore down. Silence rolled off Shawna, a deserted beach I'd washed upon alone. When her eyes momentarily flicked to the shelf of stuffed animals, I pulled them all down and assembled them on the floor in front of us: a bear, a rabbit, a lamb, a pig, a monkey.

"Let's name them," I said through the whir of my escalating panic. "What's a good name for a pig?" *Shut up, Sybil, give her room to respond.* "Maybe a 'P' name? Pitkin? Paula? Peter?"

We settled—*I* settled—on Peter the Pig, Mimi the Monkey, Ricky the Rabbit, Bobo the Bear, and Lambie the Lamb. I heard the stupidity of me and my voice and my ego. A bobbing clown, begging for attention. How naïve could I be to have thought mothering, especially this kind of mothering, would be easy? I hardly even knew any children, except for Sue's son and Sally's girls, teenagers I rarely saw.

I pulled down the abacus and began sliding the beads back and forth. "The Japanese used to use this for counting, but I just like to have fun with it."

She stared passively, as she'd been doing all along. *Aren't you curious*, I thought. She was a fawn in the headlights, and as soon as that image crossed my mind I realized *I was the headlights*, I was the whole oncoming car, the most immediate threat in her life, not the savior I wanted to be.

I escaped to the bathroom and ran some cold water over my face and thought of calling Edna, saying it was all a big mistake, that I didn't have what it took to parent, please come and get her. What if I hurt her, not by mistake but intentionally? Some people did that. What if I turned out to be one of those people? I hadn't been tested. Sure, I'd been vetted with background checks and such, but did all that vetting on paper really get to the core of who I might be under pressure?

I didn't call Edna. "We're having hot dogs for dinner," I told Shawna, ignoring the uneaten tuna sandwiches. "And ice cream for dessert." I never ate hot dogs, even without the nitrates, but I had stocked the fridge and shelves with simple all-American food I thought she was probably used to, things I sometimes lusted for myself but tried not to eat: peanut butter and jelly, mac and cheese, ramen, potato chips. And ice cream.

I pulled out plates and silverware and told her to set the dining room table. She took the things I'd given her to the dining room and hovered uncertainly by the table before dropping everything into a heap. "Like this," I said as neutrally and non-judgmentally as I could, and I showed her how to lay a place setting, thinking of my mother teaching me the same, hoping the knowledge of such niceties would help me elevate myself to a wealthier class. Knives with blades facing in, salad forks and soup spoons on the outside, butter knives above the plate. Rules for another life.

Shawna ate two bites of her hot dog. No wonder she was so thin. I wasn't particularly hungry myself, but I ate all of mine and finished hers too. She watched me eat as if she'd never seen a person eating, as if I was the featured performance inside a TV. Even the small bowl of cookie dough ice cream I served her she only sampled, while I gobbled my own bowl of chocolate without tasting it at all.

There was still light in the early summer sky when I decided it was bedtime. I thought of suggesting a bath, but the logistics of bathing, the inevitable nakedness, overwhelmed me. Modest, as I sensed she would be, she made me leave the room when she changed. When I returned to read to her she was wearing a T-shirt and had slipped under the covers with Lambie, who was to become her perpetual friend. The sight of her so tiny and at sea in that big queen bed, clutching Lambie— well, it made me glad, relieved; it filled me with the feeling of rightness I'd been seeking. I lay beside her and, thinking we needed some silliness, I read some Dr. Seuss, *McElligot's Pool*, one of my favorites. "This pool might be bigger than you or I know!" When I thought she was getting sleepy I kissed her forehead and told her I was glad she'd come to me. She wanted me to leave the light on. For Lambie, she said.

Exhausted, I fell into a heavy sleep but woke after an hour, wide awake. The apartment was quiet but I felt a difference in the air, as if every breath I inhaled was one she had just exhaled. I went to check on her. She wasn't in the bed. She wasn't in the bathroom. I tried to stay calm, knowing she couldn't have gone far. Still, I counted. 10, 20, 30, 40 . . . I found her under the bed with Lambie, eyes beaming out like lighthouse Fresnels strobing for danger.

"Were you scared?"

She nodded.

"Would you like to sleep with me?"

She nodded and padded after me into my bedroom and watched me climb onto the left side of the queen bed, a habit that remained from my years with Drew. I lifted the pale green sheet on the empty side of the bed and patted the mattress. After a moment she slid in, seamless and silent as a cat. We lay there in gauzy semi-darkness, me on my back staring ceilingward, she on her side, keeping me in her sightlines. At the corner of my vision I could see her body lightly limned by the sheet, a sylph compared to my galumphing presence. I felt on the verge of something I didn't understand, and it made me think of time folding back on itself, past and future converging. I had the strange sensation she and I had met before.

"Goodnight, honey. Sleep well," I said, and I closed my eyes in a deliberate way so she could see I was doing so, giving and taking privacy. I had yet to learn she wasn't easily fooled. She knew when adults were pretending—or lying.

Later in the night I woke again and found her curled around me, shrimp-like, her forehead on my belly a cool balm through the thin fabric of my nightgown, her belly arcing around my hip, her toes like the tips of Japanese paint brushes against my calves.

We slept like that for 687 nights.

23

A bubble quickly grew around me and Shawna, but it was hardly the warm and fuzzy lacuna I'd imaged when I was gazing at babies and mothers in supermarkets. I hadn't planned for the anxiety. I was forty-four, but until then I'd eschewed major responsibility, gliding through life as a loner, fending mostly for myself, even when I was married. Now, with Shawna, everything rode on me. Everything she did or didn't do became a report on how well I was managing the job of parenthood.

In the early days I fixated on her breathing. Often, even as she lay right beside me in bed, I could barely hear the coming and going of her breath. I worried she might succumb to the eleven-year-old's equivalent of Sudden Crib Death, an intolerable thought. I would place my ear as close as I could to her nose and mouth until I was assured there was adequate movement of air. I took great pains not to awaken her.

So much about her had the power to decimate my confidence. She rejected most of the food I made for her, often without even trying it, despite my serving her what I thought of as kid-food: grilled cheese sandwiches on white bread, hamburgers and hot dogs, pizza. Ice cream was the only thing I could count on her to eat. A couple of times, when I was desperate, I served her ice cream for breakfast.

Overhearing her gibberish conversations with Lambie also alarmed me. I knew—and Edna had confirmed—that having an object such as Lambie was healthy, a way for her to play out an array of emotions. She could love Lambie without fear of his abandonment, could confide in him, and use him as a repository for her unaddressed grief. That all made sense to me theoretically, but *in vivo* those conversations were unnerving. She spoke to Lambie in some guttural gibberish that seemed to have no roots in English. It was as if she was speaking in tongues, or channeling the Dybbuk. Often she would reprimand Lambie like a schoolmarm, sometimes screaming in a voice that was fluent and shrill and mean, the voice of someone older and more sophisticated than the timid, day-to-day Shawna. Occasionally she would cradle Lambie, crooning a monotone lullaby like the ones I sang to her, and my heart would bloom with the pride of influence. But those gentle moments often concluded in acts of violence. She would shake Lambie with both hands, or hurl him across the room. I usually interceded and rescued Lambie from his spurned position and cradled him myself, trying to model kindness and love as Edna had instructed. But when I did that Shawna would either walk away, or watch me with her normally gentle eyes becoming obdurate, bearing down with contempt.

Much of the messiest parts I've sealed away. The nights she woke up screaming, convulsed with terror, sweating an acrid, grown-up sweat, her scream shrill and alien as that of a tropical bird. She seemed not to know where she was, or even *who* she was. She scarcely seemed to be awake, instead locked in a purgatory between waking and sleeping. Words did nothing to soothe her so I would wrap myself around her quaking body, covering as much of her as I could, cooing quietly, her body frail and husk-like as an elder, her uncertainty and fear oozing into me, afflicting my heart, so I wondered who I was too, and what we were both doing there together. It seemed wrong for me, the adult, to be as uncertain as she. Those were lonely times, and I sometimes thought of Drew, wondering if he would have known what to do.

After half an hour, or an hour maybe, her crying would fade and she would gaze at me briefly, slack-jawed, vacant, before collapsing back into ragged sleep.

Sometimes fear would seize her in the middle of the day. A sound might set her off, or something flickering at the corner of her vision. "I saw . . ." she would half-grunt, half-whisper, trying to tell me. Or, "I heard . . ." but she could never put into words exactly what she'd seen or heard. I couldn't begin to guess. Edna had told me some of the things Shawna had witnessed. The sex. The shooting up. The verbal violence, and once, a knife fight. I'd rather not elaborate on the grim details. And many of the details I don't actually know. As far as Edna knew, Shawna hadn't been molested, but I wasn't sure how Edna could know this for sure. When the memories plowed over Shawna, she would want to hide somewhere, under her bed, or under the covers of my bed, or under the cushions of the living room couch, depending on where she was at the moment. Once I found her tucked behind the washing machine, arms twined around its hoses. I learned quickly to search the small spaces.

If we were out and about at those times she would dive into me, driving the crown of her head into my belly, tugging at my clothing as if she hoped to climb inside me and regress to infancy. The desperation often came over her so suddenly it assaulted me too. I felt hopelessly inadequate. There were no magic words or actions to banish the memories and calm her down. I would try to move her into a private enclosed space where it was just the two of us, a bathroom stall, a car, a dressing room, somewhere away from people and street noise and the general brawl of human life.

The worst moments, by far, were when, for reasons I still only partly understand, she turned on me, suddenly demonic, pounding me with her fists, hissing and yelling swear words she never used in regular life, scratching my bare skin, biting if she could find a place to gain traction.

I hesitated before going out, realizing these incidents might afflict us at any time. She was seeing a therapist who also met with me, and this therapist, a lively if somewhat sanctimonious woman about my age, who had been practicing a long time and seemed to know what she was doing, told me I must not curtail our lives for fear of these incidents. She told me I should take them in stride, they were part of parenting, especially the kind of parenting I had chosen, she said, eyebrows raised, nailing me with a severe look to see if I had what it took to go forward.

After the tantrums when Shawna attacked me—they weren't often, maybe once every few months that first year—she was full of remorse. She would stroke my face and hair and bring me water and tell me, whispering in her fluttery way, that she was sorry, and she'd watch me with those dark eyes of hers to see if I would strike back. I wasn't about to strike back; still, those outbursts exhausted and depressed me, and made me wonder if I could ever help her, if I was maybe character-ologically unfit for motherhood. But it was too late—I knew I wouldn't, couldn't, give up. What would it do to a child to send her back into the foster system, rejecting her once again? Besides, I was already in love.

What kept me going was a profound sense, even through her out-bursts, that she adored me. Perhaps she only needed me, but neverthe-less it felt like love. It was love of an entirely different order than the love Drew had once showered on me. If I'd been a harp, his love would have been like plucking one of my shortest strings, a high note vibrat-ing rapidly, trilling and fizzing throughout my body. Shawna's love plucked my low strings, a slow and sorrowful oscillation that glided over my soul and became the basso profundo of my life, even—maybe especially—during her tantrums and nightmares when I felt so needed and understood her to be an organism struggling to find its way to ho-meostasis, a balance that had been so profoundly disturbed in her early life that I often worried her system might never fully be set to right.

Challenging as that first summer was, Shawna and I became a comfortable twosome in those months, going on beach trips, taking picnics to Walden Pond, visiting the Museum of Science and the Swan Boats in the Public Garden, or simply staying at home reading and making grilled cheese sandwiches and cupcakes. My anger at Drew had become more distant and diluted by then, but occasionally, during those times of peace, I wished he could see us and witness how well I was getting on without him.

Despite having been born in Fall River, on the Massachusetts coast-line, Shawna had never learned to swim and was afraid of the water. Sometimes I was able to coax her in if I carried her, legs vined around my waist, but mostly she sat on our blanket in the sand and if I went to swim she watched. One day I came out of the water at Walden Pond to find her staring at a middle-aged woman stuffed into a low camp chair, apparently alone. She was wearing a skirted, brown, old-lady bathing suit and a gauzy, neon-yellow coverup, but her clothing did nothing to contain the frothy skin which drooped everywhere. Her suet-y upper arms, her dimpled thighs, her pendulous jowls all looked like empty pocketbooks that had been stretched to their limit then emptied. It was hard to believe that all that skin was attached to anything. Her thinning perm'd hair, dyed a fiery red, was divided at her crown by a wide skunk-stripe of gray. Everything about her looked ineffectively patched, unspeakably sad, as if she'd tried to improve herself but had suddenly given up. Her expression was reminiscent of the blank catatonia of department store mannequins.

As I settled onto our blanket, Shawna pointed. "That lady, see?" She spoke too loudly and I tried to hush her but she ignored me. "She's been sad for a long time."

Our days developed their pleasurable routines. Most mornings it took her a while to slough sleep. She left my bed in a daze, still clinging to Lambie, and went to her room where she took a long time dressing, always choosy about the day's outfit. While she ate her breakfast—or stared at it—I braided her hair, and after a while she would become animated and begin telling me her dreams, which provided small glimpses into her life before we met.

The dreams were narrated in a language of her own, a composite of euphemisms—*poopy-doop, potty girls, bad boys, happy pills, sleep needles*—combined with words that, coming from her perfect little mouth, sounded vulgar. *Ficky-ficky, wacked, weezer, cooty-juice.* The dreams were laced with Disney images too, kitty-cats and fairies, and a recurrent person she called *The Pink Princess,* who played a rescuing role, her version of Wonder Woman.

During the time I'd been hoping to have a child with Drew, I'd had lots of ideas about how I'd raise a girl child. She would be strong and capable and independent, a feminist. When I mentioned this to Drew he laughed. *They are what they are,* he said. *You can't force a person to be something they're not. Even a child.* It was not lost on me that he had been right. All my resolutions fell away in Shawna's presence. She was who she was, had developed coping mechanisms long before she met me. Who was I to tell her to change?

Though nothing about that time was easy, I had never been happier.

For the first time in my life I had a clear mission, a mission that wasn't all about me. Shawna was the only person in my sightlines, and gradually, over the weeks of that first summer, I came to feel I might be up to the task of mothering her.

During those summer months I assembled, with advice from my sister Sally, a team of professionals to help us—the therapist, a pediatrician, a speech therapist—and I enrolled her in the local public school where I met with the principal and several teachers and was impressed with their readiness to address Shawna's needs. She would be put in a fourth grade classroom and taken out for tutoring to address her reading and math deficits. There was a school psychologist who could help us address her behavioral issues. In a time of budget cutbacks, these amenities surprised me, and I was hopeful that things would work out. I was still in touch with Edna and she was optimistic too. She said that it was good that Shawna had spent her first four years with her parents, before they became deeply involved with drugs, and those early years had been reasonably good ones which meant Shawna's ability to bond might be more intact than if she'd been abandoned as a baby or a toddler. I tried to promote the school to Shawna, and she got on board with my enthusiasm.

She always dressed herself immaculately—even when wearing shorts and T-shirts her appearance was orderly and her colors matched. She refused to wear anything if it was the least bit dirty, and she often tried to make sure I was well-groomed too. That first day of school she was especially attentive to her outfit. We'd gone shopping and bought her several of the sashed dresses she liked (they were not easy to find!) and two pairs of buckled shoes, one blue, one red, along with pink and white socks and tights and several pairs of underwear. She had me braid her hair and fasten the braids with sparkly pink elastics. I worried about her being out of step with the other kids, but she was so pleased with how she looked that first day it made me proud, and I took zillions of pictures.

We walked to school holding hands, as was our custom. The mayhem outside the school took us both by surprise. Parents and kids swarmed the steps and sidewalk, parents embracing after a summer apart, kids shrieking, small cliques already falling into place. Shawna and I took it all in from the sidelines, acutely aware of our outsider status. As I suspected, none of the other girls were dressed as Shawna was. Most of them wore pants of some kind, the few who wore skirts had leggings underneath. I felt remiss that I hadn't urged Shawna to wear clothing that would allow her to blend in. We were also the only two holding hands. I thought she would want to drop mine, but she clung tighter.

I led her through the crowd, up the school's front steps and inside, away from the heat and noise and down the cool hallway to her class-room. Alyssa, her lovely young teacher, greeted Shawna warmly and led her to her seat where she remained, wide-eyed, as the other kids entered without their parents. The teacher nodded at me—time to leave. I squeezed Shawna's shoulder. She didn't acknowledge me, and I left the classroom a wreck. There was fear for Shawna and another kind of fear for myself. Those other mothers—most of the kids were accompanied by mothers, not fathers—had been parenting, or so I assumed, since their kids were newborns. They'd spent all the intervening years getting to know their children and perfecting—or refining—the dance of parenting. I was eleven years in the red, and as a parent I had more deficits to make up for than any deficits Shawna had.

I could not get anything done that day. I sat at my computer and pretended to work on a new job, but my ear was tuned to the phone, sure a call would be coming from the school any minute, telling me Shawna was having a meltdown. The call never came.

I went to fetch Shawna at 3:15 p.m. and found her waiting outside with her backpack on, crouched against a brick wall away from the other kids but watching them intently. When she spotted me she ran over and seized my hand, squeezing messages. One squeeze. Two squeezes. Three squeezes. My heart soared. Maybe, just maybe, we'd be okay.

24

Shawna became my litmus test for measuring the state of the world's heart. Some people went out of their way to be kind. They sized us up, the obvious physical mismatch of us—me large and pale, she tiny and tawny—then took note of Shawna's breathless speech and her hypervigilant irises and, without having to know our story, they went out of their way to be kind. A number of people offered us seats on the T. At Walden Pond a woman gave Shawna an ice cream sandwich from her cooler. On a Swan Boat ride a couple from Iowa engaged Shawna in conversation and admired her beauty. These spontaneous moments of kindness, well—

There were other kinds of people, of course. People who dismissed us with a quick but unmistakable sneer as if we posed some threat—two females alone, not linked in appearance. A woman in line behind us at the Science Museum whispered, sifting her words through a rigid smile, "What's wrong with her?" A father at Parents' Night wanted to know if my husband was black and had abandoned me. In the lobby at the Boston Pops Christmas Jamboree a woman ushered her children away from us as if we were Ebola carriers. Did I seethe? Yes. But there was little I could do except draw Shawna close.

Shawna herself understood such slights more than most people realized. It was a primary skill of hers to scope out the presence of hidden danger, particularly danger residing in other people. She would have made a great wartime scout. I could imagine her having been the person stationed atop a medieval citadel scanning the surrounding landscape for concealed enemies on the move. I could see her as a spy traveling innocently through crowds, sniffing for treason. I constructed scenarios of her learning to be like a town crier, warning everyone, traveling abroad like Paul Revere with news of imminent danger. Perhaps she would speak truth to power like the boy who called out the Emperor's nakedness. Her capacity for sensing what was wrong with the world made me hopeful for a future in which she would be self-reliant and equipped to survive whatever hazards she encountered. The world needed people like Shawna, needs them yet.

A month or so into the school year it began to worry me that Shawna hadn't mentioned any friends. I asked her if she'd like to have a play date. She didn't answer, acted as if I hadn't spoken. I let it go, but the reaction worried me, confirmed my fear that friend-making was not a skill in her kit bag. I let another few weeks pass before I asked again, and once more I got the brush-off. So I stopped by the school one midday when I knew the students would be in gym class. I found Shawna's teacher, Alyssa, in the classroom standing at a table, puzzling over squares of fabric. Her look of surprise at my interruption quickly morphed into sheepishness.

"Do you have a minute to talk?" I asked, knowing I was being forward, fully aware I should have made an appointment in advance.

"I've been meaning to get in touch," she said. Her voice was breathy, as if we were at great altitude.

"Is everything okay?" I said.

"Yes, fine. I mean, well—" She gestured for me to sit. As we settled into chairs built for small bottoms, she tucked the same strand of hair behind her ear again and again.

"Fine given who Shawna is, you mean?"

"Yes. I'm sorry I haven't been in touch. The beginning of the school year is always crazy, but I've been wanting to talk to you."

"Well, here we are now, talking."

Her smile came and went. I'd never had the experience of making anyone so nervous.

"She gets scared sometimes, as you know, but we're working on creating a safe place for her in the library area where she can go and snuggle in a beanbag when she's afraid. She's such a good little girl.

She does her work. It's not always perfect and she daydreams a lot, but she tries. The math and reading, we have to be patient, it might take a while. It hasn't even been a couple of months."

"Then what worries you?"

"The social thing."

"Exactly why I'm here."

"Her speech is a bit of a problem, of course. Sometimes she's hard to understand. She likes to watch more than join. Sometimes she tags behind a group of girls hoping they'll include her. But girls at this age can be very cliquish. Sometimes downright mean."

"They're mean? What do they do?"

"It's more of an attitude, you know? They try to outwalk her on the playground. Or they whisper to each other, laughing, clearly talking about her."

"You let this happen?"

"No! Definitely not. I've talked to them, asked them to include her. But it hasn't worked very well. They roll their eyes. They tell her they can't understand her when what she's saying is perfectly obvious, to me at least. I've never—"

She sighed in a riffly way and let her eyes close for a moment so I thought she might cry, but she continued talking through a face that was a bleak, blank pancake of helplessness. She was so damn young. "I've never had this before. I've always been able to find a solution, you know?"

"Then it's a bad fit for her in this classroom?"

"No, no, I'm not saying that. There's one girl, Cora, who tries to bring the other girls into line. I'm kind of hoping she and Shawna will become friends."

"You've encouraged them?" I hated my interrogating tone. I knew Alyssa was out of her depth. But she was the teacher, after all, and Shawna was my child.

"It's delicate, you know?"

We fell silent and her tears came. I'm sure she thought I was judging her, but I wasn't, not really. I understood that managing a classroom was hard, trying to regulate so many developing young brains and bodies and egos, especially being so young herself, but I was doing what mothers do, must do—advocating for my daughter. I needed more than good intentions.

From the eerie sinkhole of Alyssa's weeping rose the sound of a hallway stampede, the kids, amped and oozing adrenaline and hormones, were returning from the gym. She wiped her eyes. "We'll talk, I promise," she said. "I'll be in touch."

"Cora?"

"Yes, Cora."

We picked Cora up one Saturday afternoon. A tubby girl with an austere short haircut in gray sweatpants and a navy hoodie, a stark contrast to Shawna's lavender jumper and white tights. Cora and her mother were as mismatched as Shawna and I were. Her mother was a slim, yoga-pants type who greeted us with too much enthusiasm, too many exclamations about how happy she was I'd reached out. In the car on the way home, Cora chatted nonstop, mostly at me, leaning forward between the gap in the seats while Shawna gazed out the side window. Cora told me about learning polynomials (surely Shawna was not doing that); she said Joe, one of the boys in their class, was often "acting up"; she said she loved the beach at Wellfleet where she and her family went for a month every summer; she said she adored bodysurfing.

"Have you ever been to Wellfleet?" Cora asked Shawna.

Shawna's eyes pushed out to me from the rearview mirror, as if I were the repository of all her history. "Wellfleet is beautiful," I said. "Maybe we'll go next summer."

"You'd love it. But you have to watch out for the riptides," Cora said with chilling junior authority.

At home I left them in Shawna's room while I, ears pricked, went to fix them a snack. Cora was motoring around Shawna's room, commenting on everything. Then her narrative ceased and, just as I was about to investigate, I looked up to see her standing in the kitchen doorway.

"What's up?" I said. "Where's Shawna?"

Cora shrugged. "In her room."

"Did something happen?"

"No. She's just—you know. She's a little boring."

"You don't have to talk. You could play a board game? Or do a puzzle?"

Cora looked at me as if I was defective.

"You could play dress-up. Shawna loves dress-up."

"Dress-up is for babies."

You're the girl who *defends* Shawna, I thought? God help us. "I love to play dress-up sometimes too."

"My mom says dress-up is bad for girls. It makes you think clothes are everything."

"What do you and your other friends do?"

"Oh, we talk and play games on our phones. Why doesn't Shawna have a phone?"

"I don't think it's necessary for girls your age."

"I'd be dead without my phone. I text my mom all the time. I tell her what I'm doing after school and stuff."

I handed her a bag of cookies, animal crackers decorated with pink frosting and covered with sprinkles. "Open these, please, and put them on the plate."

She did as I told her, dumping the cookies into a hodgepodge at the center of the plate with none of the precision and pleasure Shawna would have brought to the task.

"What would you like to drink? Milk? Orange juice? Apple juice? I could make chocolate milk too. Shawna likes that."

"My mom says sugar is addictive. It gives you inflammation."

"True. But a little is fine."

"I'll have mint tea." She took a seat at the kitchen table as if we were peers and watched as I set the kettle to boil and dug into the back of the cabinet for tea which I rarely drank myself. No mint.

"I tell the other girls to be nice to Shawna but they forget." She paused. "What's wrong with her anyway?"

I whirled. "There is absolutely nothing wrong with Shawna." My voice faltered.

"But she doesn't talk well and she's very immature. That's what my mom says. I think so too."

"Please get Shawna and tell her your snack is ready."

Cora complied and went to Shawna's room. "She's not there!"

We found Shawna under the covers of my—our—bed. "Why is she hiding?" Cora said, as if Shawna was not present. I banished Cora from the room and, with the promise of a movie, coaxed Shawna from her refuge. She insisted I carry her to the living room where I set her on the couch in front of the TV. Cora watched us in disbelief. "My mom never carries me," she said wistfully.

As I set up the movie Cora dug in her heels. "I don't want to watch a movie. I'm only allowed to watch an hour a week and my parents have to be with me."

I placated Cora with a brand-new unopened Lego set of a Martian outpost. She tore it open like a hyena anticipating a feast and ripped into the multiple bags of cellophane-wrapped parts, spilling them on the floor without regard for their commingling. I gave Shawna a pad of paper and colored pencils. Then I brought them separate plates of cookies and PB&Js on white bread cut into quarters, with chocolate milk for Shawna and chamomile tea for Cora. For an agonizing two hours before Cora's mother came, the girls coexisted in the living room as *The Lion King* played. Cora abandoned the Legos and allowed herself to be mesmerized by the movie, devouring her plateful of food then asking for more, despite having pronounced the cookies too sweet and waxy. Shawna shuttled between watching and drawing, sipped some of her chocolate milk, ate nothing. Their faces were blank, every scintilla of energy fully deployed to blot the other out.

25

Around the corner from us Shawna spotted a sign about a litter of kittens being given away for free. We went to have a look. It was mid-November. School had been in session for nine weeks by then. There had been two meltdowns when she'd gotten scared and I'd had to pick her up early, but otherwise things had gone relatively smoothly. I wasn't overly impressed with teacher Alyssa, but the school psychologist had been encouraging, saying the situation would improve with time. I'd decided to place my faith in him, at least temporarily; I certainly was no expert myself. Still, the disastrous play date with Cora had exacerbated my concern about Shawna's social life. Since I'd promised her a kitten from the get-go, and she hadn't let me forget it, it seemed a good time to act on my promise. Kitten as stand-in friend.

They were four weeks old, five tiny animated puffballs encased in mottled gray fur so abundant it obscured the shapes of their heads. They bounced around the room looking more like battery-operated Disney toys than flesh-and-blood animals. Shawna was drawn to one with white facial markings that made him look as if he'd had a run-in with some bleach. He was the most exuberant of the litter, somersaulting from couch to chair, sidestepping drunkenly across the carpet, pouncing onto our tapping fingers. Nothing appeared to scare him as he hurled his featherweight body here and there. His antics made Shawna weak with laughter. She giggled and screamed and chased him from room to room. Her delight made me happy, of course, but I was suspicious of something about the kitten. It worried me that he couldn't walk in a straight line, and his high energy seemed unnatural, borderline psychotic, if such a concept applies to cats. The youngish woman who was trying to offload the unexpected litter—she had three young kids and hadn't realized her cat was pregnant—assured me that this was perfectly normal kitten behavior. Shawna was attaching to that one kitten quickly and exclusively; I couldn't force her to pay any attention to the others, who were, admittedly, listless in comparison. By the time we left the woman's apartment with this high-energy kitten in our possession, Shawna had already named him Giggles.

We visited a pet store and outfitted Giggles with a litter box, a bed, food and water dishes, and various overpriced kitten toys decorated with feathers and bells. At home we set the litter box in the bathroom and established a corner of the kitchen for his food and water. In the days and weeks and months that followed Shawna devoted herself to Giggles. Her devotion had surprising staying power (I remembered my sisters and I being similarly excited about a new kitten that we ignored after a couple of months). I had to remind her to empty the litter box, but she was good about making sure the food and water dishes were full, and the attention she lavished on Giggles did not flag. She made little houses for him out of pillows and blankets where she would situate Giggles and Lambie. She made him "dresses" out of the old T-shirts I had relegated to rags. Occasionally she would squeeze Giggles too hard, unaware of her own strength and brimming with a ferocious, willful love, and I would have to remind her to be gentle. She didn't mean to harm him, I knew that. I loved watching them together, seeing her develop a sense of responsibility for someone other than herself. Giggles seemed to flourish in the bath of her love, and he took to following her around the apartment with the slavishness of a dog.

Our first full year together came to a close just as her school year was ending. Things had, indeed, gotten better. I was astonished we'd made it through that difficult year and decided we should celebrate both accomplishments: her successful completion of a year at school and our anniversary as a family. We concocted a plan for an afternoon movie, followed by a trip to her favorite ice cream parlor in Porter Square.

Never much of a sleeper and still on her school schedule, Shawna woke early, slipped out of our bed, and puttered around her room while I allowed myself to luxuriate in more sleep. When I woke the second time, it was almost eight. I could hear her scuttling about in the living room, talking to Giggles. I basked in the sound of her whip-speed chirping. She sounded manic, but basically happy, as was I. We were unquestionably a family now. We had survived the most difficult challenges we would be asked to endure. Of course it had been hard, but we were both tough. And what child was not happy when school let out for the summer? Listening to her conversing with Giggles, I knew she was learning one of the most important of human tasks, how to navigate relationships. After a rough start in life, she was finally becoming well-adjusted, and if things became difficult again, we now had each other.

The scrape of furniture being dragged across the floorboards roused me from bed. I robed myself and hurried out to the living room. The window to the left of the bay window gaped open, and Shawna was kneeling on the sill, pitching forward, head and shoulders partway out, gazing down.

"Shawna!" I hurried over.

I grabbed her waist and pulled her to me, but she wiggled free.

"What're you doing?!"

"He wanted to fly. He told me he wanted to fly!" She stood by the window, pointing down. "He's down there. We have to get him."

We rushed outside. Giggles—no longer a featherweight kitten but a rangy adolescent cat—lay on a patch of hard ground just below the window. He had landed belly-down, legs splayed as if he had, indeed, attempted to fly. His eyes were open and, though his heart was still beating, he did not move or make a sound. Shawna stroked his back.

"It's gonna be alright, Giggles." Condolences delivered with the intonation of a skilled social worker, "You're gonna be fine."

With as much gentleness as I could muster, I lifted Giggles into his soft portable cat bed. He snarled then collapsed into the fleece, eyes glazed as those of a junkie. Shawna sat with Giggles in the back seat. She petted him and sang the songs I sang to her. *Peace, I ask of thee oh river . . .* I watched them in the rearview mirror. Had Giggles leapt to the ground himself, or had she pushed him? What did it mean if she'd pushed him? Was it an act of hostility, or did she really believe he could fly? Either answer was disconcerting.

Giggles was not, as you can imagine, fine at all. His pelvis was broken and he was hemorrhaging internally. Even if his pelvis could be mended, the vet told us, it was unlikely his organs could be restored to health. The vet hooked my gaze. Shawna was so immersed in comforting Giggles it was unclear what she heard. The only real option, the vet said, was to put Giggles down.

Shawna wept the whole way home, silent tears that painted her face and made it glisten. The stoic nature of those tears seemed to announce that she'd been wronged. She had been wronged—not that day, but over the years preceding that day. The losses she'd seen had accumulated and compounded and now, with Giggle's death, they all roiled together.

We skipped the movie but went for ice cream. She ordered three scoops—peppermint stick, chocolate, and cookie dough. She slathered the mountain of ice cream with various toppings—marshmallow, nuts, jimmies, M&Ms, gummy bears. She took a single bite then jabbed each scoop with her spoon, making multiple fissures. She picked out the gummy bears and stood them upright on her napkin, then stirred the gooey mess into a soup.

"Did you encourage Giggles to fly?"

"He wanted to fly."

"You helped him?"

"He needed a head start."

"Did you really think he could fly?"

She kept her focus on the table where she was arranging the gummy bears in a ring around her bowl like witnesses. Her elegant black lashes fluttered. I thought about all she'd witnessed and knew, things I would never know or understand.

I could have punished her. I thought I should. Then I thought I shouldn't. How did I know what it meant to live in a world in which you believed cats could fly? But shouldn't she take responsibility for doing something wrong?

I ate my bowl of coffee ice cream bite by bite in the dutiful way one performs a penance. I had never punished her before—how could I start now? By the time we left the parlor I'd said nothing. Giggles' death seemed punishment enough.

26

When Shawna was not in school or at an appointment, we were constantly together, a happy twosome. At home we cuddled and baby-talked. On weekend mornings we stayed in our bed and watched cartoons or Disney movies. I'd bring us breakfast there, toast and eggs, or leftover apple pie which was one of her favorites. I thought of us as moles or badgers, sharing an underground den, exchanging heat, protecting each other, all our needs satisfied in that one place.

When I did various chores around the apartment she often followed me. *What's that, Sibbie? What are you doing, Sibbie?* She'd never seen a coffee maker. She'd never seen eggs being separated. When I showed her a double yolk and explained it was twins, she couldn't stop laughing. So much of the world was new to her and, through her eyes, it became new to me too.

The second summer she was with me I rented a cottage on the Cape, not far from Wellfleet, for two weeks at the end of August. (No, we did not look up Cora and her family.) Those weeks were nirvana. We spent part of every day at the beach. She had stopped being so squeamish about getting sandy, and I was sometimes able to coax her into the water if the waves weren't too high. By midafternoon we were usually out in the backyard of the cottage, eating popsicles, doing puzzles, drawing. Sometimes we went into town for ice cream, or went for a sunset walk on the beach. She'd begun eating more and was finally growing a little in height and weight, though no one would have noticed this but me and her doctor.

We returned to the apartment on the Friday before Labor Day. The following week Shawna would start at a new private school more equipped to give her one-on-one attention. It was late afternoon and as I unpacked and started a laundry, Shawna went to her room and also unpacked, a satisfying sign of her growing independence. At dusk I told her I was going to take a bath before starting supper. I left the bathroom door ajar to remind her I was still there. She didn't like not knowing where I was. I heard her fiddling around in her room and it comforted me. Lulled by the hot water, I drifted into thoughts of the upcoming week, my to-do list and hers.

I was drawn back into the present by her Lilliputian face at the edge of the door. She looked terrified. Electrified by a kindred terror, I splashed to sitting, oblivious to my nakedness.

"Mumma," she said. She nudged the door aside and stepped into the bathroom, carrying a plate she extended gingerly before her. Her solemn face twitched with mischief. "Mumma," she repeated as she laid the plate on the ledge of the tub. "I made this for you." She spoke slowly, enunciating as if her speech therapist was listening.

A piece of white toast lay on the plate, soggy with butter, sprinkled with cinnamon sugar and cut in half, exactly as I made it for her.

What does a naked, overcome body do? It beams with more watts than it's ever put out before and reaches for the toast. It takes a bite and closes its moist eyes. *Mumma.*

Shawna turned thirteen on February 13, when she had been with me for twenty months. We celebrated with just the two of us. I had thought about throwing a party for her with my sister Sally's family. Growing up, Sally and I had been close; we hadn't been quite as competitive as Sue and I had been. But Sally's daughters, who were seventeen and fifteen at the time, saw Shawna infrequently, and when they saw her they were not kind. They couldn't see what she might have to offer them, and they couldn't—or wouldn't—find ways to invite her into their private teenage lives. They were annoyed by her tendency to follow them around, and burdened by the expectation that they should entertain her. Even Sally was condescending, questioning me about pouring so much money into Shawna's schooling when it was unlikely that she, such a "damaged" child, could ever live a "normal" life. Only Sally's husband, Dave, seemed genuinely interested in Shawna. He once spent an entire afternoon teaching her how to toss a Frisbee.

So, for the thirteenth birthday celebration I decided to take her to New York City for a couple of days. We stayed at the Plaza Hotel (I had read her the *Eloise* books) and marveled at its ornate furnishings. It was eye-wateringly cold, but we didn't care. We walked everywhere, window shopping, people watching, entranced by everything. We visited Sue in her law office. We skated in Central Park, ate whatever and whenever Shawna wanted. In a boutique on the Lower East Side she spotted a fur coat she fell in love with, and impulsively, happily, I bought it for her. It was faux ermine, fluffy and white, and it came with a matching hat. She looked like a little Russian princess in that coat, its white the most perfect contrast to her black hair and hazelnut skin. Passersby stared in admiration and the attention was not lost on either of us.

The only bad moment was when we came upon a homeless man in Midtown, wedged against a building, covered in mounds of sour blankets. We had passed other homeless people, but for some reason this man was the first who'd snared her attention. His face was red and mangled as ground meat; his bloodshot eyes stared up at the sky with the vacancy of a corpse. As soon as I saw him, I tried to steer Shawna away, but she weaseled away from my guidance and went to him. She laid her mittened hand on his face. He jerked as if electro-shocked, and she skittered back to me. "He's going to dead, Mumma. He's going to dead."

"Someone will come for him soon. Don't worry."

"Call," she told me. She dug into my purse, found my cell phone and pressed it into my hand. "Call."

In the cacophony of Midtown, I faked a call to 911, describing the situation quickly and giving a made-up address. I was able to convince her to leave after that, but for a couple of hours she was distracted and eerily silent. It took going to the Central Park Zoo and observing an orangutan moving objects around his enclosure to rouse her back to responsiveness again.

The image from that trip I hold front and center is that of us standing in Central Park's Great Meadow. The cold had chased people away so we were alone, not a single other person in sight. We looked south across the snow-whitened field to the iridescent high rises of Midtown piercing a dove-gray sky. I told Shawna to step out in front of me for a photo and, as she did so, a few snowflakes began to fall, and she lifted her face to the sky and stuck out her tongue. I flashed the picture while her tongue was still in the air, the side of her face angled toward me. The white fur of her coat and hat melded into the snowy background so what the camera caught was her black hair, her tawny face, her happy pink tongue, all at safe remove from the world's cruelty.

27

For over a year I'd lived in Somerville without knowing my neighbors, but the summer Shawna came to me two families popped into view, one next door to us and one across the street. Perhaps they were curious. Maybe they felt sorry for a mother and daughter without male "protection." Whatever the reason, suddenly the two mothers, Alice and Maude—both kind, self-effacing, stay-at-home mothers—lingered on the sidewalk to engage me and Shawna in conversation as we moved from car to house. Alice had two boys and a girl, the eldest a teenage son named Jeff; Maude also had three children, two girls who were five and seven and a teenager, Dan. Jeff and Dan were inseparable. Both fifteen when we first met them, they were about to be sophomores at the same local high school.

All summer Shawna and I would watch the boys from our living room window as they skateboarded in the street. Jeff was the leader and the bigger risk-taker, setting up jumps that lofted him several feet off the ground. Occasionally other boys stopped by, but mostly it was just the two of them. Sometimes they took off for the swimming pool on bikes, bodies curled over the handlebars with swashbuckling bravado, impervious to the possibility of damage to themselves or anyone else. Those bodies made no sense to me, their joints unnaturally loose but legs and arms stiff as pick-up sticks. Some days they slouched against parked cars like baby gangsters in training, not smoking, but wishing they did. Other days they tried to be the good boys their mothers wanted them to be, carting groceries into the house and being attentive to their younger siblings. When school started, we often spotted them arriving home at the end of the day, shouldering their backpacks like unwanted appendages. At first I wasn't sure what to think of them, coming as I did from a world of girls and having avoided boys throughout high school. But I could see their mothers adored them and wanted to mold them into good men, and it seemed as if the boys were trying their best. I appreciated the way they addressed Shawna—*Hey, Shawna, how's it going?*—without condescension.

Alice and her family, including son Jeff, lived in the building adjacent to ours and a couple of times that summer Alice told Jeff to help me carry my groceries upstairs. He complied politely. Nevertheless, I was taken by surprise when both boys appeared on our second floor landing one Saturday in early fall, offering help. Usually I had to buzz people through the bottom door before they could mount the stairs to the second floor, but apparently the bottom door had been left ajar.

They were taller than I was, and they crowded the small landing, and a glandular scent of boy-ness engulfed us. Jeff, whose body evinced a slouching, aspirational hipness, was their spokesman.

"My mom said you could maybe use some help. So—" He looked at Dan who was nodding. "So, we're, like, whatever, if you need something—" He shrugged, as if it didn't matter to him one way or the other.

"Hm," I said, trying to think if I had any odd jobs for them to do. "I can't think of anything right now, but I'll let you know if I do."

"That's cool," Jeff said, peering behind me. "Hey Shawna, what's up?"

I turned to see Shawna hovering a few feet away. She said nothing, but sidled forward until she was directly behind me and I could feel her hand grazing my rump. The boys turned to go.

"Wait," I said. "What would you think of cleaning out my trash barrels? It's not a pleasant job, but it needs to be done. They've become a little stinky." This was not make-work. The barrels had been smelling rancid for a while, and I'd been avoiding the task of washing them.

The boys shrugged, a gesture I took to mean assent.

"What's your rate?"

They exchanged a look. "My mom said we're not supposed to take any money," Jeff said.

"We'll see."

The job turned out to be bigger than I expected. It entailed a trip to the hardware store for an extra-long hose which we attached in the building's basement and threaded up a flight of stairs to the alley where the barrels lived. The boys took over after that, and Shawna watched from our apartment's small balcony that overlooked the alley where the boys were working. They sprayed and mopped and disinfected the barrels, then they sprayed each other. From my post in the kitchen I heard Shawna giggling, and by the time I joined her on the balcony both boys were soaked. I went down to inspect their work—Shawna trailing behind. Work approved, I offered them each ten dollars. They hesitated. It could be our secret, I suggested, their mothers didn't need to know. They exchanged a series of encoded looks, then grinned and thanked me profusely, pocketing the cash.

The boys continued to do odd jobs for me. I can still see Shawna hovering nearby as they worked, gaze averted, hands busy with her drawing, but listening intently as I chatted with them about school and their hopes for the future. She never said a word in their presence. The light of those older boys was too bright for her to absorb. *What nice boys,* I'd often say after they'd left, expecting a response from her which never came.

She was always close by when they assisted me. Once they helped me empty all the kitchen cupboards and drawers and line them with shelf paper. She sat drawing on the floor, not in the kitchen but just outside, still within earshot. Only days later did I find the drawing she'd made of us, the two boys, prophetically, twice the height of me.

28

Adolescence took her overnight. Without warning—or none that I noticed. August 18—13 years, 6 months, and 5 days old. Late for girls these days, but not surprising given her diminutive size. I'm not talking here about her period—that wouldn't come for another six months—I'm talking about a new world view.

The night of August 18. I had gotten into bed as usual and heard her in the bathroom, brushing her teeth, flushing the toilet. Then the apartment fell to silence. I waited, sitting up, keeping the light on. I let five minutes go by before I called out. No answer. I let a few more minutes pass before getting up and going to her room. She lay under the covers on her back, the bedside light off, the night light glowing, eyes open.

"I'm staying here," she said, intransigent, though her voice was deliberately babyish. She squeezed her eyes shut, a protection from any plea I might mount.

"Oh." I stood there, waiting for something. She turned to the wall, facing away from me.

I returned to my own bed, still in waiting mode, still thinking she'd reconsider.

She did not reconsider. I hardly slept. The following night the same scenario was reenacted. It took me weeks to realize she wasn't going to sleep with me again. This was the new norm. She had discovered a need for secrecy, for privacy. I hadn't seen it coming. Well, I suppose a part of me had seen it coming, but had chosen not to look. She stopped clinging to me and holding my hand in public. All predictable, healthy developments, sure, but that doesn't mean it didn't hurt. I took solace in the fact that she still, sometimes, when we were at home alone, availed herself of my lap. And when she had nightmares, she would always call out, summoning me to her bed to hold her.

A month or so after Shawna started sleeping alone, I woke to pee in the middle of the night and, out of habit, stopped to check on her. She wasn't in her bed. She wasn't under the bed. A slight sound lured me to the end of the hallway where a door led to the balcony that overlooked the alley. But for the attached fire escape, it was a useless balcony, tiny and sunless with an unremarkable view of the side of Jeff's house.

There was Shawna in underpants and tank top, leaning over the railing, hair cascading beneath her, a modern-day Rapunzel. She startled when she noticed me. "I was hot," she said, preempting my question. She clamped her mouth shut and pooched her lips forward in an expression I'd never seen her make.

"Get back to bed," I said, more sharply than I intended. "It's very late."

She obeyed, but defiantly, taking her time to slink down the hallway and into her bedroom where she closed the door. And locked it.

29

I should never have let her buy those clothes. The hip-hugging spandex. The siren-y necklines. The black padded bra that sponsored faux cleavage. Those clothes were an invitation to some shadowy womanly place I had no idea she knew about. They were brash advertisements that the wearer was seeking sex, clothes for a mature woman, not an underdeveloped girl in middle school. I should have kept her girlhood sealed in sashed dresses and white tights, but one day she wanted different clothes and, as always, I bent to her will.

We found ourselves at the Burlington Mall. She went to the dressing room by herself, refusing my assistance, carrying mostly her own selections, a few from me and the clerk. She emerged transformed, in black leggings and a black V-neck sweater over one of the padded bras. She had become, in a matter of minutes, a slim Japanese brushstroke of a body, with small but exquisitely contoured breasts, the outfit perfectly synchronous with her black hair and black eyes.

"Gorgeous!" raved the clerk.

I couldn't speak. The shift from girl to woman was too quick. Furthermore, it was a lie. She was thirteen, yes, but she wasn't a woman in any way. She hadn't even started her period.

"Please," she begged, reading my resistance. "Please!"

If only I'd had the foresight to say no.

30

There was a park, not far from where we lived, with a baseball diamond and a dog run and play structures for kids, the stuff of solid American cities trying to encourage healthy living. Shawna and I had gone there frequently during our first summer, to play on the swings and slide. Jeff and Dan went there for baseball. Shawna loved to keep tabs on them, and we often watched them from our second-floor window heading off with bats and gloves. Sometimes, if they looked up, we waved. Sometimes we waved even if they didn't look up.

One spring Saturday, a couple of months after Shawna turned thirteen—those very months when things were changing under my radar—we happened to be on the sidewalk chatting with Alice, Jeff's mother, when the boys came out of Dan's house across the street with bats and mitts. Jeff called out to Alice that he'd be back in a while, and Shawna called out to them, "Can I come?" I was shocked by her boldness—it was not her habit to be so forward, especially not with them.

The boys shrugged. Alice and I exchanged a glance. "I don't think so," I said. "They'll be busy playing ball."

"I wanna watch," Shawna insisted.

Alice beckoned the boys closer. "Would you boys keep an eye on Shawna if she came with you?"

Jeff nodded. "Yeah, sure."

"When will you be back?" I asked.

"A couple of hours."

"That's a long time," I said to Shawna. "You'll be bored watching for a couple of hours."

"No, I won't." She was hopping on one foot, bursting with energy.

I was dubious, but Alice seemed to like the idea as much as Shawna did. Alice, a practicing Catholic, was determined to make Jeff into a virtuous boy. Taking Shawna to the park would be a way for him to exercise his charity.

"You promise to keep an eye on her?" Alice said, as if the decision had already been made.

Both boys promised, and within moments, before I'd approved the plan, the threesome was heading down the street, Shawna a mere sylph between the two boys.

"It'll be fine," Alice said. "They're good boys." As if I was an incorrigible worrywart.

I thought of going to the park after an hour, to bring her back myself, but I was working against being the hovering helicopter mom, the anxious worrywart everyone thought I was. My sister Sally was often on my case about that, telling me I should be doing more to encourage Shawna's independence. I made myself wait.

The boys delivered Shawna back to my doorstep after the two hours they'd promised. She was manically happy and completely unscathed. I was so relieved I wanted to pay them, but I couldn't do so in Shawna's presence. They were nonchalant.

"We had fun, didn't we?" Jeff said.

Maybe they really were the good boys Alice wanted them to be.

I thought of Jeff and Dan as babysitters but, after accompanying them to the ballfield where she sat on the bleachers, a loyal and obedient fan, Shawna saw them as friends. That spring and summer they began taking her to the park on a regular basis and, while I did not think of their motives as entirely pure—I was fairly sure Jeff was doing his mother's bidding—I decided it didn't matter. It was the first time Shawna had had friends since she'd been with me. Her speech was noticeably improving—it was slower and less breathy—and I thought that might have to do with her desire to be understood by those boys.

In late May Dan turned seventeen and he invited Shawna to his co-ed bowling party. I doubted she would have fun with a group of seventeen-year-olds. I tried to tell her it would be different than being with Jeff and Dan alone. Nevertheless, she wanted to go, really wanted to go. After much haggling, I agreed to take her.

It was exactly as you might imagine: a dim, neon-lit building crawling with screeching adolescents. Video games and vending machines flashed and beeped. A pizza concession was selling soda and greasy slices. Shawna and I shared a lane with two girls, Felice and Clara, who mostly ignored us in favor of taking selfies and flirting with the boys in the lane beside us. We were all pathetic bowlers, most of our balls ending in the gutters, but Shawna didn't care, electrified as she was by the flash and zing of the place and the presence of so many older kids. Between sets she scooted to the lane where Jeff was playing. He gave her quick smile as she sat on the bench to watch him, and she clapped and squealed each time even a single pin went down. At home it took me hours to calm her down.

I braced myself for Jeff's birthday, three weeks later. It was to be a video games overnight, boys only, but Jeff had invited Shawna to come for cake. I cleared this with Alice and we went over at 8:00 p.m. Alice greeted us at the door and ushered us into the living room which had been taken over by the boys, seven altogether, including Dan and Jeff. Each boy had staked out his own turf, crouching with his console under a cave of sleeping bags and blankets. The lights were off when we walked in so we saw only hunched, blanketed silhouettes, scarcely human looking, and the bluish illumination of screens and consoles knifing through slits in the blankets, accompanied by explosions and cracking gunfire. It was like being an anthropologist and exhuming an ancient culture, one you'd never known existed but was apparently, surprisingly, still extant.

Alice turned on the overhead lights and shouted, something I'd never heard her do. "Time for cake! Shawna's here!" Alerting them to clean up their acts and be nice.

Gradually, one by one, they shambled out from beneath their blankets, limbs wobbly, expressions dazed as if they'd just awakened. Jeff and Dan acknowledged Shawna with feeble smiles, but they weren't exactly overjoyed to see her.

Alice lit the candles and she and I belted out *Happy Birthday* while the boys muttered along and Shawna watched. Adolescent boys were, I'd begun to see, poor conversationalists and lame singers and they weren't the least bit interested in cake. Alice and I sat at the table and ate our slices dutifully while the boys remained standing, took a few bites, downed some soda, and one by one disappeared back to their shrouded outposts. The explosions started up again, and Alice and I exchanged a look.

"Sorry," she said. "It's a force bigger than I am."

I dragged Shawna away. It didn't bother her that she'd been ignored. It appeared she hadn't noticed. She revered those boys and would have done anything to remain in their presence.

31

I didn't know until later that she was sneaking out. She'd learned early in life to be stealthy, to move soundlessly through rooms, out doors and windows, evading the notice of others.

Of course I would have stopped her if I'd known—she was only fourteen, for God's sake.

32

It took weeks for the boys to confess. Initially I had suspected their involvement, but as time passed—me in a coma-like daze, hermitting up in my apartment, struggling with my culpability and ignorance, irked that the police weren't providing any answers—*How had Shawna gotten into that vacant house? How had she come by the fentanyl?*—and all that time the boys said nothing and attended the memorial service, solemn-faced and ostensibly close to tears, embracing me afterwards and muttering of their sorrow. So I gave them a pass. I should have given more weight to how they and their mothers had been avoiding me on the street, radioing quick false smiles when our paths crossed. In retrospect, it should have been obvious. But grief, like love, is often blindered.

One evening in early July, exactly seven weeks after the night in question, the boys materialized on my upstairs landing, their mothers standing behind them like sheepish guardian angels. I knew as soon as I saw that cowering foursome. None of them smiling, Jeff and Dan's shoulders bowed and boneless as scolded dogs, Maude and Alice greeting me in unison sotto voce.

"Go away," I said.

Alice seized my forearm. "Let them talk. They need to talk."

We went to the living room. I sat in my usual chair by the window and closed my eyes as they settled without direction from me, Jeff and Alice on one side, Dan and Maude on the other. I thought back to all the times Alice had pushed the boys at me, goading them to help me, guilting me into accepting their help. As if Shawna and I were mere pawns in their oh-so-important development.

The boys took turns speaking, their low voices tapping on my brain, begging for entrance, pausing frequently, backtracking, using phrases they'd obviously been fed by their mothers, interspersed with their usual teen jargon, the abrasive intrusion of their speech swelling to fill the room, polluting walls and furniture like overflow sewage. Sometimes they stopped speaking altogether and, out of the room's slab of silence, had to be exhorted by their mothers to continue. Oh, those mothers with their modulated voices and pasted smiles and irreproachably good intentions—what stupid stoicism they evinced. I wanted to be assured that they'd yelled at their sons, cursed them in horror.

In the months leading up to high school graduation, Jeff and Dan had been restless. Even with only weeks remaining, school seemed endless and rife with obligations. They were done with being responsible students, done being yoked to anything. They had lined up summer jobs as day-camp counselors and would start community college in the fall; with a busy schedule like that, weren't they entitled to a little bit of freedom first, a little bit of celebration? Unbeknownst to either family, they'd begun sneaking out after everyone was asleep, meeting friends at the park and hanging out, drinking alcohol pilfered from the parental stash, smoking joints. That night they invited Shawna to join them. Apparently it wasn't the first time she had sneaked out to see them after I was asleep. The boys would hoot three times and she would descend from our balcony on the rickety iron fire escape. Where was I on those nights? How could I possibly have been so oblivious?

That night they ran into some baseball boys they knew from another school. Those boys also had flasks filled with mixtures from the family liquor cabinet. "Whiskey, vodka, whatever," Jeff said. They offered sips to Shawna while they were fooling around on the swings. The alcohol made her silly. She couldn't stop laughing. The other boys thought she was cute and she loved the attention. She wasn't drunk, not really. Well, maybe a little.

The "other boys"—Jeff and Dan didn't know their names—announced they were going to a party a few blocks away. Who knew such underworld parties ran rampant while the rest of us slept? Jeff and Dan and Shawna followed those other boys. They arrived at a building with a "For Sale" sign out front. One of the boys, whose mother was a realtor, said he knew for a fact that the building was not being lived in. They entered the basement from the backyard through a broken window. Once inside, you had to jump from the window ledge to a dusty bookshelf, then to the basement floor. In the midst of this dark scramble, Shawna cut her arm on a piece of broken glass.

The basement, lit only with the jittery arcing beams of cell phone flashlights, was thick with people dancing and drinking. They first thought there might be thirty or forty people there, later they decided it was probably only twelve to fifteen. Low music oozed from the shadows, and people were trying to remember to speak quietly, aware of the late hour, aware of the danger of awakening people in adjacent houses. Every once in a while, a shout went up and the shouter was quickly hushed. The dark, the erratic light, the presence of bodies whose faces couldn't be seen, all of it scared Shawna. Plus, her forearm was bleeding.

"I knew she was scared," Jeff said. A long silence ensued in which Shawna's bulging eyes appeared on my closed lids, and her familiar fear inflamed my body.

"Go on," said Alice.

"We were worried about her," Jeff said.

"We really were," Dan echoed. As if they'd memorized this important fact of their worry, a badge of nobility.

Shawna clung to Jeff. *You're good,* he kept saying. *You're gonna be fine.* But he was nervous, they both were. It wasn't their scene. They decided to leave. They were scoping out the bookcase that led to the window ledge, trying to work out how to scale the distance—harder going up than coming down—when a girl came out of the shadows. She wore a tube top that exposed her midriff. "She was a little sketchy maybe, but nice," Dan said. *Who's she?* the girl asked, indicating Shawna. *A friend,* Jeff said. *What happened, honey?* the girl said. *She cut herself,* Jeff explained. *Let her talk,* the girl said. Shawna didn't talk. She rolled her marble eyes from Jeff to the girl. The girl knelt in front of Shawna and laid a flap of her short skirt over Shawna's bloody arm.

You press to stop the blood. See? The girl regarded Shawna sweetly. *You have pretty hair,* she told Shawna. Shawna said nothing. *You're adorable.* The girl hugged her. *I'll fix her up,* she said to Jeff and Dan. She led Shawna away and Shawna did not resist.

Jeff and Dan had no idea where their baseball friends had gone, no idea where the girl had taken Shawna. They should have followed, they conceded, but the girl would probably have shooed them away and anyway, she was so nice, helping Shawna in that special girl-to-girl way. They waited and drank from their flask and looked around at the other people. In the wavering darkness faces couldn't be seen; there was only a swarm of bodies moving like a gigantic octopus.

The girl's scream sliced the hubbub. *Fuck!* They heard scrambling. *Fuck. Fuck. Fuck.* The music stopped abruptly. People thronged past them, a torrent of hot bodies. The girl appeared, running, growling over her shoulder as she headed for the exit. *I gotta go. She's back there.* A stampede as people struggled to climb back up to the ledge, back out the window, shoving Jeff and Dan out of the way. "It was like the Holocaust," Jeff said, apparently citing the worst thing he could think of. "Very bad."

In a few minutes everyone was gone. Jeff and Dan were mired in darkness, kicking themselves that they'd neglected to bring their cell phones. How could they have been so stupid? *Shawna?* No reply. *Shawna!*

They traced the wall and found Shawna crumpled in a corner on the concrete. She wasn't breathing. There was no discernible heartbeat. Jeff put his lips to her mouth as he'd seen people do in movies. He filled his lungs and huffed the air through her lips, whispering pleas between each breath. After several minutes nothing changed. Dan took over, leaning all his weight on Shawna's chest, pressing and pressing as rhythmically as he could. *Fuck,* they both said, over and over. *Fuck, fuck, fuck.*

They discussed lifting her back outside, but couldn't figure out how to raise her limp body, even small and light as it was, up to the window ledge. Getting themselves up there would be hard enough. It was dark, you see, and they were high.

They left her there—yes, it was stupid, they shouldn't have done that, hangdog faces, a smidgen of real remorse sprinkled in with its fake acted cousin—telling themselves they'd get help as soon as they got home, and they walked through the streets, drunk and dazed, the birds beginning their morning chorus, sunlight arriving before they were ready for it, serving up new volleys of panic. How could they explain what had happened? Their lives would be ruined. It wasn't their fault anyway, not really.

"I knew we were wrong—"

They pinky-swore to mutual silence and scurried back to their respective beds before their families awoke.

Shortly after ten on Friday morning—thirty-one hours later, as best as I can mark it—the realtor arrived with a prospective buyer. By then the smell was too pervasive to be ignored. The buyer was disgusted, the realtor mortified. The building, if you're curious, went off the market for a full year. Bad juju.

The fentanyl had been snorted or sprayed, the medical examiner concluded. There were no signs of injection. The level measured in her blood was well beyond fatal, even for a much larger person.

In my living room the boys swore they hadn't done drugs that night—well, they'd smoked a little pot, that was it; they had no idea people in that basement were high on dangerous drugs. Alcohol, yes, but not bad drugs. They didn't even know those people, except for the baseball guys, and even the baseball guys they didn't know well. Now, of course, they saw things differently. Maybe they should have known, but how would they? The thing was, the girl seemed nice. She was trying to help Shawna.

"Just because she was dressed that way didn't make her a bad person."

A few of the other partygoers were found, questioned, let go. No one knew the girl's name or how to find her. No one was charged. When I left town over a year later, the police assured me it was still an open case. Yeah. Okay. Sure.

When I finally opened my eyes that evening, I saw Jeff and Dan and their mothers waiting for me to speak. Their faces, deadpan as monks at prayer, wanted so much from me. *Please understand. Please believe how sorry we are. Please forgive us.* My pores opened, gushed sweat. Those careless boys—I wanted nothing more than to hurt them.

PART THREE

33

I have no idea how long I was speaking, but it felt like hours. There was no full stop on my story, only a petering out. I closed my eyes on a continent of stillness. Drew hadn't interrupted, which I appreciated, but now I wondered what questions he would ask. *How are you doing now? Did they find that girl? Could you ever forgive those boys?* I became aware of a rustling and when I opened my eyes I saw him getting out of bed.

"Oh Sybil," he said, standing above me, tall and naked, perfect as ever. "I just remembered—this is my day to hike with Gaylene and the gang."

He hovered. I blinked.

"I'm supposed to meet them in half an hour."

I blinked again.

"If I don't get going now, I'll be late . . . The timing is terrible, I know, but . . . We'll talk about it when I get back, okay?"

"You're going hiking now?" I said, my voice ironed thin and flat.

"It's too late to cancel. They'll be waiting."

"Of course. Go," I said, taking inventory of all the things I'd said that I should never have said, all my cells retracting, portals closing.

He hadn't moved, was waiting, it seemed, for me to release him.

"I'll be fine without you, if that's what you're wondering. I've been fine for a lot of years without you."

"I'm so sorry." He scurried away, dressed without showering, and was out the door in ten minutes.

I'll always wonder—was that the turning point? If he'd stuck around that Sunday morning asking questions, curious to know more about Shawna, would things have turned out differently?

I closed my eyes and squirreled deeper under the covers, but couldn't mask the sound of his car disappearing down the street. A wintry mix of hurt and fury overtook me. Why couldn't he cancel the hike, or find one of his outdoor friends to lead it. Gaylene and her cohort couldn't possibly need him then as much as I did. But another thought bubbled up: Even if there were no hike, he might not be capable of giving me what I needed. The fury was mostly at myself. How impulsively I'd spilled my guts, my grief. How foolishly I'd trusted him.

Desperate to talk to someone, I made plans for an early dinner with Val. She'd been my friend for years. A history teacher at an alternative high school, she advocated for unruly students and tried to coax them onto a less rebellious path; she was also a lesbian and an advocate for local LGBTQ rights, and I'd always thought of her as my advocate too. Which is to say, she was outspoken and liked giving advice. Other than my sisters, she was the only person I confided in. I'd told her about Shawna, but I hadn't seen her since the trial began.

We sat on the back patio of a popular burger spot, reveling in the tail end of yet another broiling summer day which I'd spent inside, doing the *New York Times* crossword puzzle and watching *Taxi Driver* then the first of the *Godfather* movies. It was one of those balmy evenings you wish would go on forever, the neutral temperature making you feel you could walk through walls. As you have probably guessed by now, I'm an aficionado of sunsets, the precious and fleeting time when the day begins to languish and cease its urgent forward motion. It's like stepping off a rollercoaster full of relief that you're still alive and haven't catapulted off track. Drew, as you can also imagine, revels in sunrises, while I can't stand their bugle-like call to action.

There were others with us out there on the patio and, though the tables were not excessively close to one another, I felt as if all those people were in my living room, and I worried they would eavesdrop on our conversation. We ordered beers and burgers. I tried to embrace the moment of relaxation with an old friend, but my mind was on fire.

As soon as we were seated Val pointed to the bandage that covered my tattoo. "What happened?"

"A tattoo," I said, hoping my face didn't speak of regret. I was still lucky, wasn't I?

"You're kidding. You're forty-nine, almost fifty. Plus that's not your style."

"Maybe my style is changing."

"You gonna show me?"

"In due time."

"Jeez, Sybil."

Someone arriving hailed Val—she was somewhat of a public figure in town—and they chatted briefly, shouting across tables. When they were done, Val leaned forward. "Someone I work with." She waved the woman into inconsequence. "I've been meaning to tell you. I saw Drew in the grocery store last week. I'm surprised I haven't run into him more often. We didn't talk—we haven't talked for years—but I watched him fondling the avocadoes as if they were a lover's breasts and I thought, *That guy is so fucking full of himself.* I think he saw me, but he didn't say hi. Didn't even acknowledge me."

"Oh," I said.

"It's kind of old business for him to still hold a grudge after such a long time, isn't it? I mean he could have said hi—what did I ever do to him? Best thing you ever did is to ditch that guy."

My seat was facing westward and the lowering sun descended a notch, blinding me for a moment and bringing with it an image of Drew on the trail, hand-in-hand with Gaylene, probably singing, the entire gang of teenagers held in his charismatic thrall.

"That's not exactly what happened," I said.

"Who cares? He's gone. I never liked him in the first place."

Her judgment summoned me to defend him. He was leading these hikes—didn't that prove he was a good person? Though it was true I hadn't succumbed to him again because I'd learned he was good, or because I'd discovered his latent paternal streak; I'd fallen for him a second time for all the wrong reasons: because I was weak and needy. I couldn't admit this, even to Val—or to myself either.

"There's no need to be pissed at him on my behalf."

"It's not just you. I can't stand his energy. With him everything is hopped up and sexualized. It's guys like him that make me glad I'm a lesbian."

She was confusing me. I'd been furious at him that morning when he left so abruptly, but the anger had eased somewhat, and now I had no idea what degree of anger was justified—or what degree of anger I truly felt.

It sounded so easy, deciding to be a lesbian, but having sex with women had never appealed to me. I ordered a second beer and changed the subject, telling her the bare outlines of the trial without violating the judge's orders. Then I cut the dinner short, claiming I had things to take care of. I'd show her my tattoo when it healed, I promised.

It's true I was somewhat addled and I'd had two beers, but I wasn't inebriated and I wasn't speeding and I definitely had the right-of-way.

It was a two-lane, one-way street, and I was in the left lane. The other car shot out of a side street on my left, oblivious to the stop sign, oblivious to my steady advance. When I saw the vehicle, a fiery red RAV4—a rental, it turned out—which was traveling at the speed of an absconding criminal and blind to the minor inconvenience of a stop sign—it was too late for me to stop. Hoping to avoid contact, I accelerated then reversed course and slammed the brakes, but the subsequent thud struck the chord of my miscalculation. We ricocheted off one another, the RAV4 clipping the left side of my aging Toyota and continuing into the center of the street. My car came to a standstill at an angle; a plume of smoke floated up from under its hood. I didn't move for a moment, annoyed and trying to modulate my annoyance so I wouldn't yell.

I expected the other driver to get out first and hurry over to apologize, but there was no movement in the other car. I dug for my registration and insurance card and got out to inspect the damage. My bumper had been dislodged and the hood was bent. The smoke was a sure sign something internal was awry.

The other driver approached. I expected to see a young man, one of the college boys who were the scourge of this town's streets, but it was a grown woman. We halted about ten feet apart, and I spread my legs spread in battle position. "What the hell were you thinking?" I said into the messy twilight.

Mascara ran from her lower lids, forming bogs beneath both eyes, but the rest of her face was so blanched she appeared phantom-like. She was of late middle age, and her pink skirt and sleeveless white top looked too youthful for her, exposing the loose skin of her upper arms and her sun-damaged décolletage. She glanced away, stuttered, silenced herself, and glanced back, swaying a little and gulping breath so her shoulders rose and fell and the label of her top, which was on inside-out and backwards, fluttered. Seeing her derangement, my anger dimmed a bit.

"We should exchange information," I said, wanting to be done with this. I took a few steps in her direction and thrust out my insurance card, but she didn't take it and, in that moment, I understood she was drunk. I also saw she was deceased Eric Hotchkiss's mother, the prim woman I'd been watching every day in court. Both of these things came to me simultaneously. She looked nothing like the woman I saw in court, and yet it was unmistakably she.

"The trial? Eric's mother?"

She nodded.

"Do you recognize me?" I said.

She nodded again. A car came up the street behind me and slowed to assess the situation before moving on.

"Let's get out of the street," I said.

We drove our cars to the curb and parked. Her car was barely nicked; mine had acquired new and foreboding sounds. We stood on the sidewalk. Her shoulders were still quaking, and she clutched her midriff and glanced around as if someone was in pursuit of her, though the sidewalks were deserted and only a single car had passed. Dusk had arrived at the hand-off to night and mosquitos whined up around us.

"I need your information," I repeated, seeing she was still empty-handed.

She swayed from foot to foot then stilled herself and jutted her chin forward, unnervingly reptilian. I had a few inches of height on her and stared down at the slab of her hair which looked felted. Her face glowed white in the blue-black air.

"Please," she said quietly.

"Please what?"

She waved her arm toward my car, flicking her wrist. "I'll take care of it. Whatever it is."

"You're drunk," I said.

"Maybe I am." She looked away again. Each time she glanced away she appeared to depart the scene entirely. "Maybe I have a right to be."

"Whatever you're suggesting, I'm sure it's illegal."

"What do you care?" she said sharply.

She started to cry, unguarded as a young child. At first I thought it was a performance designed to elicit sympathy, but as I watched the muscles convulsing along her neck, I saw it was genuine. Between sobs she tried to speak.

"You. Couldn't. Know."

I bristled. What could she possibly know about what I knew or didn't know?

Mosquitos were demolishing all my exposed patches of skin. Face, arms, shins, ankles. I listened to the sound of her body trying to normalize. Fading light blurred the specifics of her so she could have been any woman. Surprising myself, I reached out and placed my hand on her shoulder. I thought of pulling her into an embrace, but I didn't. Her son was dead and I understood that, but she also repulsed me.

It was fully dark by the time she returned to her car and pulled away, making her way down the street glacially, as if expecting trouble to spill from every alley.

The phone rang as soon as I got home. I saw it was Drew and didn't pick up.

I thought we would see each other tonight, but I haven't heard from you. Are you mad at me? Call when you get this. I'd like to come over . . . And by the way, the hike was good.

34

That night I slept fitfully. In the penumbra of sleep, I kept picturing Eric's mother in the street, spectral, disheveled and drunk, the drooling mascara making a mess of her face, completely incapable of performing the post-accident protocol of information exchange. I, who knew better, had allowed her to get away with it. For the duration of the trial I'd regarded her with derision. *There's the mother of an asshole. She looks like an asshole's mother.* But in that twilit street, just the two of us there trying to make sense of our random encounter, I saw things differently. Her child was dead. She was a grieving woman. She'd loved Eric, regardless of what others thought of him, and she'd lived to see him die. Killed. She, like me, was a mother bereft.

Once sleep took me I entered a dark catacomb. Aliens swayed like sea grass, strobe-lit, their bodies eely and blue. Shawna was there, but I couldn't locate her. She had to be in one of the back rooms. Trying to find her, I pushed through air that resisted me like water. The ground beneath me softened, threatened to open. I soldiered on, recoiling each time the snaky arm of one of the aliens grazed me. In a far corner I spotted two humans bent towards each other. A sexy woman in a tube top. A beefy man I was sure was Eric. *Shawna!* I yelled. *Watch out!*

I woke to frantic knocking. My neighbor Brenda was at the front door, saying she'd heard screaming, wanting to know if anything was wrong. I reassured her I was fine and sent her away.

In the clarion summer light of Monday morning the pieces of my current life fell into place slowly, a jigsaw puzzle beyond my humble ability to complete. Shawna was still dead. I'd slept with Drew. I'd told him about Shawna. Poor judgment all around. Furthermore, my unreported collision with the dead man's mother who seemed to want to silence me put me in a tenuous legal situation. The one consoling fact was that today the defense would finally begin to mount its case and soon we'd be hearing from Jessie.

My car would have to be serviced, but I had no time to take it in, so I borrowed a bike from Brenda and pedaled the four miles to downtown, arriving at the courthouse sweaty and addled. In the jury room Drew ambushed me at the coffee table, "accidentally" bumping my hip.

"How are you?" he whispered. "You look—"

"Later," I said, waving him off, wondering what words I could possibly find to express myself. Was it worth it to let him know how his sudden departure had hurt me?

I took a seat beside Ray, whose sullen attitude offered a wall of protection. He rested his forearms on his knees, as usual, and drank from his usual cup of black coffee. He nodded as I sat.

"Good weekend?" he asked. He wasn't smiling, but nor was he glowering.

"Okay, I guess. Pretty good," I said, surprised he'd spoken. "Except I had a fender bender last night, and I had to bike here today. And I'm no biker."

"Bummer. A tree fell on my pickup a couple months ago. Totaled it. That was a bitch."

"I bet."

Across the room Drew regarded us quizzically.

Filing into the courtroom and spotting Eric's mother, I stiffened. She didn't look good; the weekend had aged her by at least a decade. She wore a gray velour hoodie, navy sweatpants, no jewelry. Without makeup her face was pale and weirdly dented, like bleached clay into which someone has pressed thumbprints, and humidity had frizzed her hair into harridan wildness. I looked away, trying to find some place to park my gaze that wasn't Drew's neck. Everything in that courtroom had become a minefield.

The pulse of the digital numbers steadied me and emboldened me to steal a glimpse of Jessie. Her upright body still retained its commanding stoicism, but something had changed in her blue eyes. All through the prosecution's presentation they'd been laser-focused, but now they darted around the courtroom, tiny uncaged parakeets perching briefly then soaring a moment later, so restless it was exhausting to watch. Mindful of the judge's roving attention, I couldn't risk watching Jessie for long. Still, I sneaked brief glances, trying to shoot her reassurances: *It'll be fine. This is your moment. No worries.* Though there was every reason to worry.

Jessie felt me watching her and her eyes hooked mine and hosed me with such urgent need I was helpless to resist. Reeling, I returned her stare. A cold sweat erupted on my ribcage, dribbled toward my belly. I shivered, shook my head, glanced at the judge to see if she'd noticed, then slammed my eyes shut.

The mild-mannered man in the jury box spoke haltingly. Rick, Eric's EMT partner for a year and a half. An outbreak of fungal acne reddened his face, as if to tell us what his soft-spoken demeanor could not, that he still simmered with unresolved anger about what had gone down on the evening of their last shared shift.

Rick had wanted to intubate a young boy, defying Eric who claimed he was more competent. Their dispute escalated quickly—*I said, he said, fuck you, no fuck you*—then Eric punched Rick twice, blackening his eye and breaking his nose, forcing him to step back and allow Eric to continue with the procedure. Rick was pissed, but Boss Tierney advised him not to press charges. The unit had a reputation to preserve. Tierney reassured Rick he would be assigned a new partner; Eric would be placed on a six-week suspension. Rick, being a compliant employee, did not press charges. But over a year out, still furious, he wished he had.

"Did Eric get angry frequently?" Vitale asked.

"Heck yeah. He got ticked off all the time. Every day it was something. Stupid stuff like getting mad when he couldn't find a parking place, or when someone cut in front of him. Plus, he was always telling me I was doing things wrong, even when I was following protocol. He had, you know, a short fuse. That plus a superiority complex."

Eric's mother squeezed her eyes shut. Jessie lifted her chin to the ceiling.

Where is the happy midpoint between the short fuse and the morbid fear of expressing anger? Show me the person who routinely steers a healthy middle path.

Drew twisted his torso and rotated his owl neck to query me, his eyes overflowing with that signature melancholy look of his, trying to tell me he was sorry. He probably was sorry, but I wasn't ready to forgive him yet.

At the lunch break I scooted out before he could corner me, needing to be alone. I am used to dining alone without feeling defective, but that day, eating my BLT at a rickety lunch table surrounded by yammering men and women sprung for an hour from downtown offices, I felt like a pariah, locked in my thoughts, haunted. I tried to think myself back to the happiest period of my life when my mission was clear, when Shawna and I were an oasis of two, impervious to the world's chaos. *Mumma.* The memory calmed me.

Halfway through my sandwich I got up to pour myself ice water from an urn at the counter. Steering my butt carefully between the too-close tables, I took note of the high level of animation in the people around me, everyone joking and laughing, so relaxed. For a moment I wondered if a special event was taking place, and I was the only one who was clueless. Was a festival underway? Had they already begun celebrating Independence Day?

When I returned to my table, I found an envelope peeking up from beneath my sandwich plate. I pulled it out, looked around to see who might have left it. No obvious contenders. The business envelope was sealed and bore no name. I flagged down the harried waitress, who hovered by my table with her full tray.

I waved the envelope. "Do you know anything about this? It was under my plate."

"Uh-uh."

"You didn't see anyone leave it?"

She shook her head and took off, too busy to concern herself with manners.

I abandoned the remaining half of my sandwich, paid, and made my way to the small two-block-square park across from the courthouse. The benches were full so I perched on the low granite perimeter of the fountain and opened the envelope warily, unsure what to expect. An apology from Drew? Unlikely—writing notes had never been his style. I spotted the corner of what was unmistakably a check and widened the envelope for a better look. A Post-it note said: *So sorry. Hope this helps.* The check was made out from the account of the Elise Hotchkiss Trust in the sum of ten thousand dollars, signed in the spidery hand of Elise Hotchkiss herself.

I resealed the envelope and glanced around to make sure no one had seen. How could she be so stupid? A classic case of jury tampering. She must have followed me to the café and seized the moment when I rose for water. Did she really think I would cash this check? Did she really think it would cost this much to fix my car? Was this offered as some kind of reparation for the responsibility she assumed for her son's death?

I pondered the choices. I could rip the check and toss it. I could speak to the judge. I *should* speak to the judge. Maybe I would, though since I'd been humiliated by her I didn't relish the thought of another meeting. Meanwhile, I folded the envelope in half, quarters, eighths, and stashed it under my wallet and handkerchief at the bottom of my purse. As I passed back through court security, I was overcome by the stench of my own sweat.

35

Delaney Shaughnessy, radiation technician, Jessie's best friend. Her brown hair was laced with metallic red threads that glistened when she moved, like sparks threatening to set her head ablaze.

"After he was suspended we thought he was going crazy," she said. "Jessie and I both thought that." She nodded, resolute, aware there were those in the courtroom who would want to dispute, or skew, her words. "Really crazy," she repeated.

That's crazy, my sisters and I used to say as kids. It had nothing to do with a mental state; rather, we used the expression to refer to things so outrageous they could hardly be believed. Libby Monroe had been to Africa and was chased by wild elephants. *That's crazy.* A Masai man offered fifty cattle to marry Libby's older sister. *That's crazy.* Your father is a criminal. *Totally crazy.*

In these tumultuous times we're all symptomatic, we've all borrowed some of the world's craziness. There in the courthouse, crazy abounded. Walmart Kevin who talked nonstop, perhaps believing if he shut up he might cease to exist. Morose Ray who routinely disappeared into the bleak world of his black coffee. Dev, the beret-wearing linguistics grad student who grinned ceaselessly throughout the day, his version of skunk-stink to ward people off. There was no question about Elise Hotchkiss—she had spilled some serious crazy onto the pavement right in front of me. Even our squat fireball of a judge asserted her power with a decidedly unpredictable edge. Scratch the surface of anyone, even the ostensibly "normal" ones, and I guarantee you'll find some crazy. No, I don't exclude myself.

When Eric was suspended he went on a shopping spree, Delaney told us. He spent a quarter of a million dollars—*250k!* she exclaimed—on big ticket items. A Kawasaki ATV. A high-powered speedboat. A red Toyota pickup truck. A five-burner propane barbeque and complete set of outdoor wicker furniture. These purchases appeared without warning in the driveway of their humble neighborhood, dismaying Jessie, angering her. Why was he spending so much money on things they didn't need and wouldn't use, especially when he was out of a job? It was his money, he countered, his prerogative to spend it any way he wished. He was getting his job back soon, and he *did* plan to use the purchases—they were things he'd always wanted. She had no right to scold him.

Jessie set up her own bank account and deposited her paychecks there, watching the balance of their joint account plummet to zero. She would come home each day to an empty refrigerator; Eric, defiant, working his way through a six-pack of beer.

Delaney paused. From Jessie, a radical stillness. From Elise Hotchkiss (I now had a name for her), a pursing of wire-thin lips.

Delaney worried for her friend. She thought Jessie and Eric were bad for each other. When he was suspended, he became sullen and hostile, and she thought he might hurt Jessie. He often said terrible things to her, even in front of other people at parties. Humiliating things about her bad childhood, her bad family, her bad teeth, how she'd eaten squirrel. Plus, he was really, really stuck on having a kid. He wouldn't let it go. Sure, he appreciated Jessie's toughness, but he didn't like the idea that she might be smarter than he was, didn't like when people learned that she had more degrees than he did and earned more money.

Delaney shook her head. "About the kid, she wasn't going to change. It was kind of weird he didn't see that."

Vitale nodded, ceded to McCarthy.

Stay strong, Delaney. McCarthy's a bitch.

I've never been a sports fan. I'm not a cheerleader or a joiner, but as Delaney awaited McCarthy's grilling, each slight move of her head catching the overhead lights and igniting her hair, I understood that

I had unwittingly joined a team. Yes, I felt for Elise Hotchkiss who had lost a child as I had, but I was squarely on Jessie's team, Delaney's team, Vitale's team. Team of the underdogs. Team Iditarod. Team of the hardworking women. Team of the maligned and ridiculed.

"Isn't it true, Ms. Shaughnessy, that you and Eric went out for a period of six months, two years before Eric married Jessie?"

Delaney hesitated. "Yes."

"Isn't it also true that he was the one who ended the relationship?"

"Yes. But I was also done. We weren't at all well-matched."

"But you were upset, weren't you?"

"Objection. Leading."

"Sustained."

"Were you upset?"

"A little."

"Okay, you were only a little upset. But you were upset enough that you left a pizza box filled with human excrement on Eric's porch?" McCarthy raised a single eyebrow, regarding Delaney as one might regard a piece of rancid meat.

"Objection. Leading."

"Sustained."

"Did you leave a pizza box filled with human excrement on the victim's porch?"

Delaney's eyes flicked towards Jessie. Surely Jessie knew this—though maybe not.

"Well—I—"

"Answer the question, Ms. Shaughnessy," the judge admonished.

"Yes. But it was a joke, I swear."

"I rest," said McCarthy, a triumphant smirk twitching at the corners of her mouth.

36

Dismissed for the day, I hurried out of court to avoid Drew. I considered that I might be overreacting to him, but I still felt a need to protect myself. Time would tell. At home, after dark, I sat in the backyard, glass in hand, bottle of wine at my feet.

The thought of Delaney leaving a box of human shit on Eric's doorstep delighted me. Why had I never thought of doing such a thing? In the year and nine months after Shawna's death, when I was still in Somerville, I could have delivered numerous boxes of shit to Jeff and Dan's doorsteps. For that matter, I could have gone onto their porches and dropped my trousers and delivered them *un-boxed* shit. They would have known it was me but, crippled by shame, they wouldn't have pressed charges.

I floated in the night's dark ether, thinking of Shawna, thinking of Jessie, wise women who had things to teach me. A triumvirate, we held hands, squeezes traveling among us, pleasant electric shocks, hand to hand, round and round. *Ring-a-round the rosie, a pocket full of posies. Ashes, ashes, we all fall down.*

I opened my eyes on a rat evaluating me a couple of yards from my feet. I growled but the creature didn't move. I hurled the empty wine bottle, and he scrambled away as the bottle shattered on the flagstones.

A palm on my crown startled me awake. Drew.

"How did you get in?"

"The front door was unlocked. I figured you were expecting me."

"I wasn't. Jesus, what time is it?"

"A little after nine. Are you drunk? Why are you drunk?"

Why indeed. It was mostly dark out there, only the faint ambience of city light and a sickle moon. Then something scurried by—another rat, a cat, a chicken, who knows—and Brenda's motion detector startled on, spilling light into my backyard as well as hers. The light presented itself as a receptacle: *Place your answer here. Tell me why you're drunk.* He pulled the other chair next to mine and sat, leaning forward and kneading the hinge of his shaven jaw.

"Look, I'm sorry about your daughter. That must have been awful."

His words arrived like a Hallmark card. Empty and laughable. Pro forma words any stranger on a plane could have offered. He toed the shattered glass with an outstretched foot.

"What happened here?"

"A rat came right up to me and I threw the bottle at him."

He went inside and ferreted around in my kitchen until he found a broom and dustpan. He swept up the shattered glass and disposed of it in the kitchen trash. When he came back outside he stood behind me, close enough that I could feel the pulsing of his unspoken thought. What made a person good? There were things people could do that made them appear good, but deep in the muscle of the human heart few people were wholly good. Shawna was the only genuinely good person I'd ever known.

"Hey, I saw your car out there. It's pretty banged up. What happened?"

I shrugged.

"Are you really saying you don't know? . . . Look, you should probably get to bed." His voice was low and tentative.

Realizing he was right, I rose, light-headed and dizzy, but able to walk on my own. He followed me to the bedroom and stood with his posse of selves—judging and gentle, loose and rigid—at the end of the bed. I lay down and closed my eyes on the spinning ceiling. Forgetting he was there, I fought the vertigo, swallowing hard and breathing deeply, then drifting to the edge of sleep and back.

Shawna was holding my hand. Such warmth in that hand, such love. No, it was Drew's hand. He was lying beside me, on top of the covers. Life was repeating itself. Everything I had ever felt I would have

to feel again. If only something, someone, could eradicate the unre-
lenting sorrow.

37

The liminal state between waking and sleeping. The body inert, heavy, sensing a world of motion at great remove, but ascribing no meaning to it. Hands roving over breasts, buttocks, crotch. Irritation. Warmth. The flood. Then succumbing again to the obliterating vacuum of sleep.

The sound of running water woke me. I lay alone in bed, slimy with sex juice. Drew was showering. A headache pounded behind my eyes, but it didn't distract me. I was fully aware of what had transpired.

What disgust I felt. Disgust at him. Disgust at myself. He hadn't asked permission to access my body, my bed, my house. He had spent the night, uninvited, and now he was showering as if everything belonged to him.

He stood at the bedroom door, hair wet and combed, wrapped in one of my towels.

"Good, you're awake. We need to be at the courthouse in less than an hour."

"You need to leave now."

"You're still mad? I thought—I said I was sorry."

"Now!"

He hesitated for a moment, wondering whether to argue, then sighed and disappeared back to the bathroom. The sound of his puttering presence burned through me, bringing clarity through the fog of my hangover. He seemed to believe, on the basis of a few days of renewed sex, that we were a full-on couple again. But he hadn't consulted me on this matter and I had definitely not signed on.

Another thing, more disturbing: He could no longer read the language of my heart. If he ever had.

I glanced at the clock. Fifty minutes until we were due at the courthouse. I would have to ride Brenda's bike again—coexisting in a car with Drew right then was not an option.

The phone rang—my landline—and the machine picked up while I was still lying there, trying to convince myself to get up. Drew, emerging from the bathroom fully dressed, halted to listen. I could see him through the bedroom's open door, now fully dressed, staring across the living room to my phone machine as if it were a live person.

Edna Haroian here.

That familiar gravelly voice. Edna, Shawna's social worker. I'd always liked her a lot, and had depended on her wise advice during the years Shawna was with me. She'd been emailing me recently, but I hadn't opened the emails, hadn't wanted to expose myself to the wounds the emails threatened to reopen.

Give me a call. Something has cracked in the case.

"Edna," Drew reported through the doorway.

"I heard."

"Who's Edna?"

I had told him about Shawna on Sunday morning. Edna had been part of the story. Now on Tuesday morning, a mere two days later, he couldn't remember who Edna was?

"It's time for you to leave."

He sighed. "I trust you'll tell me what's wrong soon. You're acting like I've done something terrible, but I have no idea what." Then he left, noisily, unmistakably annoyed.

I rocketed from bed and got myself ready in record time. I was dying to call Edna but I couldn't take the time. It would have to wait for a court recess. I pedaled Brenda's bike as fast as I could and arrived at the courthouse with five minutes to spare. Surprised I wasn't late, I dialed Edna from a shady corner of the plaza, staring down at the rough concrete and feeling cold. I hadn't had coffee and I hadn't eaten anything the night before. A manhole haunted the corner of my vision.

A clusterfuck of people rushed by. Traffic and exhaust. Life ripping along pell-mell though the day was only beginning.

I had to plug one ear to hear Edna clearly. The Mystery Girl had been found. Ashley Finelli was her name, the Tube Top girl who Jeff and Dan had described, the one who had "helped" Shawna. She had OD'd and almost died and, full of remorse about everything in her life, she confessed to having given Shawna fentanyl.

The jury room was empty when I arrived, though I was only a few minutes late. Lenore, annoyed, came looking for me, chided me as she escorted me solo to my seat in the jury box, everyone watching. *Exhibit A, the tardy juror with the hangover.*

38

The next witness made me wary as soon as I saw her sashaying down the aisle to the witness stand. She was attractive—wavy black shoulder-length hair and svelte figure—and was dressed in what I would call *professional-bohemian* style, a red and purple flowered skirt that swished around lambent hips, a lavender blouse, and a wide purple rebozo slung diagonally across her chest. Gold hoops played hide-and-seek with her hair, and her low heels delivered a muted clap of authority on the courtroom carpet. Attractive, yes, but the deliberation behind such a put-together look has never appealed to me. It always makes me wonder what the person might be trying to conceal. You might think that's a justification for my own failure to groom myself and you might have a point, but I'm trying to report my honest reaction to that woman.

It was when she introduced herself as Dr. Melhoff and said she'd been Jessie's therapist for the last five years that I really began to worry. Would a therapist help Jessie's case? Wouldn't it imply she might be unstable? I personally didn't hold it against her, but I thought some of the other jurors would—they might think seeing a therapist for five years was an indication that she was crazy, a danger to society, someone who should most definitely be put away. Wouldn't Vitale be better off emphasizing the fact that Jessie had been raped and feared for her life?

Dr. Melhoff, it turned out, was not a real doctor, not in my view anyway. She was a PhD psychologist, no more a legitimate doctor than any of those academics at the university calling themselves doctors because they've read a bunch of history or English texts. Academics calling themselves doctors has always seemed to me like a way for them to pretend they have authority and influence in the world they'll never actually have. Yes, I know I once strove to be one of those people, but in the end I saw the folly of it.

To my mind even psychiatrists are imposters, their MD degrees allowing them to camp under the tent of science. What scientific proof is there for their myriad theories of human behavior? What hubris to act as if you understand why humans do what they do. There are, no doubt, some among the psychiatric tribe who still believe in penis envy.

But, putting my screed aside—there she was, Dr. Melhoff, up on the stand, and it was my job to listen. Vitale took a long time establishing Melhoff's pedigree: the list of degrees she had from top-notch universities, her professional training and licenses, her eighteen years of practice. It was all supposed to underscore that what she was about to say would be indisputable. I didn't *want* to harbor hostility toward a defense witness, but I couldn't help feeling Vitale was making a wrong move. Regardless of what Melhoff had to say, her mere presence could demean Jessie.

There was another problem with Melhoff. Her voice was soft and soothing, too much like the voice of a perfect mother. It wasn't wimpy exactly, but it was very *female*, so I imagined her testimony, despite the highfalutin credentials, might be sidelined and ignored. Possibly mocked. I could picture Ray raising an eyebrow in doubt, Dev the Beret Boy scoffing, and even Joanne, a mother herself, giving little weight to this maternal-sounding witness. I have nothing against mothers, you already know that, but a mother figure in that courtroom could be too easily dismissed.

"PTSD has many causes," Melhoff began to explain. Her dulcet tones washed over me. I heard and I didn't hear, not entirely reneging on my obligation to listen, but bringing to that task a healthy dose of skepticism. *Childhood trauma, abandonment, physical abuse, sexual abuse, rape, witnessing violence. Then you have war trauma, violence perpetrated—or witnessed—during military engagement . . .*

"And what would be the reason for Jessie's diagnosis?"

Melhoff hesitated and, like a victim of Tourette's, quickly hooked a hank of her hair behind one ear, another hank behind the other ear. "Well, for a period of at least three years from the time she was fourteen until she left home at seventeen she was sexually abused by her father."

Jessie had to have known this was coming—we all did—but still the revelation prompted a strong response. Her body's armature seemed to contract, as if she'd been stricken with a sudden case of rickets. Skeleton weakened, her spine curved and she curled in on herself. No matter how much exorcism she'd tried over the years, the past remained firmly lodged in her body.

"And what are the symptoms of PTSD?"

Melhoff regained her composure and her velvety voice continued as if she was reading a diagnostic manual to a child. *Fear. Anxiety. Depression. Insomnia. Headaches. Low self-esteem. Suicidal ideation. Nightmares. Aggression. Anger. Hostility.*

Aggression, anger, hostility? No! This was not the defense Jessie needed. My own hostility rose in inverse proportion to Melhoff's sweetness.

Intrusive memories, immune system dysfunction, brain changes, dissociative fugue states.

"Dissociative fugue states?"

Melhoff paused again, and her gaze skated past her visibly diminished client. "An involuntary escape from reality characterized by irrational thinking, detachment from self, out of body sensations, memory loss. Sometimes it lasts only a few moments, but in other cases for hours, days, months. In rare cases, years."

Involuntary escape from reality? Let me tell you, Dr. Melhoff, that is not unique to Jessie. Don't we all seek such escape? I know I do. Shawna certainly did. Drew too. What were his long hikes into the wilderness about but the urge to escape life's relentless corrosion?

"You've mentioned triggers. Did the defendant have any triggers for her symptoms?"

I sink away. Shawna and I stand on the bank of the Charles River. It's a perfect summer day. Sculls and sailboats drift by. Sequined sunlight winks on the water. We toss breadcrumbs to seagulls and they sail down to us, sometimes dive-bombing, sometimes catching the crumbs midair. At times they come so close, quarreling over the smallest morsel, that I am skittish, but Shawna is amused. She laughs and I laugh at her laughing. Then she hoots. At first I think it's escalated amusement—but no. She seizes my waist, butts her head into my ribs and moans, convulsed with sobs. It's not the birds that have frightened her—she was loving the birds. It's something else, but I have no idea what. I crouch, fold her into my arms and, blind to her plight, I press love deep into her, willing it to do some good.

"Having her hair touched has always been a powerful one because that reminds her of what her father did when he was abusing her—he would hold her hair back so she couldn't move." Dr. Melhoff captured her own abundant hair in one hand and pulled back her head. "Yanking it hard like this."

Jessie contorted further, as if doing an abdominal crunch. The tight bun on her neck rose into prominence.

"Small spaces are also a trigger for similar reasons—her father would often take her to a closet or the tool shed to have his way with her. And one other thing. Her father occasionally gave her sedatives in the form of pills to force her into submission, so she became aversive to taking any kind of pill, even aspirin. That includes birth control pills which has been difficult because she is also deathly afraid of getting pregnant. This is why she insisted on her husband using condoms. She can't bear the thought of bringing a child into this world after what her father did to her."

I noted her use of the present tense, bringing Jessie's ongoing feelings into the picture. She was *still* afraid of getting pregnant. She was *still* haunted by the awful sex with her father.

The past will not die. It festers in the body's cells, inflames the tissues, refuses to relinquish its grip. In the face of such intransigence, what can you do but flee?

You clutch Giggles to your chest, both of you giggling. Giggles' hair tickles the skin of your cheek. Giggles' paw twists through your loose hair so you and Giggles are, for a moment, the same creature, soft and furry and laughing, and you and Giggles both want to fly, to soar over the streets and buildings looking down on people but keeping a distance from them, airy and separate and safe. You dream of this flying every night. Giggles wants to go first. You set him up on the window ledge, give him a slight nudge, watch as his paws splay and turn into wings. You will go next.

All the king's horses and all the king's men. Where are they?

39

What did I do during the lunch recess? My primary intention was still to avoid Drew. At some point we would have to talk, but that conversation couldn't happen there at the courthouse or in the short block of time allotted for the break. I remained in the toilet stall until everyone else was gone. I emailed Edna asking her for more details. I scrolled through pictures of Shawna. I didn't eat, still too hungover to think of food.

Jessie's testimony would be restorative. Not only for her, but for me too. For all of us women in attendance who were enmeshed with unreliable men. After hearing from her, there would be no mistaking her actions that terrible night were wholly justified.

Back in the courtroom all the polarities were present. Everyone's attire made a statement. They had to have been dressed that way before lunch but, if so, I'd failed to notice. McCarthy in a killer black suit we hadn't seen before. Vitale in beige linen, a pink tie to express his solidarity with women. Elise Hotchkiss, more pulled together, clad in white like a bride—or an apparition. Jessie wore a pale blue suit, sitting in stiff readiness, eyeing the empty witness stand.

We were being cooked. It was in the high nineties outside and inside the courthouse it must have been in the high eighties. The humidity made it feel close to a hundred, the kind of heat people can die in. The AC whined and sputtered, and its struggle made it hard to hear anything else.

It was taking forever to get things started again. The judge, more irascible than usual, kept sending her clerk Lorna out to investigate something. Ululations from long-gone defendants began leaking from the walls, still quiet, but growing louder.

Vitale conferred with Jessie, but we couldn't hear what they said. Their heads bent toward one another with the intimacy of lovers.

Beside me Ray was restless. When I glanced at him, he glanced back and gave me the precursor to a smile. It occurred to me that he still smelled, but I'd gotten used to it and hardly noticed. He was an odd, opaque man—he would probably have said the same about me.

Chrystal was restless too. Crossing and uncrossing and recrossing her stockinged legs. It wasn't just Chrystal and Ray—we were all on edge. Even Neal and Karen, who had stayed at arm's length from the rest of us throughout the trial, seemed to be newly hatched into the room, more alert to their surroundings. Dev obsessively adjusted his beret; Anna braided and rebraided her hair. Walmart Kevin, afflicted by allergies, blew his nose every thirty seconds, bugle-loud. I looked around for Madame Defarge.

You see how I remember all these details? I, too, was more astute than ever.

Obscure messages flew at me from Drew's taut neck tendons. Somewhere adjacent to all those tendons were his carotid arteries and jugular veins, vessels which fed blood to and from the brain, enabling thoughts, most of which I would never know. I couldn't help thinking about how he used to narrate the human body as he stroked me after sex. The more he said, the more I saw the underlying mystery of the human organism, all the things inside us that we had no idea about but which chugged on nonetheless. At those times he became more opaque to me, and I became more opaque to myself. Most of what we do is inexplicable. All those years when we were together he might have never understood me, when all along I thought he did.

My tongue culled an archived seed from between my molars, the debris of some long-forgotten meal. I was dying to get the show on the road.

A sudden silence. The AC had quit. The judge mouthed a silent *fuck,* then gestured impatiently to Lorna. We went on the record without warning, the red numbers seething, almost out of control.

40

The courtroom becomes an island bowed down by a perversity of hot air. Everything slows.

Jessie and Vitale exchange a look and Jessie rises from the table. We've never seen her walk before, never seen her long legs. What athleticism she displays as she strides to the witness stand. She isn't tall but she appears tall. Her long neck suggests Egyptian hieroglyphs.

She settles into the chair and waits while Vitale gathers his papers. Her extreme stillness stands out in stark contrast to the other witnesses. This composure makes her beautiful. Charismatic and unassailable. All the wounds the trial has inflicted so far are repaired or forgotten. It's as if she's done what lizards do in regrowing amputated limbs. She's exactly what we want our heroines to be.

Vitale surprises just as much. He stands before Jessie smiling, a smile broad and genuine, without a hint of restraint, and this smile alters everything about him so his formerly lumbering presence becomes dashing, with charisma and command to match hers. They're both ready. What's more, it's evident they like each other, as she smiles back at him with the same glowing authenticity.

In a voice that is low and gravelly and calm, she unlocks her world. The hidden world of her thoughts, her feelings. The magic key. What it's like to be Jessie.

I liked his defiance. And his neediness. He often thought of me as his mother . . .

I had sex with him because he wanted it, but me, well, I never liked it . . .

After he was suspended his restlessness was alarming. He would some-times step in front of me to block my path and he'd stand there for a while like a big wall before stepping aside. It felt as if he was trying to scare me . . .

It embarrassed him that he'd been put on suspension. I wanted him to go to a therapist, but he didn't want to. He thought therapy was a waste of money . . .

He could be gentle sometimes, but it had begun to feel that he was more often gentle with other people than with me . . .

Every time I think of that night it feels like something I dreamed. I'd never fought with anyone physically . . .

"You have heard all the testimony, but you are the only person who was present in the apartment that night. Are there any important things that we should know that no one has said?"

A long intake of breath. "It's hard to describe, but it seemed like he was different that night. Something about him had changed. It was like he had no more use for me and I was in his way."

Vitale steps closer, leans in. She nods as if to indicate it's okay to proceed. It's a classic duet, as iconic as Rogers and Astaire, Simon and Garfunkel, The Righteous Brothers. Partners enhancing each other's performance—more intuition than choreography.

"Jessie, can you tell the court why you cut Eric's penis when he was already dead?"

She falters. Silence ensues. Panic sears and reddens her face. The jurors are knitted in a collective held breath. "I—I—I—"

"Take your time," Vitale says.

His voice restores her. "I didn't remember doing that at first, but then—"

"Then—?" Bent at the waist in an acolyte's bow, he urges her to con-tinue.

"Later I remembered that I actually did do that because—well—"

Another long melancholic pause. "Because I thought he should know what it felt like to have someone hurt you . . . down there."

I had already been in her camp, but now I was smitten. In awe. Her courage, her eloquence, her refusal to be subdued in the face of fear or humiliation.

Vitale awed me too. He'd ignored McCarthy's cruelty, her attempts to vilify his client. His legal acumen—which I had admittedly sometimes questioned—had surged to the forefront. No pyrotechnics, just human empathy. He had known all along, as I'd known, that Jessie was—is—a gem.

McCarthy's cross was brief and delivered without conviction. She displayed none of her usual eviscerating vigor, as if she was almost cowed by Jessie. Perhaps she was aware that the longer Jessie spoke, the more our sympathies were likely to swing in her direction.

The trial was over now, the verdict clear.

41

I took my seat at the jury room table, high-spirited and almost gleeful. It was after 4:30 p.m.—maybe we could acquit quickly and be done by the end of the day. I smiled at Ray and he nodded back. He and I had developed an unexpected bond.

The jury room was stifling and conversation was muted by the responsibility before us. The alternates, Joanne and Tom, were dismissed and Lorna repeated the instructions the judge had already explained in detail—selecting a foreman, summoning evidence, reporting the verdict—while I studied the faces of my fellow jurors. They displayed the spectrum of attitudes you might see in a high school classroom: Drew, on the far diagonal from me, eager and receptive as a straight-A student; Walmart Kevin with his usual arch, *don't-fuck-with-me* look. Everyone else wore expressions of solemnity or boredom.

Lorna had left the room, and scraps of paper were being distributed. I'd missed something, I wasn't sure what. Whispering, I queried Chrystal. "Foreman," she whispered back. "Kevin or Drew."

We had to choose between the two alpha males? I voted for Drew because I knew him and assumed he would do a reasonable job. Plus Kevin was a blowhard.

Two votes for Kevin, ten for Drew. That was good. Having Drew as foreman, regardless of the shaky state of our relationship, would give me greater license to express my opinion.

"Okay," said Drew, grasping for an appropriate take-charge persona, its dimensions unclear when his trademark joking style was out of line.

Kevin was annoyed by the vote that had sidelined him. "What a piece of work," he said. "As I see it, there's not much to discuss."

"Excuse me?" I said.

"She cut his penis while he was dead—that's all you need to know. Case closed."

Not surprising, coming from him. "The almighty penis," I muttered, thinking no one would hear.

"Sybil!" Drew chided. Apparently I hadn't been muttering.

"She's a nut job, guilty as hell," Kevin said, now speaking directly to me.

"Guys," Drew warned. "It's getting late. We'll take a straw poll to see where we stand and then dig into the discussion tomorrow."

I would have been perfectly happy to let others know where I stood, but no one wanted a show of hands. *Come on, guys,* I thought, *show a little courage.* Drew instructed us to write on a scrap of paper *convict* or *acquit.*

The scritching of pencils. The bailiff's bored sigh. The heat, approaching its late afternoon apex. Anna collected the scraps. Drew sorted them.

Four acquits. Eight convicts.

42

He snared me on the plaza, a swarm of people veering around us in chaotic exodus from the courthouse.

"I'm worried about you," he said. The six inches he had on me seemed like a mile, his head dangling over me like a wrecking ball. "Your car. Getting so drunk last night. What you just said in there. What's going on?"

I forced a laugh. The long day without food and begun in a hangover had made me jumpy. Someone was waving in my peripheral vision. "See you tomorrow!" Shanti called. How light-hearted she looked, how unperturbed by the decision before us.

I turned back to Drew. "You don't get it, do you?"

He sighed. "Don't make this into twenty questions."

"For one, you didn't ask to stay last night. You didn't ask to have your way with me."

"You seemed to like it. You didn't resist."

"I was half asleep! My body went along with it—not *me* . . . Do you really not remember who Edna is?"

"Oh, for God's sake. There's a lot to remember these days. We're both on overload."

"Shawna's social worker. Maybe you don't remember who Shawna is either?"

"Of course I remember Shawna."

"As foreman of the jury you should remember everything."

"So this is about your daughter . . ." He squinted into the sun. "Okay, let's just table this. We'll talk when the trial is over. You're getting overwrought."

"*Overwrought?* Priceless. You mean *hysterical?* Maybe *crazy?* There are so many delicious words for a woman with strong opinions."

"I'm done. See you tomorrow."

Off he went, always the leaver, never the left. He would no doubt be swallowed up by some social engagement, dinner with friends, maybe a movie, something to enable him to ignore the chasm that had opened between us.

I used to read to Shawna every night, snuggling next to each other in my big bed before we fell asleep. She hadn't been read to until she came to me, so I tried to read her many wonderful children's books she'd missed, many for much younger children, books that were silly and often rhyming. She had her favorites—*If You Give a Mouse a Cookie* and *Goodnight Moon*—and I had mine—*The Owl and the Pussycat* and *McElligot's Pool*—but one we both loved equally was *Ferdinand the Bull.*

Ferdinand is the story of a bull who is not like the other bulls. He is a peace-loving bull who loves to sit under a cork tree and smell the flowers, while the other bulls love showing off their aggression and strength in hopes of being chosen to take part in the bullfights in Madrid. One day, the men from Madrid come to the countryside to choose the fiercest bull to compete. Ferdinand, having no interest in being chosen, goes to settle under his cork tree. As he sits, he is stung by a bee. Startled and angry, he leaps into the air, snorting and puffing and pawing. The men from Madrid are mightily impressed with his ferocity so they take him off to Madrid. On the day of the bullfight Ferdinand arrives in the ring and sees the ladies in the stands—they all have flowers in their hair! Sitting himself down in the center of the ring, he sniffs with delight, too distracted to fight the matador. Disappointed, the men from Madrid deliver Ferdinand back to the countryside, where he settles happily under his cork tree to smell the flowers again.

"The bee poked him," Shawna would say every time we read the book, and she would stab me everywhere with her forefinger, pretending to be a bee. It became a habit with her, when something in the world bothered her—a loud sound perhaps, or a rude person—to say: "I was poked!" And she would hop around, snorting as if she was Ferdinand.

I took to doing the same thing when life irritated me. Maybe I'd had a difficult client, or maybe my sister Sally had made an insensitive remark. Explaining these things to Shawna I would leap off the couch and jump around the apartment in a theatrical display that made her laugh. "I've been poked!" I'd say. "I've been poked!" Remarkably, my performance often helped to mitigate my annoyance.

Ferdinand was one of the few books I'd kept from the collection I'd bought for Shawna. I brought it out that evening and paged through it in the fading light. I was too tired to leap and snort like Ferdinand, but I definitely felt poked, and I yearned for a cork tree under which I might rest.

My mind was on wrongdoing, the complicated rubric of responsibility and blame. The day had begun with learning about the existence of Ashley and her confession, the Tube Top Mystery Girl who had given Shawna fentanyl. In the quiet of that moment I realized I didn't care about Ashley. Her confession didn't exonerate Jeff and Dan. *They* were the ones who took her to that party—*they* were responsible. If they had acted differently, she never would have died. In order to make a judgment, you have to examine the preconditions and precursors of behavior. And in Jessie's case, it was Eric's intolerable, violent behavior that precipitated her actions. Those who wanted to convict her weren't examining the situation deeply enough.

As I sat there in the fading day, these thoughts decanted something. Elise's check was still nestled in the bottom of my purse, a sign of nascent criminality that could take me down too. Tamping exhaustion, I made myself rise. I wheeled Brenda's bike from the backyard around to the street where dusk unfurled, quiet as smoke.

Without a light or a helmet, I rode through the back streets, their summer torpor, people drinking beers on porches, kids licking popsicles on their backs in patches of scraggly urban crab grass, pop tunes curling from open windows like lassos. I sped past everything, out of sync with the rest of the city, hell-bent, cutting through the languor, purse thwapping my hip, unoiled bike chain announcing my passing with its juddering rasp. "Take it easy!" a guy yelled to me from his stoop.

The hibernal air of the air-conditioned lobby declared war on the sweaty skin of my bare arms. I looked around. The best hotel this town had to offer, supposedly, but to me it looked tawdry, a parody of old-world elegance, western-style. High ceilings. Saffron carpeting bordered with blue fleur-de-lis. Giant gilded mirrors. Paintings of cowboys, Comanches, bears scooping salmon from raging rivers, snow-capped volcanic peaks. Pure kitsch.

A few people wandered through the cavernous space. One couple sat on a crimson sofa, another checked in at the front desk. Noise spilled toward me from the bar off the far end of the lobby. I rubbed the sweat from my face, smoothed back my hair, and approached the desk clerk.

"Ma'am?"

"I'd like to leave something for Elise Hotchkiss." I took out the envelope, unfolded it, and ironed it with the side of my hand. On the front I'd written her name. Inside the flap I'd scrawled: *This is illegal.* I'd resealed it with Scotch tape. I handed it to the clerk, trying not to look furtive.

He frowned at first, then nodded and typed into his computer. "Would you like me to ring her?"

"Oh, no. It's fine."

I hastened back across the lobby, unburdened but still unnerved. Just before I got to the revolving front door, Elise herself sidled into my peripheral vision, exiting from the bar. Heart wailing, I scuttled outside to my bike and doubled over the seat in relief. Thank God I'd extricated myself from the mess of Elise Hotchkiss. Her grief and confusion were not my affair and the randomness of our accident could not make them so.

The nighttime streets were thick with phantoms. Curbs shimmied, houses sprouted eyes. The orange streetlight pulsed down ugliness, turning the plastic equipment on the preschool playground lurid. The humidity had congealed and become visible. Familiar landmarks were streaked with strangeness. Wraiths leered from windows and gaped at me from behind parked cars. I had barely escaped becoming a criminal, but now I could safely lay claim to being an upstanding citizen. Still, everything continued to shapeshift as I rode home to the edge of the world.

43

I was awake long before the birds' chorus, sure someone was in the bed with me. Drew? Shawna? I reached out. No one was there, only a memory, archived in my cells, of lying beside another human being who loved and needed me. It was dark and still. I was starkly alone. Something had to have awakened me, but it was nothing I heard or saw.

Too wired to return to sleep, I got up and began writing a list, naked on the living room couch, a lined pad in my lap. I am not usually a list-maker, but apparently I'd become one overnight.

Critical to know
Who voted to acquit? Who voted to convict?

Likely answers
- Shanti and Drew are with me, in favor of acquittal
- The other one: Chrystal or Anna? Maybe one of the young men? Neal? Karen? (overall, impossible to say)
- Kevin, Cory, and Ray all for conviction

Important things I must convey to persuade people to acquit (in no particular order)
1. She was scared to death of him, in part because he was twice her size, she was only trying to protect herself, he could easily have killed her, she had no control over her own safety, hence the wine bottle
2. He had a short fuse, a tendency to go ballistic

3. He raped her that night and was hoping to get her pregnant—which she strenuously objected to and always had

4. She had been molested by her father, had flashbacks and fugue states as a result and probably was in a fugue state that night which explains why she cut the penis

5. He was mean to her—he regularly shamed and belittled her, all their friends saw this, he came into the relationship with much more power

6. Don't focus so much on the cut penis—that was only symbolic, not the reason for his death

A screech from the backyard disrupted the silence. I turned on the outdoor light. Two raccoons were fighting, leaping at one another, locked for a moment in an embrace like lovers, then rolling over, snarling, hissing, roaring, biting. They ignored the light. They ignored the opening back door. They ignored me standing naked on the patio yelling: *Get out of here! Go on! Git!* I might as well have not been there.

I extinguished the light and retreated inside, enjoying the defiance of my naked flesh as I strode through the kitchen and into the living room. Through the front window the moon was a sharp dagger, hording its light. Lines were being drawn everywhere. A fillip of excitement. A clutch of dread.

44

I did not go back to bed. I reclined on the living room couch in an attenuated state of waiting: waiting for morning, waiting for the resumption of the trial, waiting for the chance to influence the outcome of things.

Are thinking and obsessing the same thing? I used to believe obsessing was a high-pitched version of thinking. Thinking on steroids. Now I believe thinking and obsessing are entirely different modes. Thinking can be impersonal, but obsession always has its origins in a highly personal state of emotion. Love. Fear. Anger. Humiliation.

I could so easily imagine the conversation Jessie and I might have. I would tell her all about Shawna. I would tell her how I'd always thought of death as a sudden event, but in Shawna's case it took days to unspool.

The apartment that morning was uncannily silent; the blare of absence, a fact I only registered much later. I rose from bed and went to the bathroom, cocking my ear for her movement then, hearing none, I went to investigate. Seeing her empty bed, my organs shrank. At fourteen she was still small enough to hide easily, but my bones understood she was not hiding.

I threw on clothes and went next door. Alice was in high gear, making breakfast, packing lunches for her youngest two. Jeff was sick, she said; he'd been vomiting and would be staying home from school. She cracked his bedroom door when I insisted. "Sybil's here and wants to know if you've seen Shawna."

She came back to me shaking her head. "He hasn't seen her. Sorry. I'll come over and help you look after I've dropped the girls at school."

As promised, she came by later, but she was useless to me and I sent her home. By then I'd already walked the blocks of our neighborhood, gone to the park, talked to Dan's mother Maude, learned Dan was also sick. How was I, back then, to make meaning of such information?

I could picture Jessie shaking her head. *Absolutely, how could you know?*

Midmorning I called the police and was shunted from robot to robot before I finally spoke to a person. She was kind, but in a professional way that did not reassure. She asked me to describe Shawna in detail, what she was wearing when I last saw her. She'd been wearing nightclothes, but I'd checked her drawers and found her chic black outfit missing. Was there any reason Shawna would have run away, the woman wanted to know. No, I said, of course not. She had a good home here. She loved me. When I became too insistent, the woman turned officious. Email a photo, she said. Someone would be in touch as soon as they learned anything.

I emailed several photos. I called my sisters and got their voicemails. It was still morning, everyone at the height of busy-ness, everyone but me embroiled in the ongoing workings of the world. Sue called back first. She was sympathetic but, despite being an irreproachable problem-solver, she had no idea what I should do as it wasn't her bailiwick. She hated to say so, but she had to get to court, she'd do some investigation and check in later.

Sally called back in the afternoon, but I was so tense and terse by then I'm sure I made no sense. She offered to come by, but I said no. She had always condescended to Shawna, and I could see she wasn't surprised by this outcome. Running away was not uncommon for teenagers, she said. Shawna would probably come back. I stewed and paced and punched pillows. I needed something specific and active to do.

Jessie nodding. *Oh yes, I've punched plenty of pillows.*

I walked the neighborhood again, my gaze scouring fences, edges of buildings, bushes and hedges. My eyes became dry from too little blinking. In the late afternoon, I returned to Alice's house, insisted on talking to Jeff. He lay in bed, watching a movie on his computer. The room was dark and rank with fumes of vomit and secretions of adolescent boy. It made me glad Shawna was a girl. I remained at the door and questioned him. Did she say anything about running away? Do you have any idea where she might have gone? Did you have any inkling that she was planning this? No. No. Sorry, no. How I came to hate that word *sorry*. He had muted the sound on his computer, but his eyes kept flicking from me to his screen. *Turn that movie off!* I wanted to yell. *Shawna is missing! You are supposedly her friend—don't you care?* But Alice was outside listening, and I couldn't bring myself to chide her "sick" son.

What an asshole, Jessie would say.

That night I took to the streets again. The moon was almost full, highlighting the pale green bounty of the newly leafed trees. The air's balminess, announcing the coming of my favorite season, mocked me. I didn't expect to find her, but I needed to occupy myself somehow. A raccoon approaching a garbage can turned to me with a warning glare: *Don't fuck with me.* Then, and only then, I wept.

I don't cry, Jessie would say. *Sometimes I wish I could.*

I returned home in the wee hours, empty-armed. Numb. I lay on the living room couch until light slammed the bay window.

They found her late Friday morning, May 17. With my recently submitted report of a missing child, it didn't take long to track me down. Everything about us was an easily accessible matter of public record. Still, I had to identify her.

Nothing could mar her beauty. Not the green fluorescents, nor the chilled air of the basement morgue with its gray cinderblock walls. Not the rolling gurney she lay on, nor the sheet that covered her until they pulled it back from her black-sweatered shoulders. Not the pallor of her usually tawny skin. Not her purple-blue lips and fingernails. Dead for over a day and beginning to decay in ways they had tried to cover up, she was still a stunner, her raven hair still shiny, her skin still poreless. The tiny drumlins of her budding chest suggested a child on the cusp of change. She had always inhabited a place removed from history, and now more than ever she was a woman-child out of time.

Hope flared that maybe, just maybe, she was asleep.

I asked for a moment alone with her. I had brought Lambie with me, and I tucked Lambie under her arm. I took her hand and squeezed three times: I. Love. You. I sang "Peace I Ask of Thee Oh River." I kissed her cool waxy lips, trying to summon back her mischievous Shawna-ness, but everything I did only underscored her absence. I covered her with the sheet—best do it myself—and I left the room.

Oh yes, Jessie said breathlessly. *I know, I know.*

After many days at home, subsisting on crackers, I forced myself to go out. A crow was perched on the hood of my car. Reluctant to disturb it, I waited on the sidewalk, admiring its glossy purple-black feathers, expecting it to fly away as most birds would, but it remained there, staring at me, eyes gentle and prescient, head cocking from side to side in that robotic avian way. It wasn't afraid of me. *Shawna?* I said. *Shawna?* It advanced toward me, high stepping cautiously so as not to slip, then it flew off. *Shawna!* I yelled as it passed up over the roof and out of sight.

I had been planning to do some grocery shopping, but hunger was distant—it was during that period and the year following that I lost a great deal of weight. Instead of shopping, I drove to Walden Pond and walked partway around until I had outwalked the other visitors and found solitude on a rock. I removed my shoes and sank my feet into the water, heedless to its chill. Grief as anesthesia. But some sensation persisted—a fish, large enough for me to see its undulating shape just below the surface, was nibbling on my toe. I didn't recoil as I normally would, and the fish remained there, then broke the surface briefly, but long enough to catch my eye. You must believe me—this fish was assessing me, and then, at the moment he went back to nibbling my toe, a robust red squirrel skittered across my lap. I was startled, but not alarmed. I felt as if these animals were flocking around me in the way white blood cells aggregate around a wound. They knew I needed help. Animals are always more attuned than humans. They are litmus tests, the proverbial canaries in the mine shaft, telling us when things have gone out of balance.

Oh yes, Jessie said. *My dogs sensed everything.*

The next week starlings arrived in our neighborhood, flock after flock of them appearing at dusk, swooping through the twilight in their mysterious hieroglyphic formations, first riding on thermals high above the trees and rooftops, then descending and navigating through the corridor of the street like investigating drones. I'd never seen so many starlings—multiple murmurations—nor had I ever seen them fly so low. I couldn't imagine what they were seeking, and at first I was frightened. I wondered if the magnetic compasses in their brains had been altered by some toxin. Then I understood, woo-woo as it sounds, that they were coming in search of me, knowing I needed tending, offering what they could. I have never owned pets, other than Giggles, but now animals, normally speedy wild animals were slowing themselves down and paying attention and becoming my solace.

Jessie nodded. *Thank God for animals.*

One morning, several weeks after the visit from Jeff and Dan, I glanced out the bay window just as they were heading off to their camp counselor jobs, their backward caps jaunty, their bodies careless and loose. It was unfathomable to me that someone would put such reckless boys in charge of young kids. I felt like throwing something at them. After that, I kept the living room blinds down so I would not have to see those boys going about their lives while my own was in freefall.

For a while, it was very hard to imagine going on. I wasn't about to do anything to take my life, but I wasn't thrilled about being alive either.

It is that day, May 17, that I continue to mark. Last year, the first anniversary when I was still in Somerville, I spent the day hunkered in bed. I slept when I could. I watched old black-and-white movies, Hitchcock, Hepburn/Tracy. I wanted to see movies in which nothing resembled real life, where all the actors played their roles with ludicrous exaggeration. I wanted to enter a world, any world, where nothing could surprise me.

I took three baths that day, lying in water that quickly grew tepid, feeling whalish and old, remembering Shawna's face at the half-open door, offering me the plate of cinnamon toast. *Mumma.*

This year, back in Oregon, it was different. I didn't realize I needed a ritual until I was already enacting it. I keep Shawna's ashes in a Tupperware container that seals them tightly, not wanting to risk losing them to careless dropping. A piece of masking tape identifies the Tupperware with a single letter, S, our favorite letter, Shawna's and mine. Not that I'm about to misplace the container, or mistake it for something else, but just in case.

I took the Tupperware to the backyard at dusk. The air was cool and gray and humid, the lawn sodden from recent rain. I lay on my back in the wet grass, the tub balancing on my belly, and I welcomed the moist discomfort and transgression of mud. It occurred to me that I was assuming the position in which I had last seen Shawna, lying on her back on the gurney. I closed my eyes and pictured my lips blueing like hers. I lifted my head to spread my hair across my shoulders, just as hers had been spread. If anything matched about us, it was our long dark hair. The peepers, exceptionally loud that evening, swelled around me, joining the plaint of two doves in Brenda's yard.

I opened my eyes to pry open the top of the Tupperware, and I pinched up some of the ashes, cupping my hand so as not to lose them. Most of it was silty, but there were a few chunks the size of large rice grains. I brought the ashes to my mouth, emptied them onto my tongue and, closing my eyes, allowed saliva to circulate the ash to all corners, into the crevices of gums and teeth, wanting to taste the distilled essence of Shawna, thinking of all the things that had gone into making her body, air and water and gallons of ice cream, and the fentanyl that had unmade her. I swallowed and pinched up more of her and the dry silt seemed sweet this time and I swallowed again then took a third pinch. The remains of her became a paste that covered my tongue and palate. My stomach churned, ingesting her more fully, and I felt her becoming part of my flesh, her pure spirit cleansing me, her soulfulness working on me to make me whole again.

Oh yes, Jessie whispered. Then she and I hugged.

45

What exhilaration it was to be streaking through the cool morning on Brenda's bike, bare legs kissed by the fresh air, unbound hair a dark flag sailing behind me. Perhaps it was the exercise—the joy of flex-and-release in my calves, the drumbeat of blood at my temples and neck—that imparted optimism and made me ready to conquer. In only a couple of days, apparently, I'd become a biker. Who knew sedentary Sybil could enjoy such exertion? I hadn't chosen to do this, but what a tonic it had turned out to be. Perhaps I would make a practice of this.

I hadn't anticipated the crucible of the courthouse. An alarm went off ahead of me in the security line. An altercation. A leathery-faced man was handcuffed and hauled away. The episode brewed nervousness in everyone.

The jury room, too, was riddled with tension. People couldn't conceal their attitudes in such a small room. Their faces were scribbled with undisguised anxiety. Faces like semaphores. We knew we disagreed and would have to work things out. Drew was in his seat at the head of the table, studying a small notebook, brow furrowed. Apparently he had also made some notes. Kevin was swearing at the malfunctioning coffee urn. Karen and Dev, both allergy-afflicted like Kevin, snorted into handkerchiefs.

Despite this epidemic of grimacing discontent, I felt an unexpected fondness for my fellow jurors. We'd been through so much together in a couple of weeks. I understood convincing them to acquit might be an uphill climb but, having laid out a plan and equipped with my notes, I'd never felt so sharp and optimistic. I took the seat I'd been in the day before and shot a smile at Drew. My anger at him had subsided somewhat, eclipsed by the moment's more important calling. He didn't notice me—or pretended not to. *No worries,* I thought.

"Let's get going," he called out to the stragglers at the refreshment table. "We've got our work cut out for us. I'm assuming everyone would prefer not to have to come back after the fourth."

He wanted us to air our views in light of yesterday's vote, eight to four. The room swirled with diabolical agendas. Snippy Kevin at one end of the table, close-mouthed Drew at the other. I fixed Jessie's incandescence in my head and heart, my lodestar.

Kevin, unsurprisingly, was again the first to speak, "Like I said yesterday, she's guilty as hell." How predictable he was, shoving his opinion to the center of the table as if it was the law itself, a covenant we must not violate. "I mean pummeling the guy with the wine bottle is one thing, but cutting his dick—that's just sick. And the way she threatened his girlfriend. She clearly hated him and wanted him dead. Same old story—jealous wife who went crazy."

Cory, spineless man, nodded.

I pulled the folded sheets of paper from my pocket—the lists I'd made in the wee hours—and laid them on the table before me, then paused, wondering if this was my moment. It could ruin my case to jump the gun.

"I disagree," Shanti said. "He was a dangerous, short-tempered man, and she was afraid of him for good reason."

Dev agreed with Shanti. "Rick, Eric's co-worker—what he said really got to me. About Eric not being as nice and kind as the prosecution was trying to make him out to be. It seems to me he had to be in control."

A caviling silence ensued. I was doing the math. Shanti, Dev, and I supported acquitting—who was the fourth? I assumed it was Drew but his face gave away nothing.

"Others?" Drew prompted. "Ray, what do you think?"

Ray shrugged. "Reasonable doubt. I think there's a lot of reasonable doubt."

I could have hugged him. Who knew Ray and I would see eye to eye? But if he was the fourth who voted to acquit, Drew must have voted to convict.

Oxygen leached from the room. *How could he?* While my personal disagreements with him were legion, I had always known him to be rational and principled, and convicting Jessie was far from reasonable. Short of breath, I began to swim upstream, a salmon heading to a home where I was destined to die. Ganglia on fire, full of grit. *You're wrong, Drew.*

"Okay," I began, "I have a lot to say . . ." I was about to stand but checked myself. Remaining calm was paramount. I knew that going in. I tried my best. I really did.

"We have to remember that Eric had a history of humiliating her. And that night he threatened her and raped her and broke her arm. And she was afraid he—"

Kevin spoke over me. "First, the broken arm was *an accident.* Second, it wasn't rape—they were married."

"No, no," Shanti admonished Kevin. "A husband can be convicted for raping his wife."

"Thank you, Shanti," I said, smiling my gratitude at her. "The point is, she was defending herself. Don't forget he was much bigger than she is and he might have killed her if—"

"We don't know about that," Kevin countered. "How could we possibly know that? We're talking about what *did* happen, not what *might have* happened. And we have evidence that she also *cut his penis!*"

"Cutting the penis didn't kill him," I continued. "He was already dead by then—"

"Yeah, already dead—who the hell does that?!"

Kevin kept interrupting me, but I didn't let that stop me. "The medical examiner said it was the fall that caused the brain hemorrhage that killed him. Cutting his penis was symbolic—her way of saying she'd had enough."

"Symbolic, sheesh." Kevin raised both hands in the air to tell everyone I was a lost cause.

"Listen!" I said. "Stop interrupting me."

Drew held up a hand of arrest. "Hey, guys, calm down. Sybil. Kevin. Let's hear from some other people."

I turned to Drew, irritated by his chiding, but keeping my irritation in check, knowing there were bottom-line principles he and I could agree on. I was still confident I could convince him of Jessie's innocence. And if he believed in her innocence others would follow suit.

"Let me continue," I said. "I'm not done. What I'm trying to say is that this whole trial has not been aiming for real justice. The prosecution is only interested in winning and in the process they're concealing the truth."

Kevin snorted. "Come on, you're telling me the defense doesn't care about winning?"

"Yes, but—"

Drew patted the table. "Sybil and Kevin, you're out of line. You need to let others talk. And we all need to agree on the facts before we go any further."

"But wait. Some of the evidence is abstract, like the power question," I said. "We have to look at who had the power. It's important that the power was totally out of whack between them. That was one of the first things Vitale told us—"

"Sybil," Drew said, his vocal cords so constricted they made my name into that of a stranger. "Didn't you hear me? Let. Others. Speak."

"Okay, but let's remember we're here for the purpose of justice. Let's not make this a kangaroo court."

"Stop," he said.

"Why are you cutting me off?"

"He's saying shut up," Kevin said. "Because you're being a pain."

"You're telling me to shut up?" I said to Drew, ignoring Kevin as well as I could. "Are you serious, Drew?"

"Yes," Drew said. "You need to shut up. You're dominating." By now Drew's tone was openly hostile.

"I'm not shutting up. I have a perfect right to speak."

"Let her finish," Shanti said. My heart swelled with intense fondness for her. Was she the only other person in the room concerned with finding true justice?

Drew glared at me. For an attenuated moment that summoned so much from our past, control seesawed between us. Who knew what the other jurors were gleaning from that sustained stare-down between us, but I didn't care.

I seized the reins. "Didn't you hear the shrink?" I spoke not only to Drew, but to the entire table of jurors. "Jessie's father abused her all those years and then her husband exerted his own kind of abuse." Out of the corner of my eye I could see Drew gazing into his lap and shaking his head vigorously, but I ignored him, just as I ignored the chorus of whispers bubbling up around the table. "That night she was in one of the fugue states the shrink described, not completely in control of herself because of her past experiences. The law needs to show her some empathy. *We* need to show her some empathy—"

"I'm telling you again—stop right now," Drew said. "This isn't a place for moralizing. And it's certainly not a place for you to air your complaints against your father or me."

"Oh, for God's sake, Drew, this isn't personal—"

He slapped the table. "Break. We'll convene in ten minutes." He rose and left the room through the door that led to the courtroom. In the moment of silence that followed, no one dared look at me, even Shanti. Glances were exchanged among them. Then, a general rustling as people reached for their phones, rose to get coffee, lined up for the restroom. How had they heard Drew's comments? He hadn't explicitly said we'd been involved, but even with limited information, the human brain is primed to extrapolate.

The next thing I knew Lenore was at my side, all aflutter. A bailiff hovered behind her. I had no choice but to follow her to the courtroom, directly up to the judge's bench. I expected to see Drew, but he wasn't there. The judge glared down at me, her opprobrium unmistakable.

"You," she said. "I should have known you were a fractious person back when I saw you making eye contact with the defendant."

"I'm not fractious," I said.

"Not fractious? The foreman said you were holding forth, questioning the legitimacy of the proceedings and refusing to shut up. He said he asked you repeatedly to stop talking, but you refused. In my book, that's fractious." She used both hands to rake the thick hive of her hair.

"I could charge you with contempt of court." Her gargantuan head swung from side to side like a giant pendulum.

"But, call me crazy, I've decided I'm not going to do that. I'm going to replace you with one of the alternates and let you go." Back and forth, a head made heavy with the lead weight of miscarried justice. A long, dystopic sigh.

"Don't make me sorry I'm cutting you a break."

I was not immune to the humiliation of standing before that judge, a woman with all the accoutrements of high status and power, but who was similar to me in age and bodily heft and possibly intellect, and who I therefore considered my equal. I wanted her to know I was no lightweight. I could have gone to law school as my sister did; it could have been me sitting up there meting out "justice." But I wasn't foolish enough to say this. I was half expecting her to say something about my relationship to Drew—then I realized he probably hadn't mentioned it, as it would impugn him too. Thank God I'd extricated myself from the messy matter of Elise and her check. I was thinking of all these things as I sat under the rain of the judge's condescension. I was also recalling the worst moments from my childhood when kids taunted me about my father's criminality, conflating the two of us, assuming I was—or soon would be—a criminal too.

"You're free to go," she said.

I turned and walked self-consciously to the back of the empty courtroom and out into the empty hallway. Free. I leaned against a wall, contemplating my next move. As I vacillated, something about the judge's chastising began to fortify me. I wasn't about to let that judge crush me. She could kick me off the jury but she couldn't change my opinions.

46

It was almost eleven o'clock when I exited the courthouse. The plaza was empty—all the worthy people were working inside at that time of day—and the bright light scorched, exposing me as someone who'd been banished. I felt like howling.

I torpedoed through the downtown miasma on Brenda's bike, anger percolating through my spine, spilling out and draping my shoulders like a fetal caul. Its targets were multiplying. I'd been burnishing my anger at Jeff and Dan for a long time. Now, alongside them there were the judge and Drew. Ire propelled me through currents of piss and pot smoke. Past homeless travelers hunkering on street corners with their dogs, spitting freely, accosting passersby. I could almost have joined them, sat on the sidewalk and relished offloading the social niceties alongside them. Instead I pedaled on, eviscerated, held together by the cleansing fumes of my rage.

The river sent off piercing spears of sunlight. I closed my eyes and continued in blindness, opened them to a woman's shriek. I had barely missed a toddler who had run into the path in pursuit of a bubble. Flummoxed, I pedaled on without looking back at the irate mother who continued to yell at me.

I forced my myopic field of vision to expand to take in a kaleidoscope of color and motion and human activity that made no sense. The wires of my selfhood were jumper cables attached exclusively to the things in my head. The jury room, Drew presiding, and all those other jurors, those would-be friends, those disposable affinities, people I'd never see again, who'd avoided my gaze as Lenore escorted me out. Had I really been offensive? It seemed to me I had simply stated my opinion—forcefully, yes, but had I been any more objectionable than Kevin? Drew had never known how to handle my forceful side. If he hadn't been the one in charge I might still be on that jury.

Now, I could no longer help Jessie. Would Shanti carry the torch and persuade the others to acquit? Could she convince Drew? Convincing Drew seemed paramount. He had followers on that jury, people who respected him. And he was foreman. I was still quite sure that if he argued to acquit, he could convince the others.

I lay in the grass, sucked into a ravine of loneliness. At the edge of my sac of loneliness, I sensed Jessie in her cell—or wherever she was—awaiting the verdict, meditating perhaps, or hyperventilating, refusing food, contemplating a possible lifetime of incarceration. I imagined she, an early student of anger, had learned to negotiate its cresting waves. Did anger, once born, ever die?

Elise Hotchkiss was waiting too, alone in her hotel room, the sole representative of the Hotchkiss family, Mr. Hotchkiss wanting nothing more to do with his renegade, murdered son, a blight on the family name. What was Elise doing to while away the hours? Having a pedicure perhaps? No, that would be too social. She would be lying on the king bed in her hotel room, playing solitaire or watching a movie, ordering room service she ignored, wondering what one did with a love that was no longer useful but would not die.

Immune to the lobby's chill, I took a seat on one of the crimson sofas. It was only a matter of time before Elise Hotchkiss would pass by. But after calculating how long that might be, I approached the desk. "I have a meeting with Elise Hotchkiss. Would you mind buzzing her?"

The clerk, the same one as before though he didn't appear to recognize me, obliged. He got no answer, told me Elise Hotchkiss was not in. "You can wait over there," he said, cordial, professional, but easily duped.

I was much too jumpy to sit. I ambled around the lobby, reminding myself that although I might be fractious, I was not a criminal. Nor was I a juror. There was no need to feel furtive.

The bar off the lobby was dim and nearly empty. Who went to a bar on a sunny summer afternoon? Lite rock seeped from the walls like chloroform. There she was, at a small table near the back, immersed in her phone, a drink before her. I wended my way through the sepia light as if traversing a moonscape. She glanced up, annoyed. When she recognized me she was surprised, then alarmed. I took a seat without being asked.

"There's a verdict? They were supposed to contact me."

"I wouldn't know. I've been kicked off the jury."

She frowned, not quite believing.

"Apparently I'm too opinionated. The judge said I was *fractious.*"

The waitress had approached for my order. "Nothing. Well, maybe water." She nodded and took off. I summoned her back. "On second thought, a chardonnay." She disappeared. I glanced around. I had thought there were other people in there, but now they were nowhere to be seen. Elise and I were the sole patrons.

There was nothing to say. I had no idea what I was doing there. Tom Petty had taken over the sound track now, crooning crescendos of longing. Notifications from a stalled game popped up from Elise's phone. Elise and I regarded each other frankly. We were not enemies, but nor were we friends. She was dressed top to toe in black, hipper than usual, but the image was contradicted by her wreck of a face whose doom she had tried to paper over with garish makeup.

She took up her drink and gulped. If she was not drunk now, she soon would be, slim as she was. "I have a right to this," she said defiantly, plunking down her empty glass. "Don't judge me. You have no idea." She closed her eyes as if she hoped I would leave.

My wine arrived. Elise lifted her glass to the waitress. "Another please. Dewar's." She turned to me. "This could be the last day of my life as I've known it. After this . . ."

I nodded.

"What an ordeal it's been. To listen to those know-nothings strutting around the courtroom impugning my son—God-awful. That Delaney girl. And that fat attorney sweating through his suits. Aargh . . .

"I told him not to marry her. She was just too different from him.

From us. Coming from Alaska, you know. Culturally deprived. Some differences are impossible to bridge. And you couldn't know her. She was difficult. She hardly spoke, but you could see her mind was always working away on things. Those eyes flitting around. Calculating. A gold digger. Still, you never imagine *this*. How could anyone imagine this?"

The waitress brought her Scotch, and she drank, sinking into her thoughts. We let some time pass. I saw us as we would look in a movie, two washed-up women in a tawdry western bar, addicted to alcohol and tunes of nostalgia.

The strangeness of the moment gave me the feeling I had nothing to lose. "Excuse me for saying so but—wasn't your son also difficult?"

"What are you doing here? Why did you come here if you're against me?"

I sipped my wine and it went to my head immediately. I couldn't remember the last time I'd eaten a meal, and it had been days since I'd had a solid night's sleep. I grabbed her irritating phone and silenced it then laid it back down in front of her. She regarded me with an air of resignation. I ran my fingers up and down the stem of my wine glass.

"I'm not against you. Yes, I hope Jessie is acquitted, but that doesn't mean I'm against you."

"Don't be stupid. I know what you think. You think the man is always the asshole. Well, I'm here to tell you that sometimes the woman is the asshole."

She sighed, the flame of her rage unsustainable. "What I've been through—a son murdered—and then they try to portray him up there as if he was *mean*? He was *not mean*." She shook her head violently. "It's disrespectful. To him. To me . . . You couldn't possibly understand."

I sucked air. "I understand a lot more than you think."

She looked at me warily. Her expression told me she was suddenly taking me in as a real person, not merely an obstacle.

"You're not the only one—" I stopped myself. Why would I confide in Elise Hotchkiss, a woman whose values I was sure I didn't share, a woman from another world entirely, a woman who I probably didn't even like? I stopped breathing and Elise Hotchkiss, mirroring me, stopped breathing too. Like seatmates on a plane, a seed of affinity germinated between us.

"I had a daughter. Two years ago . . ."

Elise swallowed audibly. Her eyes held the porousness of a sea creature as she scrutinized my face. "Go on."

"Fourteen years old. Someone gave her fentanyl. She wasn't an addict. Just that one time and . . ."

"She died?"

I nodded. Elise closed her eyes and shook her head slowly back and forth. "I know, I know," she whispered. "Unimaginable."

"Yes, unimaginable."

As if I'd been uncorked, words flowed from me. Elise listened and nodded and sipped her Scotch. I'd told this same story before—once to Val and then to Drew—but in neither case had I spoken as freely as I did then, there, to this stranger Elise Hotchkiss.

The lovely things. The rapture of Shawna's tiny body curled around mine. Braiding her shiny black hair. Central Park in the snow, she in her white fur coat and matching hat. Her hand reaching for mine, squeezing. Ice cream, all the ice cream we ate. *Mumma, Mumma.* Her beautiful empathetic soul.

The story was incomplete without describing the other things too. The insidious arrival of those boys in our lives. The mothers who pressed those boys into working for me. My mistake in buying the black outfit. Her sneaking out without my knowing. The day she went missing. The helplessness of having no idea where she was. The sight of her in the morgue, blue-lipped but still stunning. Then the visit from those smarmy boys seeking my forgiveness.

We ordered more drinks. The obsessive counter in me lost count. Elise canted toward me, reaching out to lay her hand on mine. She left it there for a long time, thin and cool and sentient.

"I had her only three years," I said. "But those years were a lifetime." Elise lifted her hand to my shoulder, eyes glistening.

"I need to tell you," she said. "My boy was not like those boys. I want you to know that. He had his moments, as we all do, but the things they said about him were wrong—or only a teeny tiny part of who he was.

He was a kind boy, like your daughter. He loved helping the people he rescued as an EMT. He told me so many times how happy it made him. I raised a nice, gentle boy, not a mean person. Do you understand?" Her voice, by then had turned urgent.

I nodded, maybe I understood.

"So many times I've wanted to jump up in that courtroom and set the record straight. Tell them how kind he was. Once, when he was in fourth grade, he begged me to take him to the park so he could give cookies to the poor children we'd sometimes see there. That's who he was—a *nice boy*. But I knew no one would believe me because I'm the mother. As if mothers shouldn't be believed when really they're the only ones who *should* be believed."

"I believe you."

"Really?"

"Yes."

She squinted, evaluating me for honesty even as I evaluated myself. I discovered I wasn't lying. I believed a hundred percent that she probably had done her best to raise a lovely boy, and even if he hadn't always been lovely, in her eyes he was.

We were there drinking and talking and listening to each other for hours. In the sepia light of that bar, just the two of us, we didn't judge each other. She understood and I understood. My daughter was dead and so was her son, and she and I were left to salvage whatever we could.

At some point we were both talked out. Drunk. Fatigue and heat engorged my limbs. People were entering the bar by then, intruding on our solitude. Dazed, we found our phones. 5:45 p.m. She had a text: *No verdict yet.*

We stood for a wordless goodbye. My hand on her shoulder. Her hand on my arm. Any more would have broken us both.

47

Paradigm shifts, moments when something unexpected happens and undermines all previous understandings about how the world works. All lives have them. I've always kept close count of these shifts in my own life. When the trial began, I'd had four of them:

1. Learning about my father's criminality. (Which taught me no one could be trusted, as he'd been saying all along.)
2. Drew falling in love with me. (I could, after all, be desirable.)
3. Drew falling out of love with me. (Love is unsustainable. Again—trust no one.)
4. Shawna's death. (Impermanence is the rule.)

What a surprise that my fifth and most recent paradigm shift would arrive courtesy of Elise Hotchkiss. But that is the nature of paradigm shifts—they surprise you. When I walked out of that hotel lobby after my talk with Elise, I was aware that something profound had transpired between us, and it filled me with an optimism I'd never expected to feel.

Elise Hotchkiss, at the height of her own personal crisis, had had no reason to be kind and receptive to me. And yet she had been. She had stepped out of the morass of her own despair and given herself over to listening to me. When I was close to drowning from anger and humiliation, she had tossed me a life vest and reeled me in.

Our conversation gave me such hope. Not only about my own resilience, but about the capabilities of others too. It seemed possible that Elise would eventually be happy if Jessie were acquitted, and she would, in the not-too-distant future, come to forgive her daughter-in-law. I pictured the rapprochement that would happen between them, regardless of the trial's outcome, both women keen on salvaging a sliver of good, both wanting to affirm the positive things they'd known about Eric.

And I thought of the other jurors too, the eight including Drew who had first voted to convict, and I saw them debating in a serious and open-minded way over the next few days, finding their higher selves. I was confident they would choose mercy. The people I had come to know—Chrystal and Shanti and Anna and Joanne (my probable replacement)—were good people. Drew was fundamentally good too, and he was leading them. No doubt even Walmart Kevin and his sidekick Cory had some moral scruples. Look at how I'd underestimated Ray. They could, all of them, come to regard Jessie's plight with empathy and vote to acquit. There was time for this to happen during their upcoming deliberations. The law might yield justice after all.

What a euphoric feeling these thoughts gave me, and it was entirely due to Elise Hotchkiss, a woman I'd written off for days and who had now become an important part of my personal history.

That was the frame of mind I was in as I found myself pedaling to Drew's doorstep. Standing on his porch, my skin tingled like a blinking light. I realized I was still drunk.

The door opened, Drew's body corking the opening. "You shouldn't be here," he said immediately. "There's no verdict yet." The sanctimonious side of him, the embodiment of Alma, was on prominent display.

"I know."

"How do you know?"

"I just do. We need to talk."

"Whatever you're mad about will have to wait until after the trial."

"I'm not mad. I was, but not anymore. Can I come in? Just briefly."

He hesitated, then opened the door with obvious reluctance, and I made my way to his living room couch, breathing heavily, relieved to sit.

"You're drunk again. This is getting to be a bad habit."

"The judge said I was fractious. Is that what you told her?"

He sighed. "Something weird was happening to you in that room. You weren't shutting up."

"You couldn't control me—is that what you mean?"

"It wasn't good for us to be on the jury together. I should have realized that earlier."

"We both made that decision when the trial began. It was too late to revise it." I was getting off track—I wasn't there to accuse him. "That's not why I'm here. The point is you can't convict Jessie. You mustn't." He shook his head, back and forth, back and forth, but I kept talking. "Look, *I know you*—you're kinder and better that that. After all she's been through you have to—"

"Sybil, you've already said all this. Don't you get it—it's not your prerogative to weigh in. You're not a juror anymore."

"Thanks to you. But the thing is, she was desperate. He was being violent. She had no other choice. *Show some heart!*"

"I can't discuss this. I won't." He looked toward the front door as if contemplating an exit.

"You can convince the others. You have the sway. They all love you."

"Stop!"

I did stop. Overcome by vertigo I closed my eyes, willing the spinning to subside. "You haven't asked me a single question about my daughter."

"Is that what you're mad about?"

"I'm not mad."

"Right. I see that. You're not mad."

"Jessie was just trying to survive, for God's sake."

"How many times do I have to say this—this is illegal. You coming here—it's jury tampering."

"So, report me. Put me behind bars right along with Jessie."

"Stop being so histrionic."

"Stop telling me what to do." I was breathing heavily, tasting bile. "Where's your heart? You think you're a good person because you hike with developmentally challenged teens. Hah."

"Shut. Up."

I rose, pushed back against another wave of vertigo. "I'm going to the bathroom."

I peed for a long time. His bathroom was pristine white, white tiles, white towels, white shag rug. It smelled of cleanser. There, sitting on the toilet, exhaustion overtook me. I thought of locking the door, curling up on the white rug and spending the night there, a blight on his spotlessness.

"Sybil?" He was just outside the door.

I rose from the toilet and locked the door then lay on the cool tiles. I thought briefly of Elise, the way her entire body had leaned into me as if offering shelter. It reminded me of a quality Shawna had had, a listing toward those in need as naturally as a plant grows to the sunlight.

"Sybil!" He jiggled the door handle. "Come out. Please."

Had I ever meant anything to him, even when he called me rare? My body had turned him on and given him access to a new libertine side of himself, but beyond his need for my body, who had I ever been to him?

"You have to come out! Now!"

"Why?"

He slapped the door in frustration and I knew I had the upper hand.

"I'll come out if you agree to try to get Jessie acquitted."

"Oh, for God's sake."

His footsteps creaked the floorboards. I heard him in the kitchen, opening drawers. Then, a hush. I lost track of where he was, heard only silence. Had he left the house entirely? I drifted, falling into light sleep then jerking awake into sharp consciousness.

Was this really the same man I'd once loved, who had claimed to love me?

Determined not to vomit, I swallowed hard against gas and acids bubbling up from my gut. I began to count, which always centers me, and it seemed to help. Before I reached fifty, I found I could stand, dizzy but intact and surprisingly energized. I rinsed my face and drank from the faucet. As I recall, I was not angry at that moment; I was focused, but without a plan.

A sound at the door, a clicking, metal on metal. He was picking the lock. A sound I will henceforth hear in nightmares. A sound that bespoke an attempt at ambush. A surprise attack. Not friendly. It was, to me, a declaration of war. Anger took hold again. He was planning to force me from this room, eject me from his house. I froze.

But only momentarily. His straight razor smiled at me from the bottom shelf of the medicine cabinet. So many times I'd watched him guiding that blade slowly over his limbs in search of perfection, careful not to draw blood. Beside that smug razor lay the scissors he used to trim his beard. I seized them, flexing them open and closed. They were full of agency and reminiscent of spread legs.

The door flew open. We took each other in, both wielding weapons of sorts—his screwdriver, my scissors—both arrested by the sight of the other. A galactic silence enshrined us, like the silence preceding the Big Bang.

You channel Jessie's courage, her blue eyes seething behind your brown ones. Your anger merges with hers, medicinal and empowering.

You know his body almost as well as you know your own, the toned muscles so carefully cultivated and maintained over a lifetime. They've been paraded before you so many times, flexed and named and exalted. He wears shorts and, standing in the doorway, the bare flesh of his prized calves rivets your attention.

He advances, about to grab you. You sidestep out of reach, slip, fall hard on your coccyx. He stares down at you sitting with your back against the tub. He offers no help. You wouldn't take his help anyway.

His perfectly shaved, perfectly muscular calves stand directly in front of you now and again they draw your full attention, calling you to action. You lunge, low and uncharacteristically quick, ambushing before you can be ambushed. You draw the spread scissor blade across the gastrocnemius, the solus, the peroneus longus. The flesh parts more willingly than you expect. It takes a second or two for blood to appear and then there is so much of it. Striations of muscle poke through the cascade of gushing crimson.

A guttural gasp from him. He collapses on the white tiles. He groans and swears.

You drop the scissors, leap over him, fly out the front door.

You are on Brenda's bike again, rising through the night, light and free and powerful. The cool air brushes your face. Jessie and Shawna balance on your handlebars. Your heart is clear. It is almost Independence Day and you have joined the ranks of the fractious rebels that holiday celebrates. An embolism of joy explodes in your chest and you ride to your new fate in proud jubilation.

48

So, there you are, the whole story, soup to nuts. Go to town with it. Do what you can to exploit the many loopholes of justice in my favor. I don't have false hopes. I know what I've done. Drew has significant scars, yes, but he's not *dead*—I never intended to kill him. I have no regrets. Nor do I have illusions about my innocence in the eyes of the law.

It will always be a mystery to me why human beings hold themselves in such high regard when we're all just animals, every last one of us.

Sure, I include myself. Isn't that clear from what I've just told you?

Something happened to me during the trial. My personality expanded as a body sometimes does, growing baggy and loose so it flapped around me and got stuck on things I'd never minded before. When you see the gap widening between how the world is and how it could be, you have to speak up.

Everyone wonders how I could have injured a man I'd loved. Perhaps you can't see that I did what I did *because* I had once loved him. Without the love there would have been no anger, without the anger I wouldn't have cut. They're always entwined, love and anger. Ask Jessie.

I could have done things differently. I could have continued to say: *Thank you for loving me.* I could have shut up, as I'd done all my life. I could have said to myself: *This is the way the world works. People like Jessie are never going to be cut a break, while people like Drew, or Jeff and Dan, will always get a pass.* But I'd accepted that status quo for too long, and living with those inequities had finally become untenable.

Drew is, of course, furious at me. Irate, really—I believe irate is a notch more angry than furious. Or perhaps the word is apoplectic. He says I overreacted, and many people would agree. I disagree. Extreme expressions of human rage usually breed on entire lifetimes of quietly festering wounds and slights. So, I did what I had to do and I'm not sorry. Remember, *I didn't kill him.* Face to face with him in the bathroom, scissors in hand, I could have slashed his neck. My rancor toward him drained away at the sight of his gushing blood. Does that mean my anger died? I can't be sure about that. I might, like Ferdinand the Bull, yet be stung by another bee.

A good development: Jessie is free, at least for now. Perhaps you already know this. After I was dismissed for fractiousness, and Drew was hospitalized, and I was arrested on assault charges, the other jury members were so traumatized they fought incessantly and couldn't come to any consensus. Deliberations went on for another week and ended in a hung jury. There might be a retrial at some point in the future, but for now there will be no adjacent cells for Jessie and me, no intimate prison sharing between us. Under the right circumstances, as I've told you, I know she and I could be friends.

Perhaps things will work out well for me too. Surviving is a kind of luck in itself, as my tattoo reminds me, and I am still here.

I ride through these days and nights buoyed by Shawna. She usually comes when I summon her, but I never know what age she'll be. Sometimes she's two, sometimes she's twenty, sometimes she's the elfin eleven-year-old I first took into my home. She is welcome in all her guises. She gives me advice, reminds me that survival is possible, empathy essential. She seems to have been born knowing things it takes most of us years to learn. When she leaves me—like any good mother I know it's imperative to grant her a modicum of freedom, hard as that is—she returns to a vast green field where she and Ferdinand pass the time peaceably, smelling the flowers, hoping, as we all do, not to be stung by more bees.

Acknowledgments for *Livid*

I was inspired to write this book during the Kavanaugh confirmation hearings when I was appalled by Kavanaugh's display of egotism and dishonesty, and dismayed by how belittling he was to Christine Blasey Ford. Watching, I was suffused with the rage-inducing helplessness women can so often feel in the face of men who have power and use it abusively, without the slightest regard for those they are hurting. When I began to write *Livid*, my anger was validated by reading Rebecca Traister's smart book about female anger, *Good and Mad*.

I could not have written a novel featuring a murder trial without the expert assistance from three phenomenal attorneys who generously shared time and legal knowledge that helped me shape the story. Defense attorney Laura Fine Moro invited me into her backyard one August evening, and we brainstormed about what was then a vague idea. Her questions fired me up and set me on the journey. Thank you, Laura, for your time and openness. I attended a murder trial prosecuted by Stephen Morgan, a former prosecutor, now a judge, and was blown away by his incisive intellect and unflappable manner. He controlled the courtroom, and I was not surprised when the jury decided to convict. I am grateful that he answered my elementary questions about legal procedure with grace and humor. Many thanks, Stephen. Mark Haight, a retired prosecutor, was involved in this project from its inception to its conclusion. He brainstormed with me about Jessie and her actions and helped me structure a credible case history that served my narrative purposes. More than that, his enthusiasm for the story sustained me when I had doubts, and he read several drafts and offered terrific suggestions. A million thanks, Mark.

I am fortunate to have good friends, writers and non-writers, who routinely offer me everything I need to sustain myself through the writing of a novel: sometimes it's long talks over coffee or wine, sometimes it's responses to drafts, sometimes it's simply leaving me alone, but their support always functions as a kind of cheerleading, and I am eternally grateful. Thank you Miriam Gershow, Debra Gwartney, Andrea Schwartz-Feit, Becky and Dave Dusseau, Char Decker and Don McElroy, Georgeanne Cooper and Jon Baker for all the various kinds of support you have given me and continue to give.

I will be forever indebted to two kick-ass women who helped me launch this book for the public: my long-time agent and dear friend, Deborah Schneider; and my editor/publisher and newer but also beloved friend, Kate Gale. I admire these two women hugely, for their fierce, suffer-no-fools approach, coupled with the ability to see the whole picture and find its humor. I have loved working and laughing with you both. Thanks also to Mark Cull and Tobi Harper, the bees' knees, who sustain so much that happens at Red Hen. Thanks also the tireless Red Hen staff including Monica Fernandez, Tansica Sunkamaneevongse, Rebeccah Sanhueza, and Shelby Wallace.

And Paul and Ben, what can I say? You two make everything meaningful.

Biographical Note

Cai Emmons is the author of seven books of fiction. Winner of the Oregon Book Award, the Leapfrog Press Fiction Contest, a Nautilus Award, and finalist for the *Missouri Review* Editor's Prize as well as the *Narrative Magazine* Fiction Prize, her essays and stories have appeared in such publications as *TriQuarterly*, *LitHub*, *Electric Literature*, *The LA Times*, and *Ms. Magazine*. A summa cum laude graduate of Yale College, Emmons holds MFA degrees in film and fiction. She has taught at several colleges and universities, mostly recently in the University of Oregon's Creative Writing Program. She lives in Eugene, Oregon.

9 781636 280752